THE SACRED CLAN

LIANG HONG

Translated by
Esther Tyldesley

SINOIST

Published by Sinoist Books (an imprint of ACA Publishing Ltd)
London - Beijing
info@alaincharlesasia.com ☎+44 20 3289 3885
www.sinoistbooks.com

Published by Sinoist Books (an imprint of ACA Publishing Ltd) in
arrangement with CITIC Press Corporation
Author: Liang Hong **Translator:** Esther Tyldesley
Editors: Susan Trapp and David Lammie **Production Manager:** Dawn Bailey

Original Chinese Text © 神圣家族 *(shen sheng jia zu)* 2020, CITIC Press
Corporation, Beijing, China

English Translation text © 2023 ACA Publishing Ltd, London, UK. A catalogue
record for *The Sacred Clan* is available from the National Bibliographic Service
of the British Library.
This novel is entirely a work of fiction. The names, characters and incidents
portrayed in it are the work of the author's imagination. Any resemblance to
actual persons, living or dead, events or localities is entirely coincidental.

Hardback ISBN: 978-1-83890-561-3
Paperback ISBN: 978-1-83890-559-0
eBook ISBN: 978-1-83890-560-6

Sinoist Books is honoured to be supported using public
funding by Arts Council England. This book has been selected to receive financial
assistance from English PEN's PEN Translates programme, supported by Arts Council
England. English PEN exists to promote literature and our understanding of it, to

THE SACRED CLAN

LIANG HONG

Translated by
ESTHER TYLDESLEY

Sinoist Books

Contents

A Shining Cloud Moving Over the Skies of Wu Town

A SHINING CLOUD was moving over the skies of Wu Town.

Aqing, a young boy lying in clumps of foxtail grass, sensed a change in the patchy shadows from light to dark. Feeling the temperature drop, he raised his eyes to the sky and was mesmerised by the cloud and its brightness. He got up and ran in the direction of home.

His father Wu Zhenzhong was putting up a frame for the bean plants. Aqing shouted, "Wu Zhenzhong, Wu Zhenzhong, look, a cloud that glows."

Wu Zhenzhong raised his head, glanced at the sky, and said, "Daft kid, that means it's going to rain, I'll need to get this frame finished quickly or it'll be ruined."

Aqing raced home to show his mother Yang Xiuju. "Mum, Mum, come out and look, quick." Holding the baby with one hand while she was busy cooking at the stove, Yang Xiuju thought that something had happened and hurried outside. Aqing pointed urgently at the cloud in the sky and said to his mother, "Mum, a cloud that glows."

Yang Xiuju let out a curse, "Drat you, can't you see I'm busy, quick, take your little sister."

Aqing turned round and ran, calling for Ali, Achang and Ayou as he went. His young friends came hurrying round from all sides to chase that glowing cloud in the sky with Aqing.

The sun hid behind the cloud, and the cloud moved unhurriedly along, trailing a great grey shadow behind it. The irregularly shaped cloud shot out golden light for thousands of metres in all directions, illuminating Wu Town. Its borders seemed to exactly match the borders of Wu Town, its shape seemed just the same as that of Wu Town, from the slope leading down to the river in the west to the wheat fields in the east, following the line of the twisting, vast, empty Tuan River, right the way round to the very edges of the open country. Beneath the cloud, Wu Town was caged in a golden glow, yet in the centre was a bright, vast greyness. The buildings, trees and streets of Wu Town, its mosque and its church, its big corner building at the central crossroads, all were inside this greyness, as if in the very first moment of the world's creation.

In the golden radiance that spread for thousands of metres, between Wu Town and the cloud, more clouds formed a series of gleaming, ascending staircases. The boy Aqing raced towards the staircase, wanting to find a starting point, wanting to climb, to see the mysterious sun hiding behind the cloud. He ran and he ran, and the staircase was always just in front of him, not so far off; that light was on the point of shining on his body, and yet he just could not reach it, run as he might.

———

Aqing was carrying a chunk of steamed bread which he did not eat, as he passed sick and listless through Wu Town. The trees by the side of the road, the clouds in the sky, the ants on the ground, the foxtail grass in the fields, things that in the normal way of things he could play with for ages, today he did not have the heart for any of them.

He walked to the mosque at the northern end of Wu Town, and he could not go any farther. He lay down on the flagstones in front of the building. His father Wu Zhenzhong said that this mosque was several hundred years old, older than Wu Town itself. Aqing had never understood his father's odd tone when he spoke of this mosque, it was like he was talking about another person. Aqing very much wanted to play with Hai Xiaohe who lived next door to the mosque, but as soon as he saw Hai Xiaohe's serious, unsmiling father, Aqing was a little bit afraid.

The loudspeaker on the first floor of the mosque was singing. People from near the mosque came out of their houses, towels flung over their shoulders, heading for the mosque. Aqing very much liked the sound of this song. He did not understand a word, but he liked the melody, so high, so remote, like it could carry all the way to the clouds, like it was drilling into the deepest places of his heart. One time he was lying on the steep riverbank and listening to the music from the loudspeaker, he had felt like the grass beside his body, the clouds in the sky, the water in the river had all stopped moving, and he himself seemed to be fixed in place. He did not want to move, and yet he also wanted to stand up and head forwards, following the song.

The imam with his white beard and white hat came out, saw Aqing and sat down beside him on the flagstones. Aqing thought that the imam must surely be a spirit, the kind who never got old.

"Aqing, what are you doing?"

"I'm not myself."

"If you're not yourself, why not go to the hospital?"

"I want to hear the song, if I hear the song I'll be fine."

"That's not a song, it's calling the Muslims to the mosque to bow down to Allah."

"Who's Allah?"

"Ah, Allah, He made the world and everything in it, He raises us and nurtures us."

Aqing was bewildered. "Then who gave birth to me?"

"Foolish child, your mother and father gave birth to you, but think about it, the food you eat, the wheat, the corn, the rice – the things you see, the sky, the clouds, the stars, the moon – what you walk on, the road, the dust, the big trees, the foxtail grass, who made those?"

Aqing seemed to understand without really understanding. He felt very tired. All he wanted to do was to lie down on the stone slab, watching the clouds, sunk deep in the song. If Hai Xiaohe would come and play with him, it would all be fine.

When Aqing had tired himself out playing outside, he went back home. He saw his grandmother, his aunt and some other people standing in a circle around Wu Baoguo, the Party branch secretary of South Village, shouting and arguing. Wu Town was divided into the north village and the south village, and Aqing's home was in the south part. Wu Baoguo was saying, "When we've cut down the old scholar tree, we can build a square in this place, pave it with concrete and then build a pavilion for shade. It'll be just lovely, all of this is for everyone's benefit."

"This old scholar tree is more than a hundred years old, that's no easy thing, and you're going to cut it down, just like that. And once it's chopped down, the spirit that keeps our spirits alive will be gone," Granny said.

"The shade of this tree is so nice, look, where else in our village is there a tree with leaves so wide and branches so deep? From now on, where are we meant to put ourselves to eat? Where are we supposed to go for shade?" added his aunt.

"Afterwards there'll be a pavilion here, we'll plant some ornamental trees, just like in the city, clean and neat. How can there be no place to eat? How can there be nowhere for shade?" Wu Baoguo replied.

"We want to eat and get our shade under *this* tree," Granny and Aunt said as one.

Wu Baoguo raised his voice. "What you are doing is picking a fight for its own sake, you're working yourselves up on purpose."

Granny lowered her voice again and grumbled, "If this tree goes, then I'll die too." Thinking on this, Granny was crying again. "If this old scholar tree goes, then how can the ghosts of our departed find their homes?"

Aqing seemed not to hear them quarrelling. First he sat under the tree, playing with an ant hole, then he lay down on his accustomed tree root, stretched his head into the hole under the roots and went to sleep.

Aqing often slept here, he played here with his friends, with mud, with ants, with marbles, each of them occupying a different root of the tree, telling ghost stories and jokes. At noon on summer days, the grown-ups would bring out bamboo beds and set them up all round the tree, getting shade from it, eating, chatting, having a siesta. Aqing and the others would hang from the tree's hammock-like branches, where they would dangle until they dozed off.

Wu Baoguo brought the woodworkers of Wu Town, Zhang Rongsheng and his son Zhang Changguang, and they walked round and round the tree, considering where to start sawing it down. He walked up to Aqing and gave him a kick. "Aqing, get up." Aqing did not reply. He bent down to drag Aqing out from the tree roots, but Aqing flung his arms round the roots and would not let go.

Wu Baoguo pulled Aqing over. Aqing's face was smeared with a thick layer of dust from the hole in the tree, his eyes were like a panda's, with tears cutting tracks in all directions down his face. When he saw Zhang Rongsheng behind Wu Baoguo, Aqing turned round and wrapped his arms around the roots of the tree. His head, hands, feet and every part of his body all curled round the old tree, as if he was a part of it.

With an effort, Wu Baoguo peeled Aqing's hands away, threw him down in the dust and continued to deliberate with Zhang Rongsheng and Zhang Changguang about where the first cut should go. As soon as his attention was elsewhere, Aqing came dashing over from another side and climbed up into the tree.

"Aqing, get down," Wu Baoguo shouted in a stern voice from down below. Aqing ignored him utterly. When they heard Wu Baoguo shouting, Wu Zhenzhong, Yang Xiuju, Aqing's grandmother and the neighbouring grownups all came running out in confusion, to find Wu Baoguo running round the tree with his head tilted up like a duck being throttled, choking with rage.

Wu Baoguo ordered Zhang Changguang to climb the tree to catch Aqing and get him down. When Zhang Changguang went up one part of the tree, Aqing climbed up another section; when he went left, Aqing went right; when he went right, Aqing went left. The two of them were like monkeys, chasing each other through the forks of the tree, getting higher and higher.

Very soon Aqing had climbed to the highest and furthest fork, facing south and east. The branch was starting to list under Aqing's weight and come away from the crown of the tree like it might break right off, but it was tough and highly flexible, and it sprung about, carrying Aqing with it. Zhang Changguang was too scared to move an inch, and the people down below let out gasps and cries of shock. Aqing put his arms round that small, thick branch, rocking his body, so that it swayed out a long way, back and forth in a series of ever-expanding arcs.

Suddenly, Aqing saw Old Wu Family Alley where Achang was being chased away helter-skelter by Li Xiu'e's small flock of wry-necked geese. Those geese were formidable. If anyone passed by the door of Li Xiu'e's house, the geese would chase after them, honking, and bite them. If anyone complained, then Li Xiu'e would say in her thin, weak voice, from a safe distance, plucking inno-cently at her garments, "There, you see, even with me, if I change my clothes they don't know me."

Achang was routed and fled. He took a detour round to the back of the old alley, where he saw the pig tied up outside the Lu family's house. He went down to the hollow in the ground where they kept the pig and aimed a vicious kick at the pig's head, but he slipped and fell on his bum, and then hopped around clutching his foot.

Aqing looked to the left and saw Second Uncle, flus-tered and agitated, leaving the house of the widow Lu. He did not go home either but headed for the earth slope at the end of the lane. Once he had descended the slope, he went to stand for a while in the shade of the woods that sloped down to the river, then he came back up again, looked all around him, circled round to the road to the Wu

Town Hospital, and headed for home. Aqing could not understand what on earth Second Uncle was up to.

Looking farther out, Aqing saw the roofs of the houses, high and low; he saw his playmates running around in the alleys, calling out loudly; he saw the Wu Town central primary school and junior high school, and behind them both the exercise ground in its deep hollow and the handful of houses next to it; after that it was the river slope, stretching off into the distance. He saw the endless distance and emptiness, saw light and clouds, and he saw himself: he was just Aqing, a tiny dot in that endless distance.

Aqing fell into a trance on the tree.

Wu Zhenzhong lay down on a bamboo bed underneath the tree, thinking he would wait until his son had had enough and came down of his own accord, but in the end, he nodded off himself. Aqing lay on the biggest fork of the tree's branches, looking at the moonlight, and he fell asleep as well.

At dawn, Aqing squatted down on the branch that stretched out the furthest and emptied his bowels, then wiped his bottom with leaves with the dew still on them. Shortly after five o'clock, his grandmother, who had got up early to wait under the tree, saw the mess plop into the dust and bustled up, swept up the turd and threw it onto the big dungheap in front of the gate. Achang stole a steamed bun from his house and presented it to Aqing like he was offering up a treasure. Ali spent pocket money he had been saving up for a very long time on a portion of hot pepper soup for Aqing, and dashed over, carrying the soup in a plastic bag, which Aqing then hooked up on a forked stick. Having eaten and drunk his fill, Aqing climbed like a monkey to the thin tip of the main trunk, swaying back and forth along with the flexible branch.

His friends brought Aqing presents: a favourite catapult, glass marbles, a plastic handgun, sweet wrappers, matchboxes, and they also carried over a broken door and sneaked out a bamboo mat from home. Aqing set the door between two branches, laid out the mat on top of it and spread out his favourite toys at the head of the mat.

Aqing had found himself a new home, and his heart seemed full of clouds and light as he was gently tossed about. He thought to himself that he was much closer to the cloud that glowed, standing like this on the tree.

And that was how Aqing took up residence in the tree.

People from miles around heard the news and gathered underneath the scholar tree, raising their heads to look at this strange novelty. Vegetable sellers carried their poles of produce over, passers-by bought a few things from them, then sellers of household goods trundled their wheelbarrows over for a look, gawkers made a few purchases while they were watching, then even fruit sellers and pancake pedlars turned up. People started haggling with vendors close by, and deals were being made. More and more folk arrived, a great noisy crowd; it was like market day under the old tree.

When there were a lot of people around, Aqing became very excited, and he climbed to the tips of the highest branches, thrusting himself downwards to the left and then to the right, causing the ends of the branches to sway violently like a bow, and Aqing along with them, springing back into a dazzling variety of arcs and curves. The people down below let out cries of shock and horror and sighs of admiration, their heads turning this way and that to follow Aqing as he drifted through the air.

Sometimes Aqing would wrap his arms around the tree, not moving a muscle, and look out into the distance. He saw the pork seller Limping Li injecting water into his pigs, whose meat he sold by weight, and called out loudly, "Limping Li, if you keep on pouring water into those pigs, your limp'll get even worse." Limping Li grabbed a freshly cut meat bone and lurched over to the tree to hurl it at Aqing. Aqing dodged effortlessly aside, sniggering. The bone fell behind the old scholar tree, where a dog dashed up and carried the bone away in its mouth.

He saw the self-imposed exile Grandmother Ahua, dressed all in black, standing solemn and silent in her yard. Aqing felt a sinister chill emanating from her body, reaching out all the way to his own head, and he gave an involuntary shudder. The people of Wu Town were in awe of this strange old lady, even the old doctor Chen Xian'er, who had no time for anyone, would become solemn when speaking of her. Aqing had never seen her smile. Aqing's granny said that when Grandmother Ahua was young, she had committed a grievous sin: she had caused the death of her own firstborn son. So she had sworn herself to the gods, dedicating her whole life to their service, wearing no bright colours, eating no meat, nor living with her children or her husband. By voluntarily shutting herself away to atone to the gods for her sin, she had become their mouthpiece.

Every summer, Granny would bring a gift of the best black brocade to Grandmother Ahua. Granny would say, "Oh, Ahua, you're a lightning rod for our village, with you here the ghosts and the spirits and all the rest daren't come near." Gaunt and ramrod-straight, Grandmother Ahua did not speak, cold emanating from every inch of her body as she regarded Aqing's granny in a way that made her seem very short and very small. Aqing did not know the meaning of fear, he had even tweaked the beard and ruffled the head of the venerated local imam, but he would take to his heels and vanish like smoke at the sight of Grandmother Ahua, for fear that she would see into the depths of his wicked heart.

Wu Baoguo had Wu Zhenzhong brought over. He circled the tree scolding Aqing, jabbing at him on his perch with a long fork. At last, he pleaded with Aqing in a low voice, "Aqing, if you come down we'll get a cash reward from the township, your granny will be able to buy her vitamin pills and your mum can go to the doctor."

Granny was scrunching up her face behind Wu Zhenzhong's back, by which she meant: Don't listen to him. Yang Xiuju too was muttering unhappily, "Don't drag me into this."

Up in the tree, Aqing shouted at his father, calling him by his name, "Wu Zhenzhong, Wu Zhenzhong, I saw Wu

Baoguo give you money, you've been bought! You've been bought and paid for, even though you're a grown-up."

The people beneath the tree burst into raucous laughter.

From then on, Wu Zhenzhong never held his head up in Wu Town again. His reputation had been wrecked by Aqing, his daft nine-year-old son.

———

One evening, Wu Baoguo came underneath the tree with snow-white steamed bread, delicious-smelling pressed sheep's head and a bright green soft drink, which he set down on the lowest branch of the tree.

He sat down and said, "Aqing, you don't know how hard it is for me, it's no easy thing being the Party branch secretary! The villagers curse my name, and I know it. They say I'm on the take, but what is there for me to take? I have a skinful sometimes, what's the big deal? I have to eat five or six times a day, and for each meal I have to dash from place to place. I don't want to eat all that, spending the whole day with my guts swollen to hell. The high-ups keep on at me as well, saying I'm not proactive, that I move too slowly. So you tell me, what am I supposed to do, blow up our whole township? It's easy for them to say, they can get promoted, they can take themselves off any time they want, but I have to stay here."

Wu Baoguo seemed to be both talking to Aqing and to himself, his voice rising and falling, swirling around in the shadow of the tree. As he was speaking, Wu Baoguo's mobile phone rang. He took the call and gave a fruity chuckle. "Great, that's the stuff, just tell me where, I'll be right over." Aqing felt like he could taste the hot oil and Sichuan pepper just listening to him speak.

After Wu Baoguo had left, Second Uncle came over and said furiously, "Aqing, don't you believe anything that bastard says. He loses his head at the sight of wine, and at the sight of money as well." Second Uncle leaned back, stretching out his beefy frame against the tree trunk, rolling a blade of grass back and forth between his hands. "Ah, Aqing, you've no idea, the last few days I've been the one who's really fed up. Tell me, how can your aunt be like that? She wasn't that way back in the day. I spent a lot of energy back then courting her. What's so great about that widow anyway? What made me fall for her? Why's it so hard to do the right thing?"

After Second Uncle had finished speaking, he stared into space for a while, sighed for a while more, then dusted himself off and left.

Granny came out of the house huffing with fury, carrying a little stool, and sat next to the hole in the tree trunk, wiping away tears. "Aqing," she said, "you've seen it all, you be my judge, do I treat your mother well or don't I? I gave her my son, I gave her my house, I gave her charge of the finances, why does she treat me like this? Your dad's married a wife and forgotten his mother, that's what it is." When his grandmother got to the most heart-breaking part of her speech, she called out to her dead husband, sobbing and slapping her thigh, "O ghost of mine, dead before your time – it's all very well for you, you've nothing to worry about, you've left me stuck here to suffer..."

The spreading branches of the old tree formed curved, soft, gentle shadows, and the countless leaves shook slightly with the wind, making tiny, crisp rustling sounds. Aqing sat in the highest part of those curving shadows, and the boundless, silent dark enveloped his small body.

———

Wu Baoguo arranged for a basket crane to be fetched, and had Zhang Changguang stand on it and start to saw off branches. Wu Baoguo directed him from down below, calling out, "Left", "Right", as the tree branches fell crashing to the ground. He wanted to scare Aqing down. Aqing sprang about from place to place on the tree, rolling his eyes at Wu Baoguo and sticking out his tongue, until Wu Baoguo was sweating with fury.

A sense of panic and confusion descended on the onlookers; nobody knew how this business should be wound up. Some people approached Wu Baoguo and said, Just let it go, he's only a daft kid, he won't be able to hold out for more than a few days. The bravado was starting to fade from Wu Baoguo's face, but there was no going back for him. All the eyes of the township were on him; he could not lose to a child.

The driver of the basket crane was hanging back, Zhang Changguang was hanging back as well, and they cut down just a handful of branches in a whole day. Wu Baoguo did not hurry them on either, but every day had the machine sit there rumbling and growling, lopping off a branch here, another there. He wanted Aqing to know that he would have to come down sooner or later.

Aqing ignored the crane. He put his arms round the highest, slenderest branch, and went into a daze watching Grandmother Ahua. There was a small shack in Grandmother Ahua's garden courtyard with a trestle table inside, on which was set an incense burner, and in front of the incense burner was a big statue of the Bodhisattva Guanyin, with bunches of incense sticks laid out beside it. Grandmother Ahua, still in those same black clothes, stood at the courtyard gate, facing outwards, solemn and still.

Her visitor bowed and knelt respectfully, was greeted by Grandmother Ahua, washed his hands, kowtowed to the Bodhisattva Guanyin, then sat on a stool and said something to Grandmother Ahua. With her eyes narrowed to slits and face expressionless, Grandmother Ahua shook out a single bamboo divination slip from a tube and examined the slip, her mouth opening and closing. After that, she closed her eyes again and did not speak for a very long time, as if she had fallen into a trance. The visitor bowed low to Grandmother Ahua and retreated reverently from the courtyard.

Grandmother Ahua's expression had filled Aqing with awe, he wanted to see just exactly what there in Grandmother Ahua's eyes. He had Achang sneak out a pair of binoculars from his house, with a promise that when he came down from the tree, he would give Achang all the marbles and sweet wrappers in his collection.

The scene in the binoculars shifted and wavered. When at last Aqing had his target in view, he saw that Grandmother Ahua's mouth was glistening with grease, and she was chewing quickly on something. Her chopsticks speedily rose and fell, they appeared in the lens from time to time carrying a big chunk of meat towards her mouth, then after a while, they would disappear and come back with another big lump of meat.

He looked down and saw a large bowl of belly pork stewed with bean noodles, quivering slightly, hot steam rising. Aqing refocused the binoculars and saw Grandmother Ahua's son Wu Tianyi and her daughter-in-law Xu Junmei sitting round a table, which was set out with many plates of food. Grandmother Ahua's mouth was chewing and swallowing as she chatted and laughed with her son. Grandmother Ahua's expression when she saw her son was nothing like when she looked at Aqing.

Suddenly, Grandmother Ahua put down her bowl, stood up and hurriedly swallowed what was in her mouth. Wu Tianyi and Xu Junmei hastily got up too, carried the little table into the main room of the house and shut the door on it. Grandmother Ahua tidied her garments, smoothed her hair, changed the expression on her face and stood up, now solemn, sinister and cold. Aqing looked towards the gateway door of the courtyard again and realised that someone was knocking on it. Aqing raised his binoculars again in a daze. The people in view were moving backwards and forwards, burning incense, kneeling in prayer, making offerings, requesting a divination, but he saw none of it. Everything was a blank in front of his eyes, and it felt like there was a sickness in his heart, something very, very painful. Aqing rubbed at his eyes with his hands and only then realised that he was crying.

When he looked into the courtyard again, the visitor had already left. Grandmother Ahua was walking towards that table again, she took up the money from that corner of the table, counted it, and pushed aside her black clothes to reveal a slack white stomach, piercingly bright to Aqing's eyes. She pulled out a small pouch from her black trousers, withdrew some money, placed the new money on top of it and recounted it carefully before she replaced the purse and covered it with her clothes.

Aqing went weak all over, all he could feel was giddiness and nausea. The far-off Tuan River could no longer be seen, and he no longer wanted to climb the tree. He came down from that highest branch and lay down motionless on his door. That cloud which had always been moving in his heart was gone now; that light and the cloud staircase were nowhere to be found.

After his siesta, Wu Baoguo came again to the foot of the tree and called out to Aqing in a loud voice. Aqing did not move a muscle. Wu left, cursing.

Aqing's grandmother moved a little stool over, sat underneath the tree, and once again recounted her lifetime of bitterness to her beloved grandson.

The people there for the market and the gawkers all

dispersed sometime after noon. Underneath the scholar tree there was nobody but Aqing's solitary grandmother, and Aqing himself.

As evening was coming on, Achang arrived underneath the tree and scurried up it, shouting to Aqing to look at the clouds, it was like they were on fire. Aqing still did not move an inch. Aqing's eyes were closed, he was lying flat on his back, the green branches next to the door were reaching out towards his face and body, as if they were covering him up. Achang gave Aqing a push, and Aqing still did not move. Achang let out a yell.

———

The adults who climbed the tree tried to pick Aqing up and carry him down, but it was impossible to lift him. Thin, soft twigs encircled him, binding him to the door, and there was a small, lively green seedling coming out of his mouth, sticking its head out perkily for a look around. His body was covered with mould, and tender grasses were sprouting out of the mould, also a crisp, fresh, bright green.

Aqing had become a tree boy.

Wu Baoguo called the basket crane in again and had Aqing and the door brought down together and sent to Yizhi's clinic. Yizhi put a hand on Aqing's forehead, and exclaimed, "Gracious, such a high fever." He quickly put Aqing on a drip, and said to Aqing's grandmother and

Yang Xiuju, who were crying themselves into fits, "Aqing was born to live, he won't die."

In the middle of the night, Aqing's eyes opened. He looked at the people around him, and at the furious Wu Zhenzhong, but before Wu Zhenzhong had a chance to open his mouth and start to scold him, he said, "Dad, I want to go to school."

From then on Aqing became a good student, diligent, mature and polite.

———

This was all twenty years ago. These days, the people from beside the old scholar tree are still living happily. The old scholar tree has gone, but when locals talk about this part of town they always say, go to the place with the old scholar tree.

Aqing's grandmother is over eighty now, half crippled and confused. At noon on summer days, Wu Zhenzhong will push her in her wheelchair to the pavilion in the square. The aunties and uncles all around still bring their bowls to the pavilion to sit and eat their lunch, and the children race about and play nearby. They continue to look for ant holes among the newly planted trees. When autumn comes, the concrete is covered with golden corn drying in the sun, from one side of the square to the other, filling every crack and corner, piled up thick and deep. When the sun shines down, it genuinely is a golden world. Every autumn, Aqing's mother Yang Xiuju engages in any number of open and covert struggles with the neighbours in order to win herself space on this square.

Aqing went south to work and found a wife there. He comes back just once a year, at most.

On the rare occasions when he does return, his befuddled grandmother collars Aqing's wife, holds on to her like grim death and tells her the story of when Aqing went up into the tree.

"Ah, you don't know, that year Aqing took leave of his senses and climbed up the tree, jumping about all over the place, calling out cloud, cloud, he wanted to run after the clouds, and he nearly couldn't get back down again, his bottom burst into flower, my lovely grandson was turning into a monster, I cried every day, burned incense and prayed, 'Bodhisattva Guanyin, Old Man Heaven, spare our Aqing'."

This was already the hundredth telling from the grandmother, different every occasion, this time there was the new detail added of the bottom and the flowers.

When Aqing heard this, he got irritated. "Gran, when have I ever had flowers on my bum?"

Aqing's grandmother said to his wife, "He did, they were there, I saw the shoots growing from his bottom, even his shit turned into flowers."

Aqing's grandmother pointed to a scholar tree growing in the yard, with a trunk as thick as a rice bowl, and said to Aqing's wife, "Just you look at that, this is the tree that grew out of Aqing's bum. We used to have a dungheap here, I planted the sapling in the dungheap and it thrived.

Aqing doesn't come home to see me now, and so I look at the tree, crying and crying, my darling grandson, you don't come back to see me, you're ignoring your conscience, if it wasn't for me, who knows where your soul would be now."

Aqing was horribly embarrassed, both angry and upset. "Gran, I never ate any seeds from the scholar tree, how could they grow out of me?"

His grandmother pursed her lips and did not look at Aqing, just scrunched up her eyes and looked at Aqing's wife.

From nearby, Aqing's wife gave a secret smile and said in her soft, southern-accented voice, "Oh Grandma, pay no attention to him, you just keep talking, I want to listen."

2

Drifting

AT FIVE O'CLOCK, light crept into the sky.

Yizhi, the doctor, pushed open his heavy iron door and saw the wheelchair again by the side of the road, and the old woman in the wheelchair. The doctor felt irritated and upset. The fixed smile on the old woman's face made the skin on his scalp crawl, so he walked over, pulled the wheelchair onto the street from its crack in the paving stones and gave it a sharp shove in the direction of the crossroads. The wheelchair skimmed ahead for some distance, then came to a stop in front of the doorway of Zhang Wu, who sold hot pepper soup.

The previous evening, the doctor's wife had driven the doctor out into the little shed in their front yard, saying that from now on she wanted to sleep in peace, and she did not intend to put up with any more of his nonsense. It wasn't just that he got up at half past four every morning, it was like someone had injected him full of chicken blood, waddling around the place with his bum sticking out, singing and prancing about in the yard, making it impossible for anyone in the family to sleep.

The weather was hot. The cool breeze blowing from the Tuan River had ceased by about one or two o'clock in the morning, and the landscape released all the heat that it had absorbed in the day, unchanged, until the bricks and tiles, the new saplings planted in the street and the rubbish on the ground were all hot and steaming. The flies and mosquitoes of Wu Town, all linked together and yet independent, hung motionless in space, seemingly stuck fast in the gooey air. It made an insomniac like the doctor even more fretful, restless and ill-tempered. His brain was spinning at ten thousand revolutions per minute, the air was full of dust, and any movement would set his sweat flowing and soak his singlet.

The door of Zhang Wu's house was already open, and his junior assistant was already at work. By half past six, he would have had to make up all the dough for the oil flatbreads and set it out to rest, chop the wood-ear fungus and needle fungus that had been put to soak the previous night, slice the strips of dough for the soup and knead more dough, prepare the stove and boil the water. All of this had to be done ready for Zhang Wu, who got out of bed at six to carry out the final stages.

When he saw the wheelchair at his door, the assistant ran over and pushed the wheelchair on again, to stop at the gate of the vet Liu Rongyao, next door.

This was an old road that ran right the way through

the town from north to south; another road went from east to west, forming a large, wide crossroads that marked the centre of Wu Town. On the four sides of the crossroads were the big corner building, the post office, the tobacco dealer, the granary, the old Muslim restaurant, the noodle seller, then farther on again, on both sides of the street, were rows of residential buildings. A distance of twenty metres separated these buildings from the road, and this empty ground became the prime location for setting up stalls.

Shortly after six o'clock, Wu Town gradually became more lively. First, it was the sounds of every household opening the front gate, splashing out water to lay the dust, sweeping the ground and frying food, and the rattle of stalls being moved outside. After that came the putt-putting of three-wheeled tractors, motorbikes and trucks laden with goods, coming from miles around to the market at Wu Town. It was starting to be a proper, noisy market day.

The broad crossroads had now narrowed. Every stall owner did their utmost to be as close to the inner part of the road as possible. Some three-wheelers simply pushed their way through, while a few unloaded their goods onto the ground and took possession of the centre of the cross-roads. There were stalls selling vegetables, seasonings or flatbreads, while others sold hardware, clothes, knitting wool or second-hand books. Some sold only fruits from the south, like mangoes and pineapples, while others sold seasonal fruit: plums, peaches and pears. Any long-term resident of Wu Town would become very familiar with these people. That man with a limp had changed from a delicate-faced, melancholy young man who mended shoes outside the corner building at the crossroads. Now, still melancholy and silent, he was no longer delicate-featured, only his shoe-mending machine remained the same, like a centuries-old demon, unchanging and eternal. The younger daughter of the Wang family, locked in a sustained conflict with her own daughter-in-law, had given up the chance to go to live in the big city with her daughter in order to guard her two pear trees and cherry trees. Every summer she sold her big green pears and yellow cherries at the market in Wu Town.

The people from East Village came riding in on three-wheeled tractors and set up their stalls on the southern branch of the crossroads. Every summer they became part of the Wu Town landscape. East Village was situated on low-lying land, the one place that was sure to see floods every summer, and the village had been relocated several times because of this. One year, someone in the township government had proclaimed this place ideal for planting plums. Flooding does not bother plum trees, they have a high production rate and mature quickly, they would be sure to make a success of it. So plums were brought in as a road to prosperity for East Village. Several years passed, and acres of plums ripened, but they could not find a buyer. The residents of East Village cursed the heavens and the Earth, but they did not have the heart to cut down trees heavy with hanging fruit, so every market day they would haul in a cartload to sell. When they left in the afternoon, they gave away what they could not sell and threw away the rest, determined not to bring a single one back home.

A line of bicycles and motorbikes of every shape and colour came snaking their way up the long slope that led to the river, climbing the steep incline to the north of the village and into the town. Most of these people were women whose husbands worked away from home, left behind to look after their elderly relations and children. Every second day was market day, and on these days, they would comb their hair and make up their faces, arrange to meet others like them, and come bright and early to Wu Town, bringing their children. There they would eat a bowl or two of hot pepper soup and a few sticks of fried dough, then go for a stroll and a look at the shops. At one or two in the afternoon, they would buy a bunch or two of greens, or perhaps a bottle or two of cosmetics or nothing at all, after which they would ride their bikes back home, to come again the day after next.

Around noon, more and more cars started coming down from the highway, but they were forced to plunge into a sea of people and objects. Not only was it impossible to go against the direction of traffic, but even in single file the way was still frequently blocked by a motorbike or bicycle. The driver in the car would hoot frantically on his horn, but the person on the motorbike would carry right on, unhurriedly picking over the goods, asking questions and gossiping.

————

A burst of urgent, sonorous blasts of a car's horn rang out powerfully in the space above Wu Town. It seemed like the sound had jolted Wu Town's background cacophony of honking horns into an abrupt silence. On the ground, the sounds of conversation and sellers calling their wares all fell silent, as if a celestial being had pointed a finger at them, freezing them there in an instant. A hush descended on the whole street market. The doctor, who was on the point of inserting the needle for a drip into a patient, was startled into immobility by this silence. He briefly cocked an ear to listen, put down the needle he was holding, rushed out of the clinic and looked over towards the crossroads.

In the exact centre of the crossroads, the old woman in the wheelchair had come to a halt. The doctor had forgotten about her. It was already six or seven hours since he had pushed her to Zhang Wu's door, and she had only travelled about a hundred metres. She had stopped at the doctor's door and the doctor had pushed her to Zhang Wu's door. Zhang Wu in turn had pushed her to the vet's house, the vet again had pushed her back to Zhang Wu's house, and Zhang Wu had pushed her to the other side of the street. In that way, step by step, by some unknown process, the wheelchair had arrived at the exact centre of the crossroads.

A perfect, empty circle had formed around the old woman, leaving her centre stage. On the face crisscrossed with wrinkles was a childish and unknowing smile; the combination of the wrinkles and the childishness made the smile both ugly and forlorn. Her head was twisted to her left shoulder, and a constant thread of crystalline drool flowed from her half-open mouth to hang in mid-air, endlessly replenished. Two turns of thick rope had been passed from the back of the chair to the front and tied in a knot at the left side of the old woman's waist, linking her body and the wheelchair firmly together. On the right side of the wheelchair hung a transparent urine bag with some yellow liquid already inside. The old woman had been dressed in a red shirt and pyjama bottoms with a pattern of small flowers; cheap clothing, but not completely dirty.

This sudden arrival of the wheelchair, coming from nowhere and with nowhere to go, was like a ghost abruptly appearing in the centre of the road.

A weak, mournful cry broke the momentary silence. That cry was frail and thin, tremulous, full of a heart-piercing pain, like a child abandoned by its mother, like a little bird separated from the flock. It was as if a great hammer were swinging down on a life already hanging by a thread, ready to dash out its brains. A second cry followed, then a third, piercing the hearts of everyone in the market. As if they had suddenly been startled into wakefulness, the people were assailed by a strange sorrow and fear that seemed to come from a deep, dark pit. It was like they were hearing the voice of their own fate.

The old woman seemed to have arrived here, inexplicably parked in the centre of the road, blocking all routes, north, south, east and west, causing time to stop, seemingly just so that they could hear a series of plaintive cries.

In what might have been no more than an unconscious hint, people realised that the old woman's neck was pointing to the left, and their eyes turned to follow it. This was the front left corner of the crossroads, where a long row of mutton stalls was set up by the roadside.

One of the mutton stalls protruded into the middle of the road. Two sheep were already hanging from a frame; one was dangling downwards with blood flowing over its head, the other one had been skinned, and the butcher was gutting it. Behind the stall was a basic space for slaughter and there was a sheep with all four feet trussed together. The mutton seller pushed down its head and tried to drag it to the other side of the slaughtering area, where another sheep had already fallen with its eyes still open and blood pouring from its slit throat. The dark blood flooded the ground, accumulating in layers, where it coagulated and solidified, like an oil painting, piled up layer upon layer, the differently coloured deposits over time lending variety to its textures. Ropes, bowls, knives and all kinds of implements spattered with blood, stood out from all that blood colour, making the flat surface three-dimensional and adding realism.

The plaintive cries of the sheep that was pinned to the ground were just like the sad wails of a child. It was struggling, unwilling to go where its comrade had fallen, its sturdy, rounded stomach rising and falling with the effort. The mutton seller's only option was to release it and go to deal with the sheep that was bleeding out. The sheep that had been struggling raised its head and looked over the crowd. Tears welled up in its grey-brown eyes and slowly flowed out to settle in the corners of its eyes.

The mutton seller came over from behind, pushed down the sheep's head with his hand, raised his knife, took aim at the sheep's neck and drove his knife inwards and upwards from below. The sheep let out a short cry and collapsed into the mass of thick, accumulated blood.

A shocked "Oh!" came from the awning of the old Muslim restaurant opposite, followed by the sound of something shattering on the ground. A girl was standing in front of a small table, both hands still in the shape of the bowl she had been holding, evidently having witnessed the scene opposite. Her grey-brown eyes reflected that fallen sheep and the dripping knife in the hands of the butcher.

To the right of the old woman, a black Toyota Land Cruiser was weaving its way erratically forward. Sellers of rat poison, windmills, steamed meat dumplings and clothes, and the shopkeepers whose storefronts looked onto the street, had all set out their goods in the middle of the road. In front and behind, to the left and to the right, there were people pushing motorbikes, bicycles and freight tricycles to the market. The young driver had stuck his head out of the Land Cruiser and was asking people who were moving from east to west about the conditions of the road ahead. The passers-by laughed loudly and said, "You've gone down a dead end, mate."

The Land Cruiser was trapped in the centre of the

road, squeezed in there like a useless, monstrous beast, making the road even more unbearably crowded. In front was a slightly arched bridge. From the base of the bridge to the top was nothing but clothes sellers, who had set up long, broad temporary stalls, leaving a width of just two or three metres in the centre of the bridge.

There was no hope of getting over the bridge. The driver made up his mind to turn into the residential area via a narrow street before the bridge. At the turn-off by the wall, a three-wheeled freight tricycle was blocking the way. Two big strips of reinforced steel had been welded onto the bed of the tricycle and were sticking out a long way, meaning that the Land Cruiser was bound to get scraped. The young driver sat in his Land Cruiser and called out to the girl sitting on the tricycle to shift it in a little. The girl was about twelve or thirteen, with a ruddy, healthy face, but she was slumped with her head up against the wall and her hands over her face, eyes half closed, and she did not say a word. The driver got out and explained to the girl several times what he was trying to do, but she still said nothing at all. A man and a woman also got out of the car, fashionably dressed but speaking in Wu Town dialect. The young woman smiled at the girl and asked if her parents had gone to sell things at the market, whether she was worried that they might be bad people and what village she was from, and she named their own home village. The young girl still did not move, speak to them, look at them or listen to them.

Next to the narrow street at the base of the bridge

was a stall with a moveable rack for clothes, held in place with stones to stop it from sliding away, and two big rocks that further shrank the turning space on the corner. The fat stallholder had been watching the people in the car and the young girl the whole time with cold eyes, shaking her head, a look of disdain on her face. But when the young driver and the man and woman from the car walked over, hoping she would help out by moving the stones for a moment, she promptly turned her back on them, walked to the other side and remained there, unmoving.

The three of them stood like stones in the centre of the road, shaking their heads helplessly at the crowd of interested onlookers that surrounded them. They combined their strength to pick up the young girl's freight tricycle, but it did not move an inch. The girl stayed exactly where she was.

The young driver stamped his foot, got into the car, turned on the engine, revved the motor and, honking his horn furiously, turned the car to the left and advanced. The two steel spikes on the freight tricycle embedded themselves in the left door of the car with pinpoint accuracy, inscribing two shockingly white tracks in a line all the way down to the tail. The onlookers cried out in shock, "Stop, stop, you'll get spiked." The driver turned a deaf ear and drove straight on through. Once he was past the turning place he disappeared into the residential area in a cloud of smoke.

The old woman in the middle of the crossroads still

had her face fixed in that smile, staring innocently and unknowingly at this crowd, and the whole world.

A man on a three-wheeler came over from the other side of the road. The wheelchair was blocking his way, so he pushed it aside on his way past. The wheelchair rolled to the left, right over to beneath the rack where the sheep were hanging. The butcher who was chopping the meat put out his hand and gave it a push, and the wheelchair rolled onto the turning place by the corner building, which was the territory of Wu Town's resident tramp.

Activity resumed in the street. The buying and selling started up again, the trucks began honking their horns again, as they slowly inched their way forward. The mutton seller hauled over another sheep, the young girl served herself another bowl of rice, turned her back to the street and started to eat.

The doctor turned and said to the onlooking neighbours beside him, "Heh, every day it's like this, sooner or later the time will come when the whole street is jammed solid with cars. Just look at it, scarcely a day goes by without several traffic jams, or dozens of them." The doctor returned to his clinic and resumed treating his patient.

———

By two or three o'clock in the afternoon, the stallholders had silently disappeared, as abruptly as they had arrived.

Wu Town was deserted, seeped in the peace that follows frenetic activity, and in hollowed-out exhaustion.

The doctor sat at his counter in front of the computer, chatting online as he watched a TV serial. The card room at the teahouse behind the clinic was doing a roaring trade, where a hard-fought card game was reaching its climax. It was already clear who were the winners and losers, but at this moment nobody could be the first to leave. It would not show a proper spirit for the winners to leave first, and the losers were reluctant to go.

Dequan came out of the coal yard after a morning shovelling coal, carrying a fertiliser bag that seemingly had never left his side for the last sixty years. He walked along in the shade of the street, his head lowered, moving silently forward, one step at a time. He did not demand alcohol at the doorway of his cousin the doctor's clinic, nor did he go to the door of the canteen to ask for steamed bread or soup, nor did he stop by Huanli's Cosmetics shop to look at the plump beauty Huanli. He knew that at this time everybody was drowsy and sluggish, and in no mood to deal with him. This poor man, whose brain had been damaged in a drowning, was short and skinny, with a face like a fossil, permeated with a toughness born of years of suffering. Only his eyes moved around nimbly from side to side, searching the ground for anything he could pick up. He had been wandering Wu Town for decades, begging for food, doing odd jobs, sleeping in haystacks, at the foot of walls, in the square or by the riverbank, with no fixed abode, and yet the whole time he had survived in good health.

The market street had emptied, the voices had fallen silent, and the sky had darkened. The dazzling white of the street was becoming soft and gentle, and the piles of rubbish on both sides of the road became a series of vague mounds in the twilight.

A fresh breeze blew over from the slope leading down to the Tuan River, blowing away the stagnant, stifling heat of the daytime. Cooking smoke rose, and people turned their empty, dry, swollen eyes away from the street and back to their homes, as they began to pack up and sweep up in preparation for supper.

After six o'clock, Dequan was already on his way back from the riverside, the bag in his hands filled with rubbish of all kinds. He sat down in his accustomed spot and began to sort the rubbish into categories, carefully, painstakingly and thoroughly. A while later, his white-haired old mother came to bring him a meal. The fat beauty Huanli had washed her face and was now painting her eyebrows and powdering her face behind the counter. Her Lothario of a husband would be coming back soon after loafing around the streets all day. The doctor was waddling about with his bum right out again, humming a little tune, busy at the stove. Every day at this time he was happy and cheerful, but also ashamed and full of self-loathing. He harboured hopes that one day he would be able to present his wife with a big handful of cash. But all the secret little deals he had made had failed one after the other, all suffering from an excess of poetic feeling and a lack of forethought and organisation. The loss, pain and financial woes he was currently suffering were common knowledge. His wife was always the last person to know he had run up another huge debt.

Several children in brand new clothes came charging up through Wu Town from the old street, pushing the wheelchair. They had applied a heavy layer of cosmetics to the old woman's face. Her cheeks were a brilliant red, there was thick white powder round her eyes, and a dirty cabbage leaf was tied on top of her head. Accompanied by that naive smile, she was like a ludicrous, tragic clown. They were pushing the wheelchair, passing it back and forth. The chair would roll forwards at top speed, the old woman's body leaning back as if she was about to fall, but each time she somehow came through safe and sound.

A passing adult who knew one of these children asked curiously, Who's that? The child replied that they didn't know, but that they'd found her over there. He pointed at the street behind him as if the old woman had been born out of the empty darkness there.

One of the children took a big chunk of steamed bread and stuffed it into the old woman's half-open mouth. The bread got stuck in her mouth, the old woman could neither swallow it, nor spit it out. The children stuffed it in again, hard, the old woman's mouth bulged out like a ball, choked up. Her eyes looked like they were about to pop out, and tears were forced out by the pressure. The children were getting frightened, so they worked at her face with their fingers, patted her cheeks, reached into her mouth to fish it out, and then slapped her hard on the back. A larger child caught hold of the old woman's neck and raised it repeatedly, hoping to force the bread out. Several other children swung her arms and legs about, stretching them out in different directions. At one moment, the old woman's head was being swung back and forth, at the next it was being dragged around like a criminal at a public sentencing, and her face was in total disarray from their pulling and pushing.

The rope that had tied down the old woman all this time suddenly slipped down, and her body went limp and slumped forwards. Her head descended with force to her knees, and the bread trapped in her throat was spat out. The frightened children standing in front of her instinctively caught the old woman's body as she fell, while other children dragged her roughly back onto the wheelchair. Some others found some rope and tied the old woman back down. After half an hour's work her chest, waist and legs had been lashed securely with many different coloured ropes, like sticky rice bound up in lotus leaves for the Dragon Boat Festival.

Cheerfulness descended again. The children clustered round like soldiers around a general, pushing the wheelchair, carrying the urine bag, walking through the streets in the dust, exceptionally pleased with themselves.

They went back to their game of rolling the wheelchair along. A tall, clever, assertive child in a red T-shirt and jeans, and wearing a silver chain, was the leader of this pack of children. He directed the game and chose the steersman, and he allowed no challenges to his authority. He ordered his young companions to stand at the other side of the turn in the road, and he passed the old woman over from the other side. He boasted that he could make the wheelchair roll in a parabolic trajectory, like the bullets in gangster movies. He moved several paces away from the back of the chair, stopped, spat on his hands, took a run-up and pushed the wheelchair, hard. The wheelchair deviated from its course with the strength of his hard push and careered crookedly towards the edge of the road, where it hit a protruding stone, causing the wheelchair to overturn and fall on the other side of the stone. Even then the old woman did not separate from the wheelchair. It was strapped firmly to her body, as firmly as a turtle to its shell.

The children on both sides of the road were open-mouthed, immobile, shocked at this sudden accident. Several minutes passed, or perhaps just a few seconds, then a short boy suddenly burst into tears and ran back home, crying out repeatedly for his mother. Several more children started to cry, a heartrending sound, as though they had been victimised in the worst way in the world, or encountered the worst possible pain. The ringleader child was there on the other side of the street the whole time, staring blankly at the wheelchair. On seeing his companions leave one by one, he too glanced instinctively towards his home, but he didn't dare move.

Night was approaching, and Wu Town was quiet and still, cool and refreshing. From time to time one or two pedestrians would cross over the street, indistinct in the dusk. By the roadside, lights went on in house after house, sending out curved yellow haloes into all the courtyards, crowds of flying insects came in pursuit of the lamplight and flew and danced dizzyingly under the lamps.

One of the braver children slowly walked up to the wheelchair and squatted down, picking up a stick to poke the old woman. He gestured to his companions to approach. Under the dishevelled hair covered with dust, the old woman's eyes were still open, and that naive smile was still there on her face, but now a patch of skin had been scraped away from one cheek, and a layer of thick drops of blood was seeping out.

The ringleader boy's eyes were hazy, like he was on the verge of tears, but there was a hint of melancholy and darkness there too. He mutely obeyed the orders of the other children. Turning the wheelchair over, they found the urine bag which had flown out and put it back in place. The old woman, her head hanging, was now sitting securely in the chair again, facing the empty space, smiling naively and unknowingly.

There was no debate, there were no farewells, there were no plans made by the children to meet to play again tomorrow. The children turned round and headed off in the direction of home, their small shapes moving slowly and heavily in the dusk. That older child who had once been their leader was hanging his head, a vulnerability and weary depression about him, as if he had suddenly become old before his time.

But as soon as they left the turn in the street, as soon as they left the old woman's line of sight, they broke into a run. Home was getting closer and closer, their steps became lighter and lighter, and everything became happy and bright once more.

———

At about five in the morning, as the doctor was preparing to open the metal door, he saw the wheelchair and the old woman again, still wearing that flowered shirt and flowered trousers. It was as if she had always been there, as if that period of time in which she had disappeared had been lost to him forever. If the old woman had not turned up again, the doctor would have completely forgotten that she had not appeared for over a month. He would never have known that he had possessed that time.

That's just the way life is. There are certain things, images or people, for which neither their presence nor their loss has any significance, they just drift meaninglessly through time and space. But they are still there, they have always been there, from the start right through to the finish. This makes us despair, but it also becomes a symbol that life continues to go on, reminding us that we often look on the passing of time and life and forget what it is we are seeing.

Autumn was approaching, the grapes in the courtyard were withering before the fruit was ripe. The mynah bird had died without speaking a single sentence, and Dequan was still going in and out of the coal yard every day with his sack. The doctor's wife had agreed to let him back to sleep in the bedroom, and for him to get up at half past four in the morning, so long as he didn't make a sound. But if the doctor did not make a sound, and did not let his wife know that he was getting up so early, what was the point in getting up that early anyway? The doctor had never thought that after several days had passed, he would find himself accustomed to getting up in silence. He got up and sat by himself in the yard, alone, sunk deep in his own thoughts, there was nobody in the world but him. He felt a sudden freedom and release, and realised how ridiculous all those years of foolish thoughts about his wife had been.

3

The Holy Man, Dequan

H E HAD SET HIMSELF IN READINESS to appear out of nowhere when needed, as if falling from the sky.

That was a night to make you shiver. In the moonlight, Wu Town was dim, quiet and still. The summer wind blew away some of the fierce, dry heat of the daytime. There was a faint smell of rottenness on the wind, fermented out of the daily life of Wu Town. Deep or shallow breathing; the heavy scent of stewing meat; offal, rotting vegetables, fruit and dung discarded in corners of the street, an abundance of germs and bacteria carried in from miles around on people's bodies, all came together to form a complicated, ambiguous atmosphere. You could not call it a bad smell; one might even recollect it with fondness. The moon rose very high. Looking down from the terrace of the hospital, the wide patch of interlinked shadows was cast by the wood on the banks of the Tuan

River. You could hear the sound of the water flowing from within the wood. To the left was Wu Town's exercise ground, which for centuries had been the final destination of condemned criminals. It was set deep into the steep slope that led to the river, as if to prevent the ghosts of all those who had been executed from climbing out.

Two youngsters from Wu Town, fifteen-year-old Haihong and eighteen-year-old Qingfei, were meeting on the hospital veranda. Haihong was bent backwards, as if she was about to fold up on the ground. She was clutching at Qingfei with both hands, yet it seemed like she was trying to escape, though in an unfixed, hesitant way. Their mouths were stuck together but the top halves of their faces seemed to be fighting to get free. Haihong's eyes would close for a while and then open vacantly. There was no way of knowing if this was caused by suffering and martyrdom or pleasurable intoxication. Qingfei was bearing downwards with his whole body, his lips stubbornly exploring those of the girl.

At the other end of the veranda, a black shadow was coming into view up the stairs, step by step, until at last it climbed onto the veranda and came to a halt there. This figure had its back to the moonlight, gaunt, ramrod straight, clad in a long gown, one hand holding a book, half raised, the other hand hanging down motionless. It seemed solemn and dignified, and also a little unnerving.

There he was, just like he had fallen out of the sky, paused there, frozen in mid-frame. He came down the stairs and walked over to Haihong and Qingfei, step by step, the moonlight casting a long black shadow on the ground, which came closer and closer, throwing its shade over the striving couple.

Caught up in feelings that no words could describe, Haihong suddenly saw an arrow-straight shape behind Qingfei. She could not see the person's face clearly, but she could distinguish the outline of his unkempt hair and the stern angles of his face, and she could sense his air of danger and sanctity. Haihong opened her mouth wide, her mind was a blank, but her heart was calling out to him, "Holy man, holy man". Haihong did not know where this form of address had come to her from. She did not know what a holy man was like, or what they did, but when she saw that erect, stern shadow she called it "holy man" straight from the deep places of her heart.

Qingfei, sensing that Haihong's defence was stalling and pressing home his advantage, looked round to see that a great black shadow had already engulfed his head. He let out a cry of horror, released Haihong and fled at an unbelievable speed.

The holy man took Haihong's hand, as if he was leading a little lamb that had lost its way. She followed obediently, shaking all over with a mixture of terror and shock, and yet at the same time possessed with a mysterious calm and submissiveness. He escorted her home with the ease of one very familiar with the route, evidently knowing precisely where she lived. Haihong asked no questions, she was too shocked to speak. After that, the holy man departed.

Haihong lay on her bed and very soon fell fast asleep. In her dreams she saw someone push open the window, walk directly up to her and stretch out a hand. She cried out, and the person fell from the window.

———

Dequan sat with crossed legs and a straight back, leaning into a nook of the big corner building, a wholesale market for clothes, closing his eyes to restore his spirit. His face was pallid and translucent. His thick hair was twisted up onto the top of his head, like a mass of madly dancing jet-black serpents, revealing the lack of tranquillity in his heart. That long robe, which might have been either a rain-coat or an overcoat, hung loose on him, almost concealing his entire body, but from its outline his huge bones and frame could be seen. There he sat, his whole body emitting a dark odour of mystery.

Surrounding him, in his two square metre space in the corner building, were stacked pile after pile of wastepaper, scrap metal, plastic bottles and beer bottles, all sorted by type, neat and tidy. Dequan sat in the centre of this rubbish like a king. Shortly after five o'clock in the afternoon, now the Wu Town market was over and the tide of people had receded from the streets, the sun would lose its strength somewhat, and Dequan would slowly arise from his domain and begin his work. He would start from the crossroads at the town centre opposite the corner building, keeping his back to the sun, and go into Wu Town following the old street, then turn right to climb the big slope that led down to the river, heading south. Finally, he would return once more to his domain. Along the way he would keep searching: plastic bottles from rubbish bins, plastic bags discarded on the ground, broken cardboard boxes piled at the corners of the street, strips of old cloth, all these were the targets of his scavenging. Dequan moved along, looking to the left and to the right. He would stoop to brush the dust off an article and place it in the cloth sack he carried with him, with easy, unhurried, solemn movements. His eyes were always lowered, he would not raise them to look at any person, as though he was walking through empty space.

Sure enough, this was Dequan, the famous tramp of Wu Town. But to call him a tramp would not be quite correct. He did not have the luggage that a true tramp would carry with him. He only had a book, half its edges curled up, old and ragged. His complexion showed clear signs of poor nutrition and semi-starvation, yet he still radiated the calm of those who need never worry about their next meal or how to clothe themselves. If an outsider who had found their way into Wu Town happened to see this man, they would be drawn to his mixture of the rootless exile of a vagrant and the unruffled calm of a homeowner, and they would notice to their surprise that when a ray of sun happened to shine upon the body of this tramp, his eyes would blink rapidly in what appeared to be extreme discomfort.

At noon and dusk every day, a white-haired old lady would appear on the streets of Wu Town carrying a lunch box and appear in front of Dequan, whose eyes were closed. Whenever there was a rainstorm in summer or heavy snow in winter, people lounging at the counter cracking melon seeds or sitting around the fire chatting idly would see Dequan's white-haired old widowed mother standing in the rain or the snow, calling out over and over again, "Dequan, Dequan, it's snowing [or raining] so hard, let's go back home."

Dequan's eyes were shut tight, and he did not utter a sound. The old widow would stand in front of her son for some time, wiping away tears, then get out the lunch box concealed in her clothing, set it down on the ground, and take away the rubbish and scrap Dequan had collected. People had seen her change from a graceful, lovely, seductive widow into a dull-eyed old woman, as they had seen the pitiless passing of time, carved on the streets of Wu Town and this woman's body.

———

For twenty years and more, Dequan had always been leaning up against this corner building until he became a part of it, a patch of fixed black shadow, a lump of psoriasis that could not be removed, a protuberance that people neither needed nor objected to. Pedestrians passed by him on the corner and no longer gave him a second look. They knew that his name was Dequan, but it was like they did not know it and had forgotten him entirely. But when they did chance to see the tall, bulky, pallid, empty form of Dequan wandering through Wu Town like a sleepwalker, they would experience a feeling of shock and awe.

Dequan's mother had once been a loose widow, famous in Wu Town, and she lived in its oldest street. That street was still paved with greenstone flags, run-down, narrow and winding. On both sides of the street were houses with mud walls and old-fashioned dark roof tiles, low and rickety, pitch-black inside. Every household had a rectangular open stall for goods in front of the door, set out with dried fruit, sugar beans, fried peanuts, tins of congee and a quantity of other oddly-shaped items accumulated over many years. Haihong had never seen a customer at any of these stalls and could not recall seeing anybody refresh any of the food products either. The faces of the people beside the stalls were blurred, as if they had existed for centuries, never dying and never having lived.

When she was young, Dequan's mother's good looks had drawn the attention of passers-by towards this dark, gloomy old street. Dequan's mother was an outsider in Wu Town, having married into this street, which was even more backward and lonely than her own remote home village. Dequan's father, a silent man, had died unexpectedly at thirty, leaving behind this widow and orphan. Soon afterwards, Dequan's mother opened up the side gate of her house and started to take in men, who climbed up there from the little hill covered with thorny bushes. Residents saw Dequan growing taller every day, and how he kept his mouth tightly shut and his eyes lowered; every day he would leave his house and walk to the school, and then walk back home again.

In the year when Dequan had his incident, his mother first went everywhere to burn incense and pray to the Buddha, bringing monks back home to read the scriptures and perform exorcisms, and she visited a holy mountain to pray to the Land God, the spirit of the hero Guan Yu and to her earliest ancestor, kowtowing and making intercessions to them. She brought a fat mendicant Daoist priest with his hair in a top knot to stay in the house, hoping he would draw her son out of his deep sleep. Dequan just sat wordlessly in a corner of the house. It was only at noontime when the sunlight shone in through the door that he would show some sign of movement, blinking his eyes and shifting himself over to a darker corner.

Someone said to Dequan's mother, "The Buddha and the Bodhisattva Guanyin can't save your son, only Jesus can." So Dequan's mother started to believe in Jesus. She took herself all over the place, singing hymns, studying the Bible. After six months, a dozen or so sisters from the church started to save Dequan's lost soul. Every evening they would gather at Dequan's home, praying, confessing, singing hymns, doing Bible study, witnessing, and every evening Dequan's mother would cry herself breathless and fall asleep praying and hoping. She became enraptured by the effect this had on her soul: in the midst of her weeping, her soul was washed clean and strengthened. She broke off with her fancy men and devoted all her heart and will to saving Dequan.

Dequan sat in the shadows, nobody saw his twitching eyes and quivering flesh. After he had stopped going to school, he sat in that corner of the house the whole time, refusing to leave or speak with anyone. He was scared of sunlight, scared of any light. That mad sunlight was everywhere, there was nowhere for him to hide. His mother's weeping, her hysterical outpourings, passed through his brain in fits and starts and made him crazy and fearful, just like the sunlight did. A humming noise circled around his ears, like the sharp sting of a bee, constantly pricking his eardrums with a pain that was hard to endure and at the same time incomparably, strangely, unbearably itchy.

One night, through the stubborn chaos of his mind, Dequan happened to hear his mother recite from the Bible in her weepy, confessional voice: *The light of the body is the eye: if therefore thine eye be single, thy whole body shall be full of light. But if thine eye be evil, thy whole body shall be full of darkness. If therefore the light that is in thee be darkness, how great is that darkness!* As if he had been granted divine inspiration, suddenly there was light in Dequan's brain. He saw, in the darkness, the light radiating out from his body, illuminating the street, the trees, the houses and all things in the world.

Dequan stood up, grabbed a copy of the Bible and walked out of the house. From that day, he never went home again. In the daytime he lowered his eyes, watching people moving about, arguing and talking in Wu Town's remote, grey haze, as if they were all pulled by invisible strings, playing their parts in a drab, uniform performance. He could hear the whispered secrets in every family; he could see the people inside every house and all their secrets.

Every Saturday, come rain or shine, Wanmin from the Hai family would stealthily sneak out from the north end of the village and set off on his bicycle to meet his long-time lover, Aju. Shortly afterwards, grunting and wheezing could be heard from the photographer's studio at the far end of the village. And on that same evening, Wanmin's wife invariably went to the neighbours' house to play mah-jong.

He saw the young girl Haihong in the first awakenings of love wandering around in Liangguang's family vegetable patch at dusk, and he saw Qingfei's lovelorn gaze pursuing Haihong from a distance. That summer, Qingfei had come back to Wu Town after a spell working outside, and he could see something new in Qingfei's eyes: a hint of reckless lust. And Haihong did not know that danger was already silently approaching.

He saw the residents of Wu Town cast aside the shells that covered their bodies during the day, their spirits awakening as they threw all their energy into things they would never do in daylight, with a purity of heart they could never aspire to by day. The night-time Wu Town was real and true, full of desire and restless movement.

He loved the furtive lovers, the tramps, drunks and the

late stop-outs hurrying about their business, he even liked the night-time version of the big-bottomed Caihong. Dequan detested that bottom; it was coarse, bloodthirsty, radiating naked fleshly desire. But once evening came, that handsome husband of hers returned home from putting it about all over town, and light and life would come into Caihong's eyes. He saw her intoxicated eyes.

He could clearly distinguish the whispered secret words in the deep places under every roof; he could tell from a woman's voice whose family she belonged to; he could distinguish which married couple the sounds of lovemaking came from; he could hear whether it was Auntie Wu beating her grandchildren or Auntie Li beating hers, and he could hear from the crying which grandchild it was. He could clearly distinguish any strange voices that had entered Wu Town, and he secretly followed those strange voices. He had seen a murderer who had horrified the whole country, killing people all along his route, incomparably cruel and merciless. In the darkness, Dequan at a glance saw the fear and terror in his heart: that man had killed out of fear and was fearful because he had killed. He walked out of Wu Town, never breaking stride, and never saw Dequan and all the light that was radiating from his body.

A crowd of drunken youths from outside the village were laughing loudly on the streets of Wu Town, taking liberties with a young girl who was passing by. Dequan recognised the girl as the daughter of Old Li who sold rice noodles on South Street. He moved silently to block their way and opened up his raincoat like a cape, like a wooden crucifix of skin and bone, pitiable and helpless. The result was a chorus of mad laughter and wolf whistles.

The holy man Dequan walked erect in the streets and alleys, on the riverbank and the exercise ground, collecting the voices that came from the deep places of Wu Town, and going to the rescue of those who had fallen into night-time encounters of all kinds. He stood ready to appear at any moment, as if he had dropped down from heaven. He would not allow anyone to damage the nights of Wu Town, he would permit no hint of coercion, defilement or hurt.

———

Every evening at dusk, the residents of Wu Town could hear Wu Xiaojiang sobbing. These sobs had been going on for two years. Ever since Butcher Wu's wife had run off with a stranger, Butcher Wu had been taking it out on his small, frail son. Butcher Wu hated his son's girlish looks, and as soon as he clapped eyes on his son, he wanted to give him a pasting.

Dequan walked back and forth on the river slope, listening to the sharp sound of slaps. He saw Butcher Wu's furious yet abstract expression, heard Butcher Wu's curses that sounded like weeping. "I'll teach you not to work hard at school! I'll teach you not to study!" He heard the sound of middle school student Wu Xiaojiang's intermittent crying, and he heard the still, small voice in Wu

Xiaojiang's heart: I'm going to kill him, I'm going to kill him.

The corners of Wu Town were full of voices saying, "I'm going to kill him." Yizhi the doctor and his wife each occupied their own halves of the bed, and neither had anything to say to the other as the doctor pretended to read a book, pondering how he was going to kill his wife. Even though he resented his wife's arrogance, he didn't dare to touch her at night. In the dark of the night, half-crippled Old Man Zhang was staring at a spot in space, thinking about how to kill his son. He could see from the eyes of his son and daughter-in-law that they wanted him dead. The fat beauty Caihong wanted to kill her husband, a man who had made a fool of her not just once or twice but countless times, and she dreamed of an early death for him. Qi Ding, the assistant at Wu's Thick Noodles, wanted to kill his boss, who forced him to work from when he got out of bed at five in the morning until eleven at night and scolded him constantly too.

Dequan was surrounded by these murmurs of "I'm going to kill him". He abruptly raised his head, looking at the solitary light from Wu Xiaojiang's window. In the dark night, that light was misty and indistinct, wavering with the wind. From his place on the river slope, he moved his neck along with the movement of the light; he went to the left and it went to the right, he went to the right and it went to the left like it was challenging him, but also calling out to him, hinting at something. He jumped into the river, chasing and slapping at the sparkles of moonlight, muttering, "Light... evil... Satan...", "Light... evil..." There was no way of knowing if he was saying "Light is evil" or "When light is consumed by evil it becomes Satan". He struck out over and over again, but as soon as he raised his head, that light appeared in the distance. "Satan..."

In the deep night, the people of Wu Town heard a series of long-drawn-out cries in the distance, coming closer, from the river slope to the centre of the town, from underground to above ground. Dequan, ragged Bible clutched in his hand, was charging towards the main gate of Butcher Wu's house. That iron door was closed tightly but with a very narrow crack left down the middle. With superhuman strength, he compressed his body into a thin line and squeezed in. (The next day, people from the town spent quite some time clustered round the door trying to work out what had happened. A few of the most curious tried several times to squeeze through, but not one could do it.) He made straight for the second floor, where he kicked away the lower half of the door with one blow of his foot and forced his way through. The broken wood scratched at his arms and legs, and blood flowed as he dragged the remnants of the door in his wake.

The small, weedy middle school student Wu Xiaojiang sat in front of the table and had finished copying out his characters for the day for the hundred and first time. The light above his head was swaying back and forth in the wind from outside the window. He did not dare to stop his pen, the right side of his face still ached. Butcher Wu used his left hand to cut meat, and for all other activities too, including groping women's breasts and boxing his son's ears.

In a sudden great stride, Dequan was at the table. He pulled Wu Xiaojiang up and hugged him close, shouting, "I've come to save you", as he embraced him tightly with both arms. In the light of the lamp, the holy man Dequan's jet-black hair was like a ball of black flames, covering up his pallid face with deep layers of shade, turning him into a three-dimensional shadow. The powerful light in his eyes came from the deep places of the world, cold but fervent.

The schoolboy Wu Xiaojiang was held so tight that he could barely breathe. He was momentarily stunned, then he let out a piercing cry for help. His voice was just starting to break: an adult horror was intermingled with a child's astonishment and fright, and his voice was like a crisp, clear broken gong, stridently splitting the air.

Everything happened too quickly. Before Butcher Wu, fast asleep in the room next door, had a chance to make out where the cry or the crash of breaking wood came from, cocking his ear, heard his son's shrill, pitiful scream. He was very familiar with that voice.

Butcher Wu came tearing out of his room to find that the door to his son's room was gaping wide, and a monster, barely identifiable as human, was hugging his son tightly to him with one hand, striking out at the lightbulb with the other. His son's eyes were closed, and he was still crying out.

With a "pop" the lightbulb shattered.

The moonlight shone in through the window, illumi-

nating the man and boy tangled up into a terrifying silhouette. Butcher Wu cried out loudly and ran over, trying to
prise apart the arms encircling his son, but those arms were
sturdy and strong as stones, and he could do nothing to
force them open. He smashed his iron-hard palms and fists
into the monster, but the monster did not react at all.
Neighbours heard the noise and came up. In the dark
night, all that could be heard was the sound of skin beating
on skin. The more they hit and the more they pulled, the
more Dequan's arms closed tightly in on themselves, as if
the child was no more than a bundle of raw cotton,
infinitely compressible. Some people used their shoes to
hit out at Dequan's forehead and his eyes so that the blood
ran down his forehead. Dequan was forced to lower his
head, leaving only his back exposed, as he cried out in a
loud voice, "I've come to save you."

The poor schoolboy Wu Xiaojiang at the heart of this
forceful "rescue" had both eyes rolled up so that only the
whites were visible. His breathing was rapid, and he was
on the point of suffocating. In all this chaos, somebody
produced a torch and shone it on Dequan. "Isn't this our
Dequan?" Yizhi called out loudly, as he pushed the crowd
away, approached the pair and slapped Dequan hard on
the back. "Dequan, what are you doing? Look at the child,
he can't breathe."

Dequan seemed to be struggling his way out of some
unknowable vision. He raised his head and looked all
around him. Only then did the people see his eyes. Two
fierce flames were burning in those eyes, but those flames

were not of this mortal world, with no connection to its injustices, its gains and losses or its petty concerns, and they were not shining on the people in front of those eyes, but on somewhere far, far away. The people seemed overcome with awe at those fierce flames from so far off and the madness in that great fire, and their raised hands came to a halt in mid-air. Unconsciously, Dequan's arms loosened their grip on the child, he picked up his Bible that had been kicked until it was almost in fragments and walked out of the door and out of the house like a sleepwalker. It was not until he had gone down two floors that everyone came to their senses and set off in pursuit, led by Butcher Wu. The sound of hands beating on flesh was heard once more from the street.

Dequan lay in the road, motionless. Beside him was the biggest rubbish heap in Wu Town, which by rights should have been on the very steep slope that went down to the river. One day, who knows when, somebody had taken fewer steps than they should have and tipped their rubbish out onto the road, so those who came after also took fewer steps, and the rubbish spread its way into the street. In summer, countless flies and mosquitoes danced joyously above the mound of rubbish, and wild dogs would dig and rummage through it.

The schoolboy Wu Xiaojiang was still in a daze. Butcher Wu was holding his son in his arms, sobbing like a woman. The doctor found several purple marks on the boy's waist from the squeezing, but his ribs were not broken. He took his stethoscope and listened to his heart and lungs, and found there was nothing much wrong with him. Butcher Wu was calling out his son's name with a terrifying gentleness. Wu Xiaojiang drew in a breath, opened his eyes and looked in bewilderment at his father, warm and gentle, pure as an infant. Butcher Wu let out a long howl and stuck his face to his son's, scraping hard against him with his coarse, rough beard.

Dequan was still lying on the rubbish heap. The doctor helped him up by one arm and pushed him to his own house. He washed his wounds, scolding him, "Dequan, old friend, who do you suppose you're saving? Who are you, Jesus? Did Jesus save himself? Did Old Man Heaven save you? If we weren't old classmates, I'd have half a mind to ignore you. Getting yourself injured day in, day out, one of these days you'll get beaten to death. Look at the scab from last time on your leg, it's still weeping."

Dequan, stinking all over his body, closed his eyes and did not utter a word.

Only the doctor knew some of Dequan's secrets. The doctor's home was next door to the biggest guesthouse in Wu Town, where he had encountered Dequan in the main street at night, standing erect and silent, eyes burning, staring hawklike at the travellers coming in and out. From that expression, it seemed that these people were his natural enemies. At first the doctor did not know what he was doing, but later it slowly dawned on him: Dequan was keeping these strangers under observation. Every so often Dequan would appear at the doctor's door with an injured leg, or his head would be swollen from a beating, or there would be a cut on his scalp.

From time to time at night, before he had dropped off, the doctor would hear raucous shouts or mocking laughter in the street, and he would let out an involuntary sigh, "Dequan's got himself into a scrape again."

———

The following day, a crowd gathered around the doctor's clinic. This clinic was like a news centre for the entire town. Patients from miles around brought their stories, and acquaintances who had come to market would rest there and drink tea, listen to stories and chat. Seeing a business opportunity, the doctor had built a large, partitioned area behind the clinic, put out a few tables and started a teahouse and card room. Although those who had come to drink tea could not do so for free, by paying they were entitled to stay there, get unlimited refills of water, occupy seats and gossip. Those who had come to play mah-jong or card games would not just buy tea, they were expected as a matter of course to give the doctor a percentage of their winnings, as the state of their finances allowed.

The schoolboy Wu Xiaojiang had recovered his wits, and early that morning he had shouldered his schoolbag and set off for school. Since he was fine, and Dequan was mentally ill, Butcher Wu felt no inclination to pursue the matter any further with Dequan.

Dequan had left the clinic the previous night and

returned to his territory – the building on the corner. "Ai, this Dequan." Standing behind the counter, his hands resting on the glass, the doctor let out a sigh that was pregnant with meaning. Seeing the inquisitive expressions of everyone around him, his spirits rose, his face brightened and he began to tell them Dequan's story.

"We had very strong sunlight in those days. It would make you dizzy, the way it shone on you. You might say that in spring, the sunlight was stronger than it had any right to be. After the Dequan business came out, we tried to make sense of it all. The sunlight was so strong that something was bound to happen. The Fifth Middle School classrooms all faced south, with wooden doors and windows that didn't shut properly. In winter snowflakes drifted in, and in summer the sun shone through. Cold in winter, hot in summer, as you might say. It was pretty much OK in spring, as you could warm yourself in the sun. Dequan sat over there by the window in the fifth row, which was the best place for warming yourself. I was in the back row, to the right. Every day at eleven o'clock, the sun would come all the way round, shining on us, warming our bodies. Everyone in our class was retaking the year, we were old hands. By day we put on an act of not caring one way or the other, going to class when we had to, chatting when we wanted to chat and sleeping when we felt the need to sleep. In the evening, every last one of us would find a corner and burn the midnight oil there, swotting away. Dequan was one of the daytime nappers. That fellow, he was already on this third retake, and every year his marks were worse than the last, but he still insisted on coming back. Then again, in those days plenty of students took the Senior Three year four or five times."

The doctor had a gift for storytelling, he liked to build up the suspense, drawing the story out a very long way, sometimes as far back as his characters' great-great-grandfathers' generation, or all the way to the time when the Tuan River was still just a twig in the hands of the goddess Nüwa. The stories were all interwoven with elaborate description, sensational details, exaggeration and flashy extras, then at the end he would suddenly revert to the matter at hand. His audience was accustomed to his rambling, unpredictable beginnings. They listened all the more patiently, knowing there would be a good show at the end.

"Then all in a rush, the weather turned hot. And it was still only April. The sun shone in through the cracks in the wooden windows, oh the glare of it, so dazzling it would send you into a panic. When it was past eleven, it blazed onto Dequan's face again. I saw Dequan shading himself from the light with his hand, his eyes twitching and jumping, his bottom wriggling back and forth on his seat, but he just couldn't avoid that shaft of light. You might say that something was bound to go wrong that day. Class was already over, all our stomachs were sticking to our backs with hunger, the smell of Auntie Wu's stewed cabbage and pork was already drifting over from the playground, there was always a mad scramble over that stuff. Looking at it now, it was no more than a few lumps of fatty meat, but at that time Auntie Wu was the only one selling meat for a jiao a bowl. The class teacher Teacher Zhao was giving us yet another of his homilies, counting down the days to the university entrance exams, cursing us retakers for wearing out our bottoms on his seats for nothing and spending our school fees in vain, spittle flying, you could have drowned in it.

"As I listened, I was trying to calculate the rate of Dequan's blinking eyes and shifting backside, and I could tell that he was blinking with increasing rapidity. All the fine hairs on his face were standing up, like rows of arrows under the bright light, and it looked like he was starting to lose control. I was just puzzling over this, when I saw Dequan get to his feet, grab the ink bottle from his desk and hurl it at the teacher's podium like a grenade. The ink bottle exploded with a crash against the blackboard, like a big black flower. Then he swept the books on the desk onto the floor with a crash, and swore, 'Who the hell are you calling names! I'm not playing your games.' His eyes were staring straight ahead, he did not look at anybody, but strode briskly onto the teacher's podium, walked to the door, where he paused for a moment, turned back again and mounted the podium, from where he pointed at Teacher Zhao, cursed him loudly for a good twenty minutes and then left, slamming the door after him. That air of his, honestly, it was like some god had taken over his body, it was quite magnificent."

The doctor was gesturing as he spoke, just like a traditional storyteller, only lacking a gavel for emphasis. When he had got this far, he paused for a moment and lowered his voice, saying in a mysterious tone, "From then on, Dequan turned to the dark. He couldn't even bear to see the sun. When have you ever seen Dequan lift up his eyes under the sun? When have you seen him moving about in the light? You never have. He has to take detours to avoid the sun."

The doctor gestured exaggeratedly at the sun and then brought his hands together and pressed them down forcefully, as if he was compressing the sun and the air together. "In those twenty minutes, Dequan spoke all the words he was going to say in his whole life. He's made his peace. He's been saved."

When the doctor had got this far, he couldn't help smiling. "Our class teacher, that Teacher Zhao – back then he wasn't the old lush he is today, roaring drunk all the time. He was the greatest of them all, and the one who thought the most of himself too – but at that moment he was at a loss. He stood right there listening to Dequan tear into him for twenty minutes. You should know, usually it was him passing judgment on everything, scolding each one of us in turn. That was a sight for sore eyes."

That Teacher Zhao was sitting in the extension just then, part of a group playing cards. As the doctor's tale was reaching its climax, he had forgotten that this Teacher Zhao was also that Teacher Zhao. This Teacher Zhao, busily engaged in losing money, turned his head and interrupted, "Yizhi, no more of that nonsense, Dequan's a mental case. He's genuinely crazy. If his mother died, he wouldn't be able to survive for a single day. You're playing the traditional storyteller again. If it weren't for this habit of pointless invention and your fondness for frivolous books, would you still be spending your whole life in this one-horse town, a clever lad like you?"

The doctor chuckled, hurried over to top up "this Teacher Zhao's" tea, and stood next to him for a while, suggesting moves to help him win. Once he had finished, he walked away and continued, "Talking of those years in the Fifth High School, it produced a lot of mental cases. Dequan is one, and then there's Water Buffalo Wu the hunchback. He went through the final year nine times. When we joined the school, he was in his eighth Senior Three year. Some of his classmates had gone all the way through university and come back to teach here afterwards. His mother was so worried she begged his teacher to have a word with him, to get him to quit, enough was enough. And the result, guess what? He took a brick and chased the teacher all over the school trying to bash his brains out with it. After that he went mad, thought he was the fairest of them all, and every day he'd get a mirror and look himself over, chuckling at random, the sound would make your flesh creep. And then later on again he was nowhere to be found. He hasn't been seen for years."

———

Haihong had passed Dequan's corner building countless times, but she had never given him a second glance. He had been in Wu Town for too long, he was like a shadow, and Haihong had simply been unable to see that he existed. Dequan too had never given Haihong a second glance. In his world, the things that happened in the night had nothing whatsoever to do with the daytime.

From start to finish, Haihong had no way to explain what had happened to her, but the scene on the veranda kept bubbling up in her mind until everything was enveloped in an air of sanctity. That man who had appeared out of nowhere, like he had fallen from heaven, who had taken her hand, was a mysterious symbol and also a revelation; in the future, her salvation was assured. Of course, Haihong herself was not aware that, because of the holy man's sudden, miraculous appearance, her first time touching a man had become a curse. Thereafter there was always something awkward in her relations with men. At the moment of greatest intimacy, she would suddenly twist her head away in shock, it seemed that that black silhouette was standing there once again.

———

The people of Wu Town did not understand why Qingfei always remained single. It was said that he had done pretty well for himself outside: he was a high-status chef, with certificates to prove it, and had found plenty of people jobs in high-class restaurants. He had helped his younger brother and sister to leave the village; he had bought some of the most desirable land by the highway for a house and was now the owner of a European-style villa in one of the town's most prestigious and expensive residential areas. Every year at Spring Festival, Qingfei would drive back to Wu Town in his car, where he would hand out cigarettes to all he met and smile at everyone. But he stubbornly remained unmarried.

———

It was dusk, and the lights of Wu Town gradually extinguished one by one, the dust slowly settled, and the night, full of gentleness and kindness, draped itself over the streets that had been so noisy and full of bustle by day. The wind blew through the streets and the Chinese holly trees in front of the buildings, causing the leaves of the trees to rattle together, making a noise like a low chant. Occasionally there would be the sound of a vehicle passing down from the main road, which intensified the listlessness and dejectedness of Wu Town. The holy man Dequan's eyes slowly opened, widened and glowed, his heart started to beat strongly, his thoughts became richer and more numerous. He rose up from the corner building, shook out his numb legs, stretched his neck, and started to listen and look for the night's secrets.

Dequan was unwilling to admit that he had made an error of judgment. In the last few years, his hearing had become increasingly dull. There were too many unfamiliar sounds and new things that had come pouring in, he had no way to grasp them all. It was very hard for him still to walk easily and freely in night-time Wu Town. It was also getting very difficult to hear the sounds of a family in their home calmly eating or involved in mutual recrimination, he could not even make out the sound of Granny Wu beating her grandson. A twelve-storey high-rise block had been built at the north end of the town. Its height was beyond the reach of his eyes, he could not see the people in the skyscraper or observe their lives, he no longer had any way to look down from on high on this quiet yet restless small town, or exert his control over it. A new internet bar had opened next door to the doctor's clinic, and in the centre of town there was a karaoke parlour. The neon advertisements at the entrance flickered and shone all through the night, and the banging and booming sounds shook the town, disturbing its sleeping inhabitants. He saw that the Party secretary for the South Village, Wu Baoguo, the township Party secretary and Wu Hongxing the property developer were meeting frequently, and he heard them discussing the demolition of the corner building. He was going to be made homeless.

The nights were becoming brighter and brighter, more and more of the bright sunlight was now wavering in front of Dequan's eyes, unwilling to leave. Dequan rushed impetuously through the wide streets and narrow alleys of Wu Town, ran swiftly to the deep places of the Tuan River, slapping at the light that was moving all over its surface.

If you walk the streets of Wu Town at night and see such a man, clad in a long gown of some unidentifiable cloth, holding in his hand a battered, rolled-up book, walking on the road like a shadow, whatever you do, do not disturb him, do not wear bright, sparkling clothes, do not let out lascivious, wanton laughter. Otherwise, he will follow you until he takes you in his arms, and he won't be willing to let go until he has saved you.

4

Xu Jialiang Builds a House

WANG JIGUANG THE GRAIN DEALER, Zhang Zhenguo the electrical goods salesman and Li Hongzhong who had a sinecure in local government were sitting in Dr Yizhi's clinic, watching the rain outside as they discussed the "Opening of the Lock" ceremony for Wang Jiguang's son's twelfth birthday. This was a rite of passage for children in Wu Town, and it was expected to be done in style. Wang Jiguang had already wined and dined a number of people over this matter, and now he was discussing the practical details of the Opening of the Lock, such as division of labour, guest lists and seating plans, with three of his friends: Zhenguo who was well known in Wu Town as a master of ceremonies, Hongzhong who had some knowledge of the *Book of Changes* and the eight trigrams, and Yizhi the doctor who was good at calligraphy.

The rain fell, unhurriedly and listlessly. The dust on the street, the newly planted trees on both sides, the rubbish by the roadside, all were like a waterlogged chicken, a tuft here and a pile there, soaking wet, revealing the dark skin beneath. At three or four in the afternoon, Zhenguo, who always had to sleep after he had had a drink, was slumped lopsided in his chair with his head up, snoring.

The old bachelor from the south side of Wu Town, Xu Jialiang, appeared out of nowhere and walked straight into the clinic. He went up to the place at the back where the teapots were kept and poured water into the brown plastic jar he carried everywhere, then once he had topped himself up, he turned and looked at the people who were watching him.

"I'm getting ready to go to the big city," Xu Jialiang announced with great satisfaction, jerking his head sharply upwards as spoke. His voice boomed and grated, modulating as if it were part of a traditional opera, dragging out the notes.

Xu Jialiang's face was very small, forming a wedge shape, what in Wu Town they called "three types of flat, four kinds of not round, all stuck to a gourd". His complexion was greasy and so dark it was almost black, like he had not washed for years, grease and dust smeared on in layers so thick and oily that they gleamed. His eyes were an oily black too, and they rolled and darted about with a frequency that belied his age; cunning, tense, full of fear and alertness, as if there was someone on his track trying to kill him and he might turn and flee at any moment. His body was short and slight, and when he walked he made no sound, but would suddenly appear behind you, or he'd linger in the corners of the teahouses, restaurants and card-playing establishments of Wu Town, smiling at people, bowing and scraping. When you looked at him it was like seeing prey which sooner or later was sure to end up as food for a tiger, whose survival up to now was entirely dependent on an abnormal level of alertness.

"I plan to use a flanking tactic. The last two times I didn't even get as far as Rang County train station before they got me and brought me back. This time I won't go to Rang County, I'll take the opposite direction and head south. There's a long-distance bus, 'Rang County – Xichuan – Ping'an' that goes through our village at the right time. I'll get off at Xichuan, where I'll get the night bus and transfer to Zhengyang, then take the train from Zhengyang to Beijing. It's a pretty big detour, but that bastard definitely won't have thought of it. No matter what, this time I have to make it there. Another old petitioner just phoned, saying that right now they're holding some sort of meeting in Beijing, they're keeping a close eye on everything, and officials from every province, county, town and township are hanging around the door of the reception office. They'll whisk you away as soon as you turn up and deal with the issue on the spot. Whatever requests you have, they'll satisfy them all.

"If I can get myself to Beijing, that sod is finished. I don't believe that son of a bitch will be able to hold out on me."

Xu Jialiang was standing up straight; his words were

spoken with no rest between sentences, and with considerable venom. He then stalked off, taking his big brown jar of tea with him.

None of the four men watching Xu Jialiang's small, smug form disappear into the far end of the rain-filled street had any idea how to react. Yizhi put his head on one side and asked Zhenguo, who had woken with a start at Xu Jialiang's strident voice, "You tell me, just why did Old Liangzi come and stand here? Just to pour himself a cup of hot water?"

The men chuckled.

———

Xu Jialiang's plan went without a hitch. The following afternoon, he successfully arrived at Beijing West Station, took the number 40 bus, got off at Taoranting North, went on foot for a few hundred metres, crossed at the underpass and reached the reception office of the Bureau of Petitions. He had just got to the main doorway when he saw the short, fat Party branch secretary Wu Baoguo, the little document case that never left his side clasped under his arm, yelling into his phone. Beside him stood the Wu Town Party secretary and the deputy bureau head responsible for this kind of work. Several sturdy young men were also standing there.

They were all old acquaintances.

One of them pointed, and they all came rushing over, took hold of him and dragged him towards the back. Xu

Jialiang struggled a few times for show, then capitulated and went along with them. Shortly after that, a minibus came roaring up, Xu Jialiang and the others were loaded in, and it sped off directly towards the West Station. When Xu Jialiang saw this, he began to worry. In the past, they had always gone to the courtyard owned by a Wu Town expatriate called Zhang Xingchang. They would stash him away there and then negotiate further at their leisure.

What they called the Zhang Family Courtyard was actually a handful of dilapidated single-storey huts on a big stretch of waste ground, with a large, weed-strewn empty space in front of all the huts. Zhang Xingchang had somehow managed to pull strings and smooth his way to acquire several of these buildings. There was a central open area for cooking and eating and rooms around it for people to stay in. Every room slept four, with two tiers of bunk beds. The Zhang Family Courtyard was very well known in certain circles, not only to those from Wu Town who came to intercept petitioners. Residents from other parts of Rang County and even of neighbouring counties would all get dragged here when caught bringing petitions to Beijing, and Zhang Xingchang would charge a daily rate of one hundred yuan, all in, board and lodging. Xu Jialiang had stayed here four times, eating at mealtimes, sleeping when he was tired, and when he had nothing else to do, he would compare experiences with his peers, no need to spend a cent, it was quite the indulgence.

Xu Jialiang shouted, "You've got it wrong, you're going the wrong way, it's this way, right?"

Nobody paid him any attention.

In the front seat, Wu Baoguo and the township Party secretary chatted the whole way. They were talking about a bad woman in a neighbouring county who had got AIDS and spent her days petitioning the higher authorities, demanding that the government find a job for her child, and when she was told by the government that this would be difficult, she went out into the street with a syringe, jabbing people at random, so they all fled in terror. In the end, there was nothing else for it, and they did arrange a job for her son. The last couple of days she had been out petitioning again, saying that the job they gave him was no good and demanding a different one, nothing but a state-run work unit would do for him.

They said that things were in a sorry state these days in the Bureau. If you want to get someone on your side, that would take at least two thousand. They don't even take ready cash, you send it directly to their card, which saves the bother of meeting in person for the handover. So no matter what, you can't let people go into that reception hall, because as soon as they take a number and get in the queue, they've registered themselves, and the province, the county and the township all have to hustle. By that point, you can't keep it under wraps, no matter how much money you spend.

They also discussed a crippled soldier who had been on the frontline in Laoshan during the Sino-Vietnamese

War. His successes all those years ago had made him high and mighty, he said the arrangements made for him were no good and made reports all over. One time, he finally agreed to go back home, they'd bought him his ticket and taken him to the train station. In the blink of an eye he had vanished, wearing his old-fashioned khaki uniform with a sack over his shoulders, and stood at the other side of the station, military medals held high in his hand, and shouted out, "You bastard official, I'll fuck your mother!"

Everybody snorted with laughter. Xu Jialiang was listening intently from the back seat, and forgetting his own situation chipped in with righteous indignation, "That bastard, he's got a nerve, swearing at the leaders, what a nasty piece of work. A man like that, you need to show him what's what."

The Wu Town Party secretary twisted his head round to glare at Xu Jialiang. "You say that about him, shouldn't we be showing you what's what as well? We've had to spend twenty thousand just for this one trip of yours. The last few times you came here, you've cost more than a hundred thousand of my money with your toing and froing. And what did you get out of it? We gave you four thousand in compensation, what more do you want? All for that stupid business of yours."

───────

This is how it happened. The branch Party secretary of Wu Town South, Wu Baoguo, had refused to enrol Xu

Jialiang on the Five Guarantees, a policy designed to guarantee basic living standards to the elderly and disabled. This was despite the fact that he was over sixty, childless and lived alone. Xu Jialiang was dashing around the place all day long to no purpose, he did no proper work, he had no sense of decency, he had hounded his wife to death too, and now he was old he wanted to sponge off the state. Such a man did not deserve to be looked after, let him live by himself and die by himself. Speaking of driving his wife to her death, this was a matter of grief to Xu Jialiang. When he was young and hot-tempered, he had said a few harsh words to his wife, never thinking that she would go back home and hang herself. Xu Jialiang ran away that same night and stayed away for more than ten years. After he returned his parents were already dead, he had no home to call his own, no employment and no wife, his nephews were grown up, and they stared at their uncle with murder in their eyes.

It was autumn, and all the families in Wu Town had spread out grains of sweetcorn on the concrete in front of their homes to dry in the sun. Sixty-year-old Xu Jialiang lay on the sweetcorn in front of Wu Baoguo's house, rolling about, swearing and weeping, saying that he had spent his whole life being treated unjustly, crying that his nephews treated him as an enemy, cursing Wu Baoguo for a bully and saying that he would not have a good death. Everybody was stripping sweetcorn from the cobs and putting it out to dry, and when they heard the sounds of crying and swearing, they all gathered round. Once Xu

Jialiang saw he had drawn a crowd, this lent fresh inspiration to his profanities; he kicked the sweetcorn in all directions, much of it into the ditch by the side of the road, shouting and swearing about all the shameless things Wu Baoguo's mother had got to up in her youth. This enraged Wu Baoguo, and he summoned several young men who dragged Xu Jialiang off to a deserted place and give him a beating. Xu Jialiang took several kicks to the chest and broke several ribs, and his bottom swelled up like steamed bread, and he was taken to hospital.

When he came out of hospital, some unknown person had given him ideas. Xu Jialiang found somebody to write a petition for him, and he went to the township government to lodge a complaint. Finally, in front of the township head and the township's Party secretary, Wu Baoguo threw four thousand yuan to the ground in front of him. "There you go, take it, you're just a ground rat, scooping out cavities and digging holes, and then wanting money for it."

Those red notes with their portrait of Chairman Mao scattered all over the ground. Xu Jialiang picked up the money, one note at a time, went back to his home for a short rest, and then he began the next stage of his life's journey: the lodging of complaints. First in the county, then in the province, he went all the way to Beijing, lodging his complaints as he went. Xu Jialiang could not say for sure just exactly how much money he really wanted, or how much credit or recognition he was seeking. Wu Baoguo came from one of the old, established families of Wu Town and was well-off and well-regarded. He was also not willing to back down, and the two of them became locked in a back-and-forth struggle, which they kept up for several years.

———

Twelve hours later, Xu Jialiang was back in Wu Town. They shut him up in a small square room in the police station, every day they brought him things to eat and drink, but otherwise they ignored him.

At noon on the fifteenth day, Xu Jialiang was summoned by the head of the police station to the best restaurant in town, Chen's Roast Goose. He pushed open the door to the private room to see Wu Baoguo, the head of South Village, a senior member of the Xu extended family who was an accountant, the Party secretary of Wu Town and several other Wu Town notables sitting there in a neat row. Xu Jialiang could never remember most of what they ate at that meal, or what was said. But he remembered very well how everybody placed him in the seat of honour and treated him with great respect, how those important personages spoke persuasively to him in soothing, cultured tones and toasted him repeatedly, calling him "brother" here and "Uncle Xu" there until his head was in a spin and he didn't know where he was. Moreover, Wu Baoguo, who had always been harshly overbearing towards him, broke the habit of a lifetime and prefaced every remark with "Respected

Master Liang", and also agreed both to enrol him for the Five Guarantees and to stop speaking disparagingly or angrily to him. He also took out a bulging envelope and placed it respectfully in front of Xu Jialiang, saying, "There's four thousand yuan here, take it Respected Master Liang, please accept this apology from your junior."

Furthermore, the whole table criticised Wu Baoguo, and they said to Xu Jialiang, "It's only the Five Guarantees, no great matter, Wu Baoguo has already compensated you four thousand, now he's indemnifying you with another four thousand, this shows good faith. All of us present will bear witness. If he, Wu Baoguo, dares to do anything to you again, he will get no support from us."

These important people who normally would never spare a glance for Xu Jialiang were looking at him with faces full of hope. Xu Jialiang put his head on one side and was about to speak, but before he had time to say anything, glass after glass was raised to him in a whole series of toasts.

That is how it was.

Befuddled by drink, the old petitioner Xu Jialiang was toasted to a standstill before he had a chance to say a word. Life on the run and hunger did not frighten him, nor did threats or intimidation, but respect made him nervous. He had never been treated with such deference, sitting in the best seat at the high table, with everyone around him deferring to him, watching for changes in his expression, listening to his words, drinking with him, this was an experience that Xu Jialiang had never enjoyed in all his sixty years.

As the party was winding up and the guests were taking their leave, Wu Baoguo was bustling about, seeing people off and thanking them. He had a great deal to say for himself. "I'll take care of him, I guarantee he'll never cause trouble for the township again. He's just a windbag, a ground rat, he cares more about money than face, give him a bit of cat's piss to drink and he'll lose his head."

Xu Jialiang, drunk on wine and dizzy from the gracious treatment, was squatting by the side of the road, hunched over, retching dryly. He heard these fragments of talk blown over by the wind.

At that time, many folk in the town saw Xu Jialiang pacing about in front of his home. In general, Wu Town's development had expanded to the east and west, with newly built homes stretching out in a continuous chain, extending into the territory of some of the surrounding villages. It was only the side next to the river slope that was developing rather more slowly due to the limitations of the terrain. Old Xu's home and a few dozen houses like it were built next to that slope, in a nondescript, unremarkable clump at the back of Wu Town.

Xu Jialiang's three-roomed earth house was on the last high point on this long, long slope down to the river. Behind it were bushes and weeds, in front and down the slope were three big pit ponds. Two of its three rooms had already caved in, leaving only a few sections of mud-brick wall. The one intact room was sagging to the east, shored up at one unstable corner. Xu Jialiang had propped up the eastern wall from the outside with seven or eight pieces of wood, which just about kept it together and prevented it from falling down. The short, low wall to his yard was made of sweetcorn stalks smeared with mud, and over many years it had gradually reached a state where it had shape but no substance. Viewing Xu Jialiang's house at a distance from the high slope, it looked rather like an abstract painting, with a postmodernist bleakness and desolation and just a hint of implied irony.

Xu Jialiang seemed to have vanished from Wu Town. Sometimes he could be seen leaning against the crooked wall sunning himself, his mop of hair earthy yellow with dirt, his hands and feet stretched out, weak and limp all over, letting out coarse, protracted snores. But this was not Xu Jialiang's style. He liked visiting, enjoyed a hand or two of cards and would drop by wherever there was a good dinner to be had, or when he had nothing better to do, he would go to Yizhi the doctor's card room and loiter there, holding his brown jar full of tea, standing silently behind the players, his eyes moving to follow the game. The people of Wu Town did not pay any attention to him, but whenever he did cross their minds, there he would be.

Nobody knew when it started, but people kept hearing banging late at night, highly regular, with a quick tempo, but distant and heavy, as if transmitted from the depths of the earth. One sound became ten, ten a hundred, and for a while, the residents of Wu Town were stricken with fear, worried that a great disaster was at hand. Some lay sprawled on the ground trying to listen for the source of the sound. It always arrived late at night, as if on a schedule, but by the time dawn broke and the human background noise of the town started up, it would vanish.

Wu Baoguo gathered some of his people and made a big show of patrolling the area, but could not find any clue. Their route took them several times past the ponds, where Xu Jialiang was leaning motionless against his gable. Wu Baoguo's eyes narrowed. For the last few months, the two had had no interactions at all. The day after the banquet, Wu Baoguo had enrolled him on the Five Guarantees and had told Lao Erdan to inform him that he could get one hundred and eighty yuan every month. This met with complete silence from Xu Jialiang, who made no visit of thanks for this favour, which was not a problem, but he had also stopped wandering around Wu Town and boasting of the honourable treatment he had received in Beijing and the county town. He had fallen completely silent, and this was deeply abnormal. Lao Erdan, whose job it was to keep him under observation, had nothing to report except that Xu Jialiang spent every day sleeping. Wu Baoguo suddenly felt a slight prickle on his scalp.

Out of the corner of his eye, Lao Erdan noticed Wu Baoguo's expression change, and he saw him run up the slope and kick Xu Jialiang several times. Xu Jialiang rubbed his eyes and saw the black, tower-like form of Wu Baoguo looming above him, so he stood up, a hint of alarm flickering in his eyes, and he instinctively shifted forwards, as if to block Wu Baoguo's way.

A dim light was shining from the rotting, battered, draughty door of Xu Jialiang's little house. Wu Baoguo walked over in a few long strides, opened the door, bent his head, stooped low and entered the room. He suddenly found himself encased in pillar after pillar of golden light, with gleaming wisps and motes of dust revolving slowly in the shafts of light. The brilliance made Wu Baoguo dizzy for an instant, and he staggered, knocking over a chopping board at the door, as cleaver, bowls and chopsticks all went clattering to the floor. From the chopping board to the back wall was five paces at most. Wu Baoguo put out his hand to support himself on the front wall and focused his eyes on the back wall, which was sparkling with a golden light.

This was a western wall, whose mud bricks had lost their square corners over many years' weathering to become rounded ovals, and cracks had grown between one oval and the next, so there was wind blowing and light shining in. Every time the westering sun shone in, it would cause this strange scene with its thousand points of light.

At the precise centre of the back wall, sparkling with golden light, a still more dazzling portrait of Mao Zedong loomed over him. The gold-coloured face was smiling benevolently amid the thousands of sparkles, the eyes seemed to see all the things and creatures in the world, yet also seemed to be looking at Wu Baoguo alone. The golden radiance in the portrait and outside it illuminated each other, a gold world of incomparable purity. Underneath the picture were five golden Chinese characters:

"Comrade Mao Zedong," and on either side were two vertical inscriptions that formed a couplet:

> A scholar who fights with tongue and pen,
>
> a warrior with his sword;
>
> > Full of concern for China's fate,
> >
> > with a vision bold and broad.

The couplet was handwritten in neat, flowing and vigorous calligraphy, but in comparison with that giant picture was a bit too small, and the faded red paper it was written on was coarse and thin. It was all rather dingy and tentative.

This was clearly a room that never saw visitors. There were no table or chairs. Propped against the north corner was a bed made of piled up earth bricks, on which were heaped up dark, greasy bedding, winter clothes and other unidentifiable garments. Right by the bed was an ancient chest of drawers. The chopping board that had been placed on top of it had already been knocked onto the floor by Wu Baoguo.

There was a burst of surprised shouts outside the house and Wu Baoguo rushed out. A crowd had formed around something between the ruins of the other two rooms, with heads looking down together and craning forwards so far it seemed as if they were going to fall in. Xu Jialiang stood in the doorway, dodging back and forth in an attempt to keep the crowd back, but his expression indicated that they were bound to find out sooner or later, and he did not truly restrain them.

Wu Baoguo also looked down, and then down again, as he leaned over lower and lower until he was almost prostrate on the ground. His eyes slowly became accustomed to the light inside. He saw a vast cave, deep and wide, with a wooden ladder leading downwards, and several baskets of earth near the ladder. Looking to the left and right, he could see a flat, even floor, a squared-off roof held up by several central wooden pillars, and looking farther in again, he dimly glimpsed a small table with a teapot and cups on it, an electric light bulb hanging above it and a small bed. This must be the root cellar. In earlier times every household in Wu Town had had such an underground room, used in winter to store sweet potatoes, turnips and cabbages. Nobody had used cellars like this for the last thirty years. But Xu Jialiang's was clean and neat inside, there was no smell of rotting vegetables, nor of damp, it was just like a room in a house. Above the cave, Xu Jialiang had set up a shack on the remaining half of the ruined part of the house and covered it with a layer of asbestos tiles. Surrounding the cellar was a shallow drain that ran all the way down the slope.

Wu Baoguo stood up slowly, his black tower-like body seemed to weigh a thousand pounds, and now falling directly towards the surface of the Earth, it was an intimidating sight. From this black tower came a voice, asking, "Old Liangzi, what is this?"

Old Liangzi. No more Great Master Liang.

Old Liangzi moved aside. He did not look at Wu Baoguo, but said, looking at the sky, "What? It's a rat's hole."

"What does that mean?"

"Doesn't mean a thing. A ground rat digs a ground rat hole."

"Old Liangzi, what do you mean by this?" Wu Baoguo was choking with anger. "Are you still dwelling on that after all this time? Did everybody say all those things to you for nothing? Were those promises you made in front of all those people just a fart, no more than hot air?"

"That was no fart. We've settled all the scores between us, we're quits."

"Then what do you think you're playing at with all this? Are you deliberately trying to make me look bad? You know that for a while now the people in this town have been going crazy, everybody thought it was an earthquake, that something terrible was going to happen."

Xu Jialiang put his head on one side and looked at the crowd. He seemed taken aback.

"You fill that thing in for me double quick, and we can leave it at that. If you don't, I'll organise the entire village to come and curse you. I'll break you."

———

The news of the hole Xu Jialiang had dug passed very quickly round Wu Town. Nobody abused him, they all viewed his hole as a novelty. At the start, Xu Jialiang held them back and would not let them look, but he could not keep them back for long, so he made the best of it and became a guide, standing at the centre of the cave, talking to everybody about his vision for the house: the left-hand side was to be the bedroom, the bed would go here, the wardrobe and the bedside table would be there; to the right would be storage for grain, mattocks and that sort of thing; the living room would be joined to the kitchen, he was going for an open-plan style or whatever you call it. In the centre would be the living room, and when all the work was finished, he would furnish it with a few tables and invite everyone round for a meal.

Everybody could hear that he was speaking in earnest, and they all sniggered. Some people said, "Where's the TV going to go? The cupboards? You've never managed to get your hands on those things your whole life, and once you live here you'll have them?" Others said, "This is just to put one over Wu Baoguo, there's surely no need to do it for real?" Some laughed and jeered, "All right, we'll sit back and wait to raise a glass to you when you raise your rafters."

Xu Jialiang sniggered too, and said, "I'm a ground rat, that's exactly what I am. I really do plan on moving in. Look at this house, warm in winter and cool in summer, saves both trouble and money. My house above ground, a bit more rain or snow and it'll definitely be done for, and when that time comes where will I live? Build a house? I can't build a house, but here it's all ready-made."

Everybody burst into laughter and Xu Jialiang laughed along with them. They all knew that Xu Jialiang was trying to make Wu Baoguo look bad. Once they were back above ground, they noticed that the house had developed even more of a list and that the wooden pillars in the cave had come from there. They realised that things were not as simple as all that.

Xu Jialiang continued unhurriedly excavating his hole, there was no need for him to dig at night now. People would come by, and he would get them to give him a hand pulling the earth up. In the afternoon he would go for a wander into the village, take a couple of glasses of cheap spirits and eat a bowl of stewed noodles.

One time, Wu Baoguo got together a group of guests for another dinner. On this occasion, Xu Jialiang plumped himself down on the ground like he owned the place. He would not drink the wine or eat the meat, and when they spoke of the hole, all he said was that he was doing it for fun. There was nothing Wu Baoguo could do about him.

One afternoon in spring, a journalist came by. He had heard about it, and on seeing Xu Jialiang's underground cave he became greatly excited. He made Xu Jialiang strike all kinds of poses, digging, drinking tea, narrating, and he took a great many pictures, clicking away with his camera. The journalist even wanted to chat with Xu Jialiang in the hole, but half an hour was all he could manage, after that he had to continue their talk outside.

A week passed, and Wu Baoguo came back from Rang County, swearing loudly, a newspaper in his hand. Wu

Baoguo spent more time living in the county town than he did in Wu Town; he depended entirely on Lao Erdan to keep watch on Xu Jialiang. But this time Lao Erdan had let himself get carried away with the novelty of it all. He had hung around the journalist, butting in, desperate to say more than Xu Jialiang, and as a result he had forgotten to make his report to Wu Baoguo.

Wu Baoguo flung the newspaper in Xu Jialiang's face, and said, "Now you've done it, all China knows about our town now, you really have won glory for us all." Xu Jialiang picked up the newspaper, and a headline in thick black type that took up almost half a page hit him between the eyes:

IN THE NEW ERA
A PEASANT LIVES IN A HOLE IN GROUND
Where are our moral obligations?!

That heavy black exclamation mark shook everyone to the core. Next to the title were several photographs: Xu Jialiang's cave, the bed in the cave and finally a picture of Xu Jialiang holding a shovel, about to pack earth into a basket, his eyes raised to look at the lens. Under the strong light, his startled face looked heavily wrinkled, lonely, poor and forlorn.

The report said that Xu Jialiang was an old man without a family or any support in his old age, but also a tragic hero who was digging a hole to express his rage. You might say it was a rearguard action from an impossible position, absurd, and yet there was something inspiring about it too. The cave was dark, but it retained the only warmth in the human world. At the end of the report was a doggerel that the people of Wu Town had made up:

You call me a ground rat,
The ground rat's made a ground rat hole.
I live in my hole, happy as you please,
While the black tower spins with rage.

This was the rhyme Lao Erdan had insisted on repeating word for word for the journalist, who had reacted with even more excitement than when he heard the story.

When he had read to the end, Xu Jialiang was somewhat baffled. He felt that the man in the article both was him and was not him, and clearly there were many things in it that he had never said. But he did not care about any of that, he secretly felt that his image had gained in stature from all this, although Wu Baoguo was obviously getting ever more worried and angry.

Wu Baoguo came again to look for "Master Liang". He squatted at the mouth of the cave and spoke to him, as Xu Jialiang replied from down below, calculating positions, digging away earnestly.

"There's a new government policy," explained Wu Baoguo. "The government is rebuilding unsafe housing in rural areas. There's an allowance of six thousand per household, the quota for each village is just one, and I'll allocate it to you. It's up to us who we give it to, plenty of folk have their eye on it, and some of them are even trying to pull strings to get at it. I'll give the money to you.

"Actually, there are poorer people than you in our village, like Lao Dakuan who doesn't even have a house and sleeps in a haystack, and Lao Ercai who's out on the streets all day. Who takes care of him? You're not doing too badly here – you still have a house. The Production Brigade will give you another grant of two thousand, that's eight thousand. You take it, repair the house, make a proper job of it, and *fill in that hole*.

"This time let's talk it through and make an end of it, don't you go pulling any of your tricks, otherwise I'll have that blasted hole of yours filled in."

Behind his back, Wu Baoguo added, "Windbags like him have no sense of shame, they just want money. Give him money, and everything's fine by him."

Xu Jialiang took the eight thousand yuan, bought cement, stones, tiles and wood, got them to the slope and set to work. On the gable sat a red portable music player, which Xu Jialiang had recently bought for a hundred yuan, on which he played Henan opera: *The Rolled-Up Mat* or *The Two-Bit Sesame Official*. Passers-by could hear the melancholy, sonorous, yet lively tunes as they passed.

One morning, Xu Jialiang borrowed a three-wheeled goods tricycle and went to the market in town, where he bought preserved pig's, cow's and sheep's heads, all kinds of cold snacks and side dishes and a case of wine. He also bought a live cockerel and an enormous roll of firecrackers.

Whenever he met an acquaintance, he would invite them in a loud voice, "Come to my place at noon to raise a glass with me. You must all come, I'm raising the rafters on my home."

When raising the rafters on a house, whether an old house or a new one, you always had to kill a chicken, set off firecrackers and invite guests for food and wine. Xu Jialiang visited neighbours to borrow benches and bowls too, and at each house he would invite everybody there to go to his house at lunchtime to raise a glass with him.

The people went to the yard of Xu Jialiang's home and discovered to their astonishment that the hole in the ground had been transformed into an underground palace. A wall of grey-blue bricks had been built on all four sides, the entrance to the cave had been squared off and plastered with concrete and he had piled up earth to make stairs, each layer tamped down, and every step made smooth with cement. Going down the stairs you entered his underground home with a smooth, glossy grey-blue cement floor. The space was broad and more than three metres high from floor to ceiling. Xu Jialiang had reinforced all the corners with cement and bricks, making a square room of at least a hundred square metres. Several high-wattage electric bulbs were brightening the whole room.

But the brightest thing of all was the portrait of Mao Zedong on the living room wall. Xu Jialiang had reverently transported the "Comrade Mao Zedong" portrait down from above ground, made a square frame, mounted the picture on it and hung it on the wall. The couplet was still there, but the red paper had been refreshed, written in Xu Jialiang's own hand – Xu Jialiang had finished middle school, and his calligraphy was pretty good. In front of the picture of Chairman Mao was a long table for offerings, on which an incense burner had been set out and incense lit, its smoke curling gracefully upwards.

With a red flush on his face, Xu Jialiang gathered everybody in front of the portrait of Mao Zedong, standing several rows deep, and directed them to bow three times from the waist in front of the portrait. They came over smiling and laughing, but once they started to bow, they all became quiet and serious. When they had finished, just as they were about to move away, Xu Jialiang made everybody wait a moment, saying, "Back in the day, when I went to his birthplace, Shaoshanchong in Hunan, I saw people bowing to the picture of Chairman Mao, and afterwards they would make a special wish. I asked the locals, and they said it was highly effective. Close your eyes, put your hands together and make a wish silently to yourself, and the great man is sure to protect you."

The crowd did as Xu Jialiang told them, they all closed their eyes and put their hands together. As soon as they opened their eyes, they saw Comrade Mao Zedong's benevolent smile, and for a moment they felt refreshed a hundredfold.

That lunchtime Xu Jialiang was especially happy. The firecrackers were set off on the ground, the cockerel was killed, the thick roof beam was set in place and fixed on the right-hand side of the roof. The banquet in the underground room was unusually lively, all the food was eaten up, people were calling out cheerfully to each other, and they drank up every drop of the wine as well.

Xu Jialiang drank too much, of course, and he kept toasting people, "You say this house of mine can keep me in my old age, but that eight thousand yuan, how far would that go towards building a house? You couldn't even build a single wall for that, but used here it's enough and more than enough.

"That bastard Wu Baoguo is all talk, he's got no idea how much money you need now to build a house, he just gave me this eight thousand to get rid of me. Try getting him to live in that house of mine, how would he go about fixing it?" And he shouted, "Lao Erdan, go and get Wu Baoguo to come over, say I'm inviting him for a bite to eat and a drink, but first I'll teach him how to bow to Chairman Mao. I'm under Chairman Mao's protection, let's see if he dares to destroy my house!"

Lao Erdan was befuddled enough to actually phone Wu Baoguo. Wu Baoguo drove his car at speed all the way from the county town to Xu Jialiang's home, and when he went down into the magnificent underground palace he was struck dumb. Xu Jialiang tugged Wu Baoguo over, lit a stick of incense and insisted that he bow to Chairman Mao. Wu Baoguo twisted away and refused. "What's the matter? If you're not even willing to bow to Chairman Mao, what sort of Party member are you?" asked Xu Jialiang.

"This is feudal superstition."

"What feudal superstition? The portrait in front of the Tian'anmen Gate, the portrait in the Chairman Mao Mausoleum, the portrait in Shaoshanchong, are these feudal superstitions? Have you never visited the Mausoleum, never made your bow there? That's respect, that is. I was in Shaoshanchong, and there was nobody there who didn't bow, they all made wishes, and some people had come there with thank-offerings after their wishes were granted. This is powerful stuff."

The wine had gone to Xu Jialiang's head, his tongue was loosened and he grabbed Wu Baoguo's sleeve, saying, "Kiddo, right from the start it's been about putting one over on me, you were picking on me, and me practically old enough to be your grandfather. What's this then, you think I'm too old, you get people to beat me up, your grandfather. Getting old doesn't mean a man's got no right to live! You called me a ground rat, I heard that loud and clear! No human should live the way I've lived, and so you look down on me. Ground rat, so what, I am a ground rat, fine, so I've gone to live in a hole in the ground. Say what you like, go on! Now I'm really not trying to put one over you. You saw it, there's only one room left in that house of mine, a bit more heavy rain will finish it off. Where d'you expect your granddad to live? Is that eight thousand yuan enough to build a house? You know everything, you have to leave your grandfather with something to live on. Isn't that right?"

Xu Jialiang was in full spate, and by now Wu Baoguo

had lost patience. He stood up and said, "Master Liang, I've given you the money, and you've shown me up, I think we'd better leave it at that. That house above ground won't fall down just yet, it's been that way for the last decade and more, and it's still that way now, so it won't collapse. If you don't want your grandson to be at odds with you, you destroy this hole. If this gets in the papers again, the two of us will be at daggers drawn."

Everybody said that Xu Jialiang was unstoppable, after years of miserly and solitary existence, he had changed. Bit by bit, he moved his bed, cooking pots, bowls, spoons and basins into the underground cave, and he would invite anyone he met to come over and sit for a spell, make their bows to Chairman Mao, close their eyes and make a wish, and then eat a few chunks of stewed meat and take a glass or two of cheap wine. Gradually, a few people started going to his place on purpose, and they brought their own wine with them. But they were not drinking the wine, it was brought especially to bow to Chairman Mao and make a wish.

Wu Baoguo came to inspect several times and drank wine there several times, each time he would both persuade and scold him, "You really are a ground rat, you've certainly got a knack for scratching out holes and making caves. Don't think I'm afraid that you'll tell on me, what do I have to be scared of? Go on, make your report, what would you even say? It's only out of consideration for us both being from the same village that I'm not coming down too hard on you."

Several times Wu Baoguo brought a few toughs from the town, who would make a play of being very drunk and use it as an excuse to kick over Xu Jialiang's shabby furniture or cut his electric cables. On one occasion, one of the young men grabbed the incense burner from the offering table and smashed it to the ground. Drunk as he was, Wu Baoguo shrieked at him to stop, in an urgent, shrill voice that shocked even Xu Jialiang.

They went through several rounds of this. Xu Jialiang did not demolish his home, and above ground the officials did not pursue matters. Wu Baoguo carried on with his official duties, and the matter came to an end without really coming to an end.

Every day, Xu Jialiang would fiddle around with his underground house. He started to work on the outside as well, clearing earth away from the end that was closer to the river slope to open up a window there, so it was a bit brighter inside and the air could circulate. He told Wu Baoguo that this meant it no longer could be considered a hole in the ground, it was now a semi-basement.

Gradually, visitors coming to the market in Wu Town from far away would make a small detour to see Xu Jialiang's underground house, burn incense, bow to Chairman Mao and make a wish. Xu Jialiang casually let fall a few banknotes in front of his incense burner, one or two yuan, ten or twenty. He never said anything, but others would drop a few notes there too. Xu Jialiang thought, It looks like their wishes have been granted. He polished the portrait of Chairman Mao with even more reverent care and prayed to it daily.

When the end of spring came, the journalist came again too, bearing a big box of White Elephant brand instant noodles and two bottles of Tuo brand wine. Xu Jialiang told him, "I was just thinking of getting in touch, you'll need to do another report on me." He dragged the journalist all around his underground house on a guided tour, describing excitedly to him the quality and composition of the soil, its structure and its functions. He spoke of how this place was warm in winter and cool in summer, and how he intended to live out his old age here. The journalist listened with a neutral expression, appearing neither to assent nor dissent. When taking photos again, Xu Jialiang did his best to show a happy, smiling face, sitting in front of the portrait of Mao Zedong. The journalist shook his head and left.

Over the next few days, Xu Jialiang went every day to Yizhi the doctor's house to wait for the papers. One morning the long-awaited newspaper arrived, only for him to see a row of small characters before the headline, "Peasant living in a hole in the ground – update", straight after which came a row of shocking words:

FORCED TO THE BRINK OF MADNESS:
Peasant living in a pit thinks he's gone to heaven

Xu Jialiang rubbed his eyes, not quite believing what

had been written, and continued to read. The Xu Jialiang in the report was dressed in a dark blue jacket straight out of the 1970s and yellow canvas shoes, his smile was twisted, with unfocused eyes and yellow, protruding teeth, presenting a crazed, unnerving appearance. The portrait of Chairman Mao behind him had been blurred out. Two other pictures were of Xu Jialiang's small, listing house above ground and a full picture of the underground house. The journalist carefully described the psychological changes that had taken place in Xu Jialiang since he first began to make his petitions, and was at pains to stress that Xu Jialiang's happiness was a fake, empty thing, that it was mental confusion, the after-effect of persecution, and he thought that this was the greatest possible satire on society. In the piece, he used countless exclamation marks and very many words that Xu Jialiang had never even seen before.

Xu Jialiang took up his mobile phone and spoke to the journalist for two hours in an argumentative voice, repeating over and over, "Comrade Journalist, you have to change this back for me, that's not the way it is, how could you write it like that?"

Xu Jialiang dawdled about the town, had some noodles at Li Hongsheng's Pulled Noodles and downed glass after glass of cheap wine, with an uncomfortable feeling in his mind that he could not quite articulate. At four or five o'clock in the afternoon, in the golden sunlight, Xu Jialiang staggered drunkenly back home.

A great mass of people were milling about in his yard.

Some were walking here and there holding cameras and making videos. Wu Baoguo was in the crowd, nodding his head and bending his waist and respectfully offering cigarettes around, but everyone ignored him. He also saw the Party secretary of Wu Town, and the township head in the crowd, standing around awkwardly. As soon as those people saw Xu Jialiang they came surging forward, like vultures that had caught sight of their prey.

Xu Jialiang was shocked into immobility at the scene in front of him. He stood stupefied for a moment, then rushed towards the site of the underground house. In front of him was a great pit, sloping steeply downwards: his underground house had vanished. Xu Jialiang walked round and round the sides of the big pit, looking everywhere, like a madman. "Oh, my hundred square metre home," he exclaimed. "Oh, my Chairman Mao!"

He looked to his left and discovered that the door to that old tumbledown house was standing open, and rays of gleaming golden light were shining out. As he walked inside the house, golden light shone out to meet him, and the old man in the golden light gazed down benevolently at a bowl of mincemeat for dumplings on Xu Jialiang's chopping board.

It would appear that "Comrade Mao Zedong" had been respectfully transported back again and hung squarely on the western wall. Underneath was the table for offerings, and there was even a stick of fresh incense burning in the holder on the offering table, sending up a winding trail of smoke. On both sides of the room were all the odds and ends that Xu Jialiang had moved into the underground house, including the stuffing for his dumplings. He had made a great bowl of filling the day before so that he could eat dumplings that day.

Xu Jialiang stood there for a while, then dashed out of the house, shoved the gawpers aside, stood on the slope, set his hands on his hips and cursed hysterically, "I'll fuck your grandmother! And all her ancestors too!"

5

Swimming in the Second River

IT WAS HIGH NOON, and the weather was burning hot.

In the morning she had gone from Wu Town to the village where she grew up, where she and her brother had visited their mother's tomb to burn paper money for her "Two Seven", marking the end of the second week after her mother's death.

Lu Village happened to be one of the places moved to make way for the big new river, part of the South-North Water Transfer Project, alleviating the long-term water shortages in northern China by bringing water in from the south through canals and aqueducts. She had watched as the crops were flattened, the houses pulled down and the inhabitants moved away, and seen a series of big road rollers, diggers, huge trucks full of sand and earth, and low loaders carrying all kinds of machinery driving back and forth, as the empty space was gradually transformed into big roads, concrete ground, riverbed and river embankment. People in orange helmets, people driving vehicles and project workers, were all labouring busily away here like ants, spring, summer, autumn and winter.

Two years passed, and a great, tall river had arisen. The protective barriers on both sides of it were eight or nine metres high, winding their way forward from south to north. The horizon had been altered. Lu Village, Wangying, Lijia and the neighbouring villages were dwarfed by it, pitiable, sunk on both sides of the large embankment. The trees had become low, the houses small, and people standing at the entrance to the village or walking on the road looked as if they had been discarded, thrown into the far distance. The rumbling trucks driving by were like toy cars. Viewed from the main road, they seemed to be tiny ants beside a giant python, too small to be worthy of notice.

Kneeling in front of her mother's tomb, she pulled the paper money apart, folded it and put it into piles. When the fire touched the loose, fluffy, flammable paper money, it immediately spread its way outwards. She watched the fire start to take, the flames licking at the willow branches in front of the tomb and crawling upwards. The ash from the paper was blown up by the wind and the fire, circling up and down, drifting and scattering far away. She got down on all fours and kowtowed nine times, three each for herself, her husband and her son.

Without waiting for the others to depart, she got onto her electric motorbike and left. Her younger brother and sister-in-law had already bought their return tickets. That afternoon they would go to Wu Town and catch a minibus to Rang County, then in the evening they would take the train back to some town or other near Guangzhou, where they worked in a clothing factory. She did not want to watch her nephews weeping and wailing for their mum and dad, she hated to see that, nor did she want to see her dad, drunk and stubble-faced, she despised him too.

She headed towards the wall at the back of the old village. Just beyond was the Tuan River. The old boundary wall had fallen into disrepair over many years, people had been taking bricks and wood from it for longer than anyone could remember, but its height and overall structure remained intact and it still encircled half of the village. The residents of Lu Village had kicked a path through, leading directly to a small bridge by the Tuan River.

After passing the village wall, the view broadened out and opened up. The ground gradually dropped away and the river slope extended downwards. First, it was wild bushes and silk trees, followed by a whole stretch of white poplars and patches of sandy ground planted with peanuts, watermelons and other cash crops, criss-crossed by white sandy earth roads, and then lower again was the broad riverbed.

The bridge was broken. The centre had caved in on itself, and the concrete slabs on either side poked up very high, like a vast bird with broken wings that had crashed headfirst into the river.

This came as no surprise to her. From her earliest

youth to the present day, she had seen a broken bridge many times in exactly this place. When she was little, there was only a narrow wooden plank bridge here. A few dozen logs were driven into the middle of the river, lashed together on both sides with ropes. In the centre, a layer of rare wood planks was laid down on top, and that was the bridge. The people on the north side of the bridge coming to Wu Town for the market, and those visiting from the south side, all had to cross this bridge. The bridge was privately owned, built by a single family. When Spring Festival came and the numbers crossing back and forth for the market or to see their relatives were the greatest, there would be someone on both sides of the bridge collecting money, one jiao, two jiao, five fen, any small sum would do. In summer the first big rainstorm would generally carry the wooden bridge away. She had seen wooden planks and rope rolled along by the big waves and the family that owned the bridge running along the riverbanks with bamboo poles to fish out the wood and other flotsam. Once the storm was past, the family would push out a tiny ferry from a small hut nearby to transport people back and forth, and they would not ask for money at all. But at autumn harvest they would visit all the households in turn, asking for a scoop of sweetcorn, half a bag of sweet pota-toes, a handful of soybeans, mung beans or chillies, they would accept any autumn crop.

Afterwards the government built a bridge, which broke every few years and was then duly rebuilt. This bridge had been built the year she came back from

Chongqing, cast in a single layer of concrete from the piers of the bridge to the surface, broad and sturdy. When the bridge was completed, an official came from the township government to cut a ribbon and make a very long speech. All the villagers had been summoned to listen to him.

Underneath the broken bridge, blackish-green water flowed downstream, making waves of white bubbles. It still seemed to have a little momentum, but the momentum did not sustain itself for long. On the other bank of the river, a sand pile rose up like a cliff, and next to it was a dredger, rumbling and growling as it sucked up the bottom of the river. When the water reached this point, it was as if it had suddenly been sucked into a hole, and it became unnaturally calm. Farther down again, the water started to flow in an ever more confused, disorderly way along the increasingly shallow, branching riverbed. Although it was summer, the Tuan River would struggle to produce large quantities of water, so the reeds no longer lined the water's edge but formed a clump here and a stand there, chaotically distributed on both sides of a newly trodden path. The riverbed was a stretch of exposed oval stones of all sizes, between which a narrow flow twisted its way forward.

The Tuan River was retreating farther and farther away.

As her father would say, "thirty years to the east of the river, thirty years to the west": things flourish in one place for a while, then they decline in favour of somewhere else, that's just the way life is.

Even the river was changing, getting farther away for no reason, diminishing for no reason and adding another river out of nowhere for no reason.

A little bit farther on, an aqueduct was suspended above the Tuan River. A mass of thick concrete pillars stood vertically above the Tuan, and the enormous waterway was set horizontally on these thick pillars. There was a rumour in Wu Town that just this one pipeline had cost six or seven hundred million yuan.

She looked towards the aqueduct. The Big River suspended high in the air and the Tuan River down below formed the shape of a cross, one arm pointing north to south, one east to west. Under the grey sky, the Big River was lofty, majestic and solitary, like the indulged young master of a wealthy family; the Tuan, on the other hand, was feeble and humble, horribly shabby, like a woman of good family who had aged, lost her looks and been abandoned.

As if she had suddenly understood something, she set her electric motorbike in motion and headed off towards the Big River. It was far from easy to approach the embankment, which was protected by a long chain link fence roughly ten metres away. Inside the fence were new-planted trees and flowers, and all kinds of plants that she could not name. As the electric bike approached, all the sparrows sitting on the fence fluttered away. A dense, black mass that seemed to block out the sky.

She drove along the track outside the fence. She knew that near the road beside the fences and ditches, there were some small green corrugated iron huts, with watchmen inside to keep out trespassers. There would usually be a small gate for the people who took care of the trees and flowers to go in and out.

Several hundred metres beyond was a little hut. An old man was sitting on a chair inside, snoring, head lolling to one side. The small gate next to him was standing open. She went through, quietly pushing her electric bike, and rode on along the small path that was close to the embankment. It was not really a path, but a track trodden out by workmen on their way to work. Wild grasses had grown up again in the centre of the track, completely covering it in places. She stopped the bike and looked around in all directions.

The village was already far away, but here the crown-shaped ornamental small trees were growing green and strong, filling the eyes with a cool, refreshing green, and bright flowers were blooming. The sparrows resting on the chain link fence, pecking for food or ambling on the ground appeared not to have seen her, but kept on pecking on the ground or staring into space. A light wind blew over, and all the folds and layers of tree leaves moved gently without making a sound. It was all extremely peaceful.

She locked the bike, took off the bag she had been carrying across her body, put the key inside and set the bag in the front basket. She also took off her dripping wet black silk raincoat, folded it nicely and put it on the seat. Then she started to climb to the tall embankment. With the aid of the protruding criss-cross pattern of the concrete surface, shifting herself from left to right, she climbed nimbly to the top of the eight- or nine-metre-high embankment.

The top was a broad platform. She stood there, looking behind her at the road to the village, the distant village that seemed so low that it was under the ground. She stood on tiptoe, and with an effort looked back, wanting to see her mother's tomb, but her view was blocked by all the trees and bushes of the village. To the right, she could see Wu Town. The red twelve-storey landmark high-rise building was now just a perfectly ordinary residential block. Her family's stationery shop was in the street in front of this building. No doubt her husband was sitting in the shop, in front of the computer, playing card games online. Looking ahead, the high river and the platform stretched away as far as the eye could see. To the left, a dusty red sun was hanging high in the sky, now already starting to dip to the west. The sunlight did not seem particularly strong, but it was unreasonably hot.

She took off her white, flat-heeled leather sandals. The soles were very soft and the quality was not bad either. The summer was almost over, but neither straps nor soles were worn or damaged. At the start of summer, she had seen them in Fengli Clothing next to her house, so she had bought two pairs, one for herself and the other one she gave to her mother. Mum had worn that pair of shoes on the day she died.

She set the shoes down, left and right placed snugly

together. She liked to be tidy. Then she sat down on the high, high embankment and looked down at the surface of the river for a while, before raising her eyes to look ahead.

After a while she got up, and half stooping, pressing down with her hands on the sloping concrete surface of the dyke, slowly slid herself down. She dug her feet hard against the concrete, both hands clutching hard at the surface to stop herself from tumbling downwards.

Her feet touched the surface of the water, so cold. Icy and uncompromising, there was no trace of softness or detachment. She hesitated for a moment but lost her grip, her body dropped straight down, and immediately she sank into the water. She choked several times, and a burst of panic hit her, her hands flailed instinctively in the water, and very soon she floated up again, but she was not dead. She took a moment to adjust her posture, pressed both hands tightly against the sides of her legs, held her breath, closed her eyes and made a concerted effort to sink. After a short while, her body once again floated up slowly.

The water flowed exceedingly quickly, smooth and regular, and with a high buoyancy. Then she once again was dragged down, little by little.

———

She was still alive, lying on her back and drifting along in the direction of the current. She opened her eyes wide and saw the sky. A bluish-grey cloud was following her.

Everything was so peaceful. She thought, It's actually quite nice, floating along like this.

Someone drifted by, just like her, lying flat on the water, facing upwards. It gave her a start. It was a man dressed in black, with clothing inflated and full of air so that it covered most of his face, with only the eyes showing. The man gave her a glance and floated on, utterly expressionless.

After a while, another person floated over. It was a fat old lady. On seeing her, the old lady kicked the water a few times and slowed down to follow on behind her.

Another woman came, dressed in a pretty, colourful dress that the water had made bulge with air, stretched taut like a little flag bellying out in the wind. That woman drifted past the old lady until she was abreast of her, then turned her face and looked at her, all smiles, as if she had known her for a very long time.

"How did you get here?" the woman came straight out and asked her. It was like they were meeting on the street having only just parted, with a kind of exaggerated happiness and friendliness.

She did not know this woman, but she felt it would be awkward to rebuff her friendliness.

"My mum died. She took poison, *maiduling* it's called. Today's her two-week anniversary, so I went to burn paper money for her, then I came here."

"Oh dear, that is a pity. Why did she do that?"

Why did she do that? She looked at the sky, that long,

long cloud above her, with a little bit of grey and a trace of blue in it, neither far nor close.

"She was too ruthless, she ground a whole packet of the stuff into fragments, mixed it in with water, there was nothing left over, she drank the lot. There was nothing left over at all, all she wanted was to die quickly, to get release, she didn't care a bit for me."

It was as though she was replying to that woman and talking to herself at the same time. She thought, If it wasn't for her, what would I have come back for? I had a husband and a son, it was only for her that I came back, and married again, I even abandoned my son. I thought that, so long as Mum was there... But she died first.

She continued telling the woman, "My mum was always going on about dying, saying, 'Dammit, I don't want to live any more, I'll take poison and die and that'll be the end of it.' It was like an opera, an opera she'd been singing for over a decade, we all just regarded it as a joke, nobody took it seriously. She was straightforward and plain-spoken, always fierce and full of energy, things would loom as big as the sky, and then in a while, it would all be fine.

"The day she left us, she went straight to the bank, took out ten thousand yuan my younger brother had told her to save and gave it to my dad. My dad was still groggy from the booze, and she was worried he'd forget, so she went over with me which families my dad still owed money to, and whose weddings or funerals I should go to with gifts. When noon came, she made a big batch of steamed bread and divided it up for all my nieces and nephews to eat. She took her own piece to eat while she walked and went to the old house in the village.

"On the way, she bumped into my Grandmother Hua. Grandmother Hua even asked her, 'Xiulan, what are you up to?'

"My mum was eating her steamed bread, and she said, smiling, 'Dammit, I don't want to live any more, I want to drink poison and die.' Her voice was cheerful, who could tell that these were the words of someone who wanted to die?

"So my Grandmother Hua replied, 'What foolishness is this?'

"Mum said, 'I've had enough of living, I don't want to live any more.'

"And she walked on. When she came to the old house, she got the *maiduling*, crushed it into smithereens with the rolling pin, mixed it with water and drank it. She drank it clean up, there wasn't a drop left.

"It was only when my niece went looking for her granny that she found her collapsed on the ground. It was before she was dead, she was still twitching and could still speak. She told everyone, 'I've taken poison, I don't want to hold the kids back.' My dad was digging into her mouth as hard as he could, slapping her face. He said, 'What possessed you, you were living, you were fine, but you had to go and die.' People who die by poison usually have bulging eyes, staring. When she went, her eyes were nicely closed, very peaceful. She'd wanted to die with her whole heart. She got her wish."

The river water dragged at her, she floated stably on the surface. The grey-blue sky poured into her heart. She was speaking slowly, she could feel tears trickling down. She had not cried for a very, very long time, not even wept openly at her mum's funeral. She reproached her: You were too ruthless, you went to your death cheerfully, you took no thought for me.

The woman she was talking to was shedding tears and sighed loudly, "It's good that she's dead, when you're dead everything is fine." The old lady who had been following behind her the whole time kept on sighing, "Ai!" and sobbing quietly.

"Why did she kill herself? For no reason at all, you might say. She had a hard life when she was young, she and my dad worked in the fields from dawn till dusk in order to raise me and my two little brothers, and they sold their blood too. Still, in those days everyone in the village was selling blood, so nobody thought anything of it. It was at that time that she got a gastric ulcer, she didn't dare eat anything too hot or cold. As soon as it started hurting she'd say, 'Dammit, I'd be better off dead, I won't be a burden to the kids.' Still, that was just a thing she said, she was pretty easy-going.

"My two brothers grew up, built themselves houses, got themselves wives, and they treated her pretty well, at home she was still the boss. My brothers and their wives both went away to find work in the cities, she and my dad farmed an acre of land at home and took care of the grand-children. Whatever she wanted to eat, they could buy.

"Sometimes the grandkids could get her down with their goings on, her stomach hurt too, and she would shout, 'Dammit, one of these days I'm going to take poison and die.'

"When I came back from Chongqing my mum was happy, laughing and crying like she'd lost her daughter forever and found her again. She'd thought I must have died out there. I did what she told me, I married again. I was a good daughter. Who'd have thought that she'd be so ruthless?

"She only thought of herself, never considered me. I've been wanting to die for a good while too, but I didn't dare say the words out loud. I was afraid my mum would be sad. *She's* all right, though, nothing to worry about or take care of, she didn't bother about anything except freeing herself first."

———

Slowly, the other people floating on the river gathered together, listening to her talking, drifting onwards together. She was wearing a black, short-sleeved shirt with a pattern of tiny flowers and a pair of black cropped trousers. That woman was wearing a pretty, brightly coloured dress, and beside her were men and women, old people and children too. Everybody's clothes floated around them like bubbles as they bobbed along, like a crowd of inflatable dinghies, cheerful but disconnected from the world.

She suddenly felt a desperate need to speak all the words she had never said.

"I've not wanted to live for years. My mum's dead, so I've come to die. When I left the mountains, the husband I had there bought me a gold necklace and a gold ring, he even went with me as far as the train station in the county town, and he brought our son with him. Why didn't he say he'd let the child go with me? His idea was to use the child to tie me down so that I'd be certain to go back. And he was a fool, he didn't consider coming back with me. When I think of that day, I want to cry. My son was fair-skinned and chubby, his eyes were so black, he waved his hand and said, 'Bye-bye Mama, come back soon Mama.'

"The husband I have now is very fond of me, he already has a daughter with his first wife, but he got his parents to take her. He runs a shop in Wu Town and doesn't make me help out. I sit in front of the computer all day, looking at my son's pictures on WeChat. You don't know how good-looking my son is, sturdy as a rock. When he had nothing else to do, he used to call out to me: 'Ma...Ma...' I haven't seen him for four years, he must be ten now."

"How could you be such a silly girl, why did you have to get married to that man? Couldn't you go back to Chongqing and bring your son here with his dad? It's not as though you've never been away from home, or couldn't find some way to make a living wherever you go?"

She did not reply to that woman's sharp interruption, she just kept staring at the grey-blue sky.

"The train drew away, and I knew then that I wouldn't be going back. The mountains are too big there, you can never get away from them no matter how far you walk. I don't know what I was thinking, I'm ruthless too, deep down. I'd been thinking, this is just the way it's going to be, for my whole life. But as soon as I got on the train, I knew I'd never return to the mountains."

She looked at the clouds, and it suddenly dawned on her that she had not just come back because of her mother, but for herself. She had abandoned her son of her own volition and put all the blame on her mother, the better to forgive herself. In recent years she had glowered at her mother whenever they met, to make sure her mother knew that it was she who had made her abandon her son.

"Mum, I was wrong. Mum, I want to call your name a few more times. I want to go back to your tomb again to kowtow a few more times."

"Then your son's dad didn't come looking for you?"

"I don't know if he did or not. It seems I didn't leave an address for him, he only knows that I'm from Henan Province, but definitely not where in Henan. I didn't know where his home was in the beginning either, we met while working in Guangzhou. His finger got caught in a machine and he couldn't work, so I went back to his home with him. After taking the train you take a bus, after the bus you take a three-wheeled tractor, after the tractor you have to walk. It wasn't until then that I realised his home was deep in the mountains. I hated him too, at the time he stopped me from leaving until I got pregnant and couldn't leave.

"Later on my mum told me to find a husband, and so I did. She told me to get married, so I got married. The two of us don't quarrel, but we don't have anything to say to each other. Normally he's in the shop. I don't work so I spend every day online. He's not happy, though he never says anything."

———

This was the first time she had spoken of her own affairs to other people, the first time she had spoken for so long. Before, she had never told anyone. Not her mother, not her friends, still less her current husband. She had hidden them away, hidden very deep. She thought she had forgotten them herself. But they were like seeds, planted in her heart. She had always blamed others: her mother, her father, and later after marriage, she blamed her husband too. She thought that it was all down to them that she no longer had her son.

She was wrong, she had driven her mother to her death. But that was not the main thing. Mum was dead and there was nothing to hold her back. It was a fine time for her to die.

"There's one way in which I'm different from Mum," she declared to everyone. "I don't want to cause a lot of fuss and bother. I don't want to be like Mum, having everyone faff around me once I'm dead, I want to die far away, so nobody can find me."

Somebody laughed and replied, "I'm the same, ever since this cement river began to flatten our fields and roll over the ground with its roads and concrete, I watched it every day, waiting for the water to start running."

"Just look, a tall concrete embankment like this," added someone else. "If you're looking for death, you can't miss, nobody could fish you out, no matter who. Now the wire mesh on all sides has been raised even higher, but over there in Handong, at Wang Village, the wire fence came down, and I climbed up from there. I don't want my sons to find me."

The woman who was always crying now stopped and said, "In Wu Town we have a joke, that as soon as the water began flowing, this river started to kill people, and it floats the dead all the way down to Beijing." The old lady's voice carried unexpectedly, and her tone was firm and decisive, with a hint of a smile, like she was afraid that someone else would steal her punchline.

Everybody started talking all at once, about how they had had the good fortune to get past the chain link fence, stand on top of the tall dyke and jump in this river. They all seemed very pleased with themselves.

Her mouth split open in an involuntary smile.

The other woman was getting closer and closer to her, looking at her warmly, tragic but also expectant. She felt that they seemed to know each other and yet was certain they were strangers.

She had to ask, "Why did you take this path? You seem very much the cheerful type."

———

"Well, as for me, I'm not like you, I died gladly. I'd cursed everyone all I wanted, so I went to die."

That woman spoke like beans rattling in a tin, very fast and very clear, never pausing.

"I phoned Old Li twice today, bawled him out for two hours straight. We'd not been in touch for two months by that point. The one from before, that's my kids' dad, he hung himself. Before he died, he had our daughter-in-law pass on a message to me that he wanted to see me one last time. He'd always been wanting to see me. Our daughter-in-law didn't pass the message on. She didn't want me to come back because she was worried that if I did, I'd hang around, and she'd have to look after me as well as him. When that old devil died, his eyes were wide open, he wouldn't shut them for anything, which shows he died with unfinished business. Our daughter-in-law got scared, she was afraid the old devil would hang around her as a ghost. On the first week's anniversary, then the second, then the third, she kept yelling at me to go back and burn paper money for him. I didn't go back. We'd been divorced for ten whole years, what would be the point of going back now?

"Once we'd divorced the old devil really went to town, boozing every day. He poisoned himself with drink, if he hadn't hanged himself, he'd only have had days to live."

She glanced at this fast-talking woman. The woman was absolutely without grief, as if she was discussing some other person's business.

"I went to find work outside the village, and me and Old Li got together. He was senior chef and I was a waitress. Actually, we knew each other back home, we were from different parts of the same village. I didn't divorce the old devil straight away, I was out earning money the whole time, I must have paid for ten houses for the family. I kept my son until he was eighteen, and I took nothing away from that marriage. The old devil had nothing to complain about.

"Me and Old Li, there was no keeping us together either. He was a gambler. Last year we opened a hot pepper soup restaurant in Wu Town, and business was pretty good. He went gambling every lunchtime. I thought, how can a small business like ours support your losses? We quarrelled every day, I started throwing things, then I upped and left, and the restaurant closed. He went to be the main chef in a restaurant at the entrance to the village, and he phoned me, telling me to go back. And where would I live if I went back? We didn't even have a house. I had a proper go at him, scolded him in text messages as well. He told me to go back and stay at his son's house, but how was I supposed to go and live there? And I wasn't going to my original house either. It's not like my son missed me."

She looked at this woman, puzzled. "Why did you scold him?" she said. "Couldn't you rent a place and live there, like a proper family?"

The woman chuckled. "I just wanted to scold him, I can do that if I want. Once I'd had a proper go at him, I felt good inside. If I rented a house, what would they say about me then, living right next to the village? As soon as the neighbours found out, I'd be a laughing stock, wouldn't I? I wasn't going to live in his son's house either, how could I? I wasn't taking care of my own son, but I was supposed to look after his? I wasn't even willing to get pushed around by my own daughter-in-law, but I was supposed to let his boss me around?

"When I'd done bawling him out, I felt tons better, and there was nothing to hold me back. So I jumped in the river."

————

She was looking at her companions up ahead and behind. They were lying in the water in their own positions, floating onwards, as if they had come together by arrangement to view the scenery.

As the poet Yang Qingxiang wrote,

All of those who drown in the world,
it's their own decision to swim.
All deaths in the world,
are fellow travellers on the same journey.

She suddenly realised that the person she had been talking with seemed to be her younger aunt. This aunt did not have a good reputation, and after Mum died nobody had thought to inform her about the funeral. She had never imagined that her aunt would be floating in this river too.

Her aunt was good-looking. When she was small, she would often stay in her grandmother's house, and they would share a bed. Aunt had long plaits and rosy cheeks, and she was always chuckling. No matter who she was talking to, it seemed there was always something to get her laughing out loud. She married into Zhaojia, which was a few kilometres away from Lu Village. When she went to middle school in Wu Town, her aunt and uncle were going through a messy divorce. Everyone in the village was gossiping about her aunt, saying that she had gone to find work outside and picked up a wild man. And as if that wasn't enough, the man was from right next to her own village. Afterwards, she herself had gone out to work, and then far off into the mountains, farther and farther away from her aunt.

"Auntie," she called out to her.

Her aunt let out a chuckle. "Daft girl, you've only just recognised me."

"Why are you here?" She looked all around her, a little bit puzzled. "Where are we now?"

Her aunt laughed again. "We've reached the world of the dead, Little Xi."

She did not believe it, she knew she was still living, she

could see her aunt and the river, see the sky and the cloud that had been following her the whole time.

———

Her aunt, still as lively as ever, looked in front and behind, left and right, at the people surrounding them and listening to her talk. She turned her head to chat with some of the others.

"Hey, what's going on with you? You're so young, how could you not get over it?"

She heard a low, hoarse voice say resentfully, "I have got over it." This was a young man's voice. Beside him a young girl angrily broke in, "You're still blaming me, even now, you're always so petty, wherever you go." She turned her head to look: a young girl was struggling to get her hand loose, to free herself from that boy, but their two hands were lashed together, and the saturated rope kept them ever more tightly bound together. The girl said in a loud voice, "It's not too late to take it all back." The boy replied, "I'm a dog if I take it back, I'm a pig if I take it back!"

She heard a roar of laughter from all around. She suddenly felt agitated and irritable, and wanted to find a peaceful, secure place, to go and die in peace. But there was no peace here either. She wanted to float along a bit more quickly and leave this crowd of people.

She was thinking, Where should I go now?

They had already been drifting for a while; they must

have left Wu Town by now. In front of Lu Village was Zhaojia. She remembered that the Big River turned to the south here, passing the village of Wangying. Her good friend Hongcai was from Wangying, they had been at the same school, and at sixteen they had gone together to Guangzhou to find work, but after moving several times between factories they had lost contact. After she came back from Chongqing, she had gone to Wangying to look for her. Hongcai's mother said she had got married and gone to live in Hubei Province and only came back every few years. After that came Xieying, where there was a winding, twisting stream at the entrance to the village. People said it was shaped like a dragon, a sign of powerful feng shui. She had been there when she was very small and seen a big tree that had fallen at the curve of the stream and lay rotting there, sinister and terrifying, a very impressive sight. Farther on again was Li Marsh. It was a big village, with an old temple near the entrance. The temple was dark with thickly planted pine trees, and the ancestral records of the old village families were kept there. Farther on still was Xiaying. A classmate of hers from middle school was from Xiaying, and she had drowned saving a child swept away in a flood. Her father had tried to get her listed as a hero by the government, but with no success. She had forgotten the girl's name, but every time she passed through Xiaying, she would think about her.

After that came Wanglou, Xihe, Guolicun, all villages she knew very well. She had visited relatives there with her mother, or gone with her father to sell fried peanuts, or to visit girls from her class at school. After that, they would leave Wu Town behind them and cross the boundary into Wenxiang.

Once she had left Wu Town, she should be able to sink down and die properly.

She twisted her head to the left, and there was a grey concrete slope; she turned her head to look to the right, and there also was a grey concrete slope. She felt a sudden panic, she did not know where she was, she could not find her location. She felt like she was in the Chongqing mountains again: nothing but mountains, to the right and left, in front and behind, no landmarks at all. She had wanted to escape from those mountains, even leaving her own son behind. Now she found herself in that same situation again.

If she was floating in the Tuan River, then it wouldn't be like this.

She was familiar with the Tuan, every bend, every reed bed, every whirlpool. The reeds that bent over the water, long, long grasses swaying in the water, the mud and sand that were washed and scraped away, gradually lost and moved on. She knew which places were deep and which were shallow, where there were big fish and where there were softshell turtles. One year when she was washing clothes in the river, she saw a turtle swimming slowly in the shallow water. She gathered it up in her garments, and it did not move. She put the turtle in her basket, and it still did not move. When she was about to go home, she let the turtle go.

In the middle of the day in high summer, she knew the places she could swim, where there would be no passers-by. Even if someone did happen to pass, once she was out of the water there was a wood of silk trees for her to hide in, nobody would see. She knew the shape of the Tuan River behind every village, which trees there were on the riverbank, how many melon fields, peanut fields and how many newly planted trees.

If she was floating in the Tuan River then it would be clear as day to her, as sure and solid. She would know where she was, and where the Tuan was. She would know where she would get tangled in water weed, where clumps of reeds would block her way, and what bend she would stop at. But nowadays, the water of the Tuan River was too sparse, the riverbed was too jumbled, and she was afraid she would get washed up onto the sandy shore before she had drowned, beached there like a half-dead fish, her mouth gaping wide, white belly uppermost. She did not want to be so ugly.

Her only thought had been to find a place where there was a lot of water, a place where she would not be discovered, yet she had forgotten the hard, unyielding, cold indifference of this brand-new Big River, forgotten that there was no trace of silt or sludge here. This big concrete river was dead. It had boxed up the water, tightly, firmly, powerfully, overbearingly. It had no life or growth to it, it could not grow weeds, or reeds, or fish and shrimp, it would not rise and fall, ebb and flow with the changing seasons, it would not become one with the muddy earth, the sky and the weather over time, until finally, it seemed that this river had never been, that it had always been this way, that it originated in the primordial chaos of the universe, together with its people, who were also sinking and floating, flourishing and declining and dying.

It would not be like all rivers, "thirty years to the east, thirty years to the west". It would not be like that.

Deathly still, deathly quiet waters. A great snake of a river, like a corpse. Enormous, clumsy, winding across the centre of the continent, without any feeling of life at all.

She wanted to let mud and sand fill up her ears and nose, and to sink down, to be caught up in the trailing weeds of the riverbed, and by the stands of reeds, to slowly change into mulch, and finally dissolve into the river ooze. She wanted to hide herself away like this, in the darkness of the deep places where nobody could find her. Her son, her son's father, her current husband, her mother, let none of them think about finding her. She would hide there forever, hide herself away there utterly.

But now she would be floating forever in this great concrete river, slowly coming apart, flesh peeling off bit by bit, rotting away, starting to stink, past Wu Town, Wenxiang, Rang County, gliding past unknown places all the way to Beijing. She would gradually disintegrate into foul-smelling bacteria, dissolve into the water, and at the last would reach a stranger's mouth, and then their stomach.

This was truly nauseating. Too sickening. She wanted to get herself back up and return to the side of the Tuan River again, to find a place where she could die. She was willing to go up a bit further upstream, and a bit further again, where perhaps there would be a broad body of water.

She could feel her head becoming heavier and heavier, the water slowly rising over her, pressing her down, forcing her under, to collide with the hard, unyielding concrete riverbed. The water that was pouring into her mouth was not like the water of the Tuan River; it was not water that tasted of mud, sand or stones, mixed with fish, shrimps and water weed, this water was thin and tasteless, a deathly insipidity that she could not bear.

Even death is this insipid. Well, die then.

The curtains of the sky were drawing together, the last light in the sky was packed away, the land around suddenly darkened.

The darkness had come.

6

The Beauty, Caihong

THAT SUMMER MORNING, people going past the post office on the old Wu Town crossroads on their way to market suddenly felt a moment of panic in their chests, as if something was not right. They took a second look: Caihong's Cosmetics was closed.

This was an extremely rare moment in Wu Town. Actually, there had never been such an occasion before. Since its launch in 1988, Caihong's Cosmetics had always opened its doors at eight in the morning and closed at ten at night. Even when Caihong was having a baby, or when her little sister got married, her brother was executed or her father died, no thunder or storm could stop her.

Caihong was sitting on a long bench outside the operating room of the local hospital, where her husband Luo Jianshe was lying unconscious. He had fallen from the first-floor balcony of the new house they were doing up to land headfirst on the ground and had smashed his leg against some slabs of precast concrete. A crowd had gathered around Caihong: her own mother, fat and constantly gasping for air; Luo Jianshe's mother with her white-streaked hair and twinkly, cowardly eyes; a few other not particularly close relatives who had come to enjoy the show; and Luo Jianshe's friend Hongguo who had telephoned Caihong. The noisy crowd was both watching Caihong and craning over at a girl with a dirty face and messy hair. The girl's head was bowed and she was wiping away tears, relentlessly tugging at the strap of a small black bag she clutched in her hands.

"He got up at daybreak to bring shame on us all," Caihong's mother said, slapping at her little rainbow-coloured make-up bag, quite unsuitable for her huge frame, furious that this scandal was about to become common knowledge. "For all I know, he humiliated himself so badly that he topped himself."

"That's not right either, auntie," said Hongguo, who was sitting beside her. "The main thing is—"

"What 'main thing' would that be, you good-for-nothing brat? If it wasn't for you and your band of fishy friends, would Jianshe be on the road to ruin like this?" Her eyes were slicing up that girl not far away, who she had already slapped several times. "Nobody gets to leave, and if something goes wrong, I'll see you in court."

Hongguo sniggered a couple of times in embarrassment, unable to speak. If they were going to talk about finding a bit on the side, the fault was really not with him.

His own little sweetheart had in fact been introduced to him by Luo Jianshe.

Caihong sat on the bench, a neutral expression on her face. She neither made any effort to quell the uproar beside her nor appeared particularly concerned about the patient in the operating theatre. Today Wang Huan from Li Village was coming to pick up an order of hair restorer and a feminine wash; old Auntie Chen from Wangying would be in to change the memory card in her MP3 player, leaving her old one behind for resale; a batch of new products had not yet been put on the shelves; some of the new shoulder bags had been hung crooked; the poster for children's disposable nappies had not been stuck up properly... She felt that her shop was in a state of chaos, every product had left the position she had assigned it and was wilfully making a bid for freedom, leaving them all clumped together in confusion, unable to find their proper places. She was in a freefall of anxiety and she needed to get back immediately to straighten up, put everything back in its place, to calm and pacify them. She raised her eyes, looking at everyone around her, and their eyes widened hopefully as they looked back. She glanced in the direction of that woman, knowing very well that they had kept her penned up there so as to enjoy the show when Caihong laid into her.

At six o'clock that morning, Luo Jianshe had crawled hastily out of bed, saying that the workmen were getting in early today and he needed to check on them. Caihong's family had just bought a house in one of the town's two rows of European-style villas. Caihong had never once been there. From viewing the house, to purchase, to decorating, Luo Jianshe had taken charge of everything. She did not even know the precise location of the property.

Caihong watched Luo Jianshe scrabbling around for his clothes, hurriedly tucking his shirt into his trousers to reveal his pencil-straight body, and as she listened to his earnest explanation, she felt her throat constrict involuntarily. Every time Luo Jianshe spoke to Caihong with this deadly seriousness, Caihong would know for certain that he was off to meet a woman.

Strange to say, Luo Jianshe gave people a strong impression of falsity. He was always very earnest in his dealings with others. Because he was from the countryside, and from Wu Town's poorest and most isolated village to boot, Luo Jianshe always put a lot of hard work into his social interactions with the townsfolk. Whether eating, drinking or chasing after girls, he threw himself into it all. He came across as presentable and respectable, with a refined, cultivated, sly cleverness that was seldom seen in Wu Town; he was the kind of person who fits in anywhere. However, the residents did not like him. He gave the impression of being transparently two-faced, and when he assumed his air of deadly earnestness, that was precisely the time when he was at his most fake. That falseness was written on his face for all to see. The harder he worked to get close to you, the further away you would feel he was. He was like a smooth, slippery mudfish, dapper and well-groomed, yet it was impossible to get to the core of him.

———

A long time ago, when Caihong had made up her mind to marry Luo Jianshe, her mother, a shrewd, tough, ruthless woman from Wu Town, warned Caihong that this man could not be depended on. He was too affected, and on top of that, he was from the deep countryside. In the minds of the Wu Towners, the folk who lived in those places were still rolling about in their mud-brick huts, dressed in rags.

But what girl could resist advances like those of Luo Jianshe?

Even as a young girl, Caihong's bottom was already notable for its sheer size, weighty, spreading out in all directions, giving her a lumbering appearance and a duck's walk, swaying from side to side on splayed feet. Her upper body, on the other hand, was delicate and slender, with a very narrow waist, and a long, long, white, straight neck; a little face that was both rounded and chiselled; rosy pink skin, so delicate that you could see the tiny, faintly blue veins; a pair of long, oval, almond-shaped eyes, light brown and gleaming, and a head of long, thick, healthy hair, tied up very high, which swished to the rhythm of her walk. This pure, clean beauty formed a stark contrast with her crude lower body; it was a serious mismatch. But on Caihong, this mismatch gave her an additional, coarse allure that left one bewildered and distracted.

In her third year of middle school, she and three other girls, Wang Hong, Yanzi and Caixia, were one of the sights of Wu Town. Their rosy, glowing faces, their desires, so clearly on show, and their clear, sharp laughter made them something close to goddesses, brightening the dark and gloomy skies of Wu Town. The four girls were already fully developed, and boys often accosted them, whistled at them, or passed them notes. These boys were either the charming, dashing sons of the town's leaders, or they came from old Wu Town families, with substantial family property accumulated over generations, or else they were troublemakers and pranksters. But there was another kind too: timid boys from the countryside, driven by their desires to actions beyond their station.

Luo Jianshe was one of the last kind. The eighteen-year-old had just transferred from a countryside middle school, and before the timidity, self-abasement and uncertainty had faded from his eyes, he had become hypnotised by Caihong's neck, almond eyes and enormous bottom. One day on her way home after school, Caihong happened to meet Luo Jianshe on his bicycle.

From then on, every evening at ten o'clock, several dull, heavy sounds would be heard from Caihong's bedroom in the gable of her house: the noise of a brick hitting a wall. At eleven o'clock, as Caihong was going to sleep, the thumps would sound again. Neither light nor heavy, but instead proportionate and polite, as if reminding you that there was someone there: I'm still here. In the early morning at six o'clock, Caihong would open her front door and see a pencil-straight shadow under the old willow tree opposite the pond. Luo Jianshe was standing there, gazing intensely at her as she slowly and steadily approached. He did not speak but silently followed behind her. Luo Jianshe was nearly six feet tall, and when he bent his upright form to look directly at Caihong with his serious black eyes, she felt that there was nowhere to hide.

Caihong was not going to hit that girl. That was her mother's tactic, not hers. The girl was not worth hitting. From her thin, flat appearance you could tell at a glance that she was a girl of good family, with no experience of the world, and that she had let herself be sweet-talked by Luo Jianshe, who before very long was sure to reject her without mercy.

Caihong had no time to waste attending to the anxieties, anger and urgings of all those relatives. Other thoughts were crowding into her brain, and every one of them was concerned with the heaps and piles of matters at the shop. She sent the girl packing, signed everything she needed to sign, arranged what had to be arranged and sat there, waiting for Luo Jianshe to be carried out of the operating room.

She was not furious, not grief-stricken, she did not cry or make a fuss, and so she had everyone frozen to the spot with shock. Caihong had no idea that this stillness and silence were her power, nor that her relatives were far more afraid of her than they were of her mother.

At three o'clock, she rolled up the metal shutters on Caihong's Cosmetics.

A blast of slightly hot, stuffy air brushed past her, and a hundred thousand familiar smells filled Caihong's nose all at once, vying with each other, moving around and jostling in there, squeezing, yelling, quarrelling, striving to take pride of place in her nostrils. Only Caihong could tease apart their slight, subtle differences.

She walked through row after row of brightly polished shelves, her hands reaching out unconsciously, pausing briefly on every shelf for just a fraction of a second, with what seemed to be both affection and a kind of pacification. The oily smell of Lishi washing powder, Safeguard's soapy aroma, the light fragrance of Tide detergent, Eagle brand laundry soap, smelling of phosphorus and the bold kick of Shanghai Sulphur soap, all carried the scent of cleanliness; the bright red, green and blue packs of toothbrushes hanging from hooks always had a stiff, papery smell; the toothpaste, Colgate, Darlie, Zhonghua and prickly ash for sensitive teeth, were slim, graceful and bright, their flavours of mint, green tea, spearmint, strawberry and salt seeped through the cardboard packaging as their cold aluminium tubes forced themselves directly into Caihong's view. Then there was the cool, sharp smell of Head & Shoulders, Rejoice shampoo's sticky, artificial odour, the fruitiness of L'Oreal, the medicinal smell of Bee and Flower, Clairol's springtime tree-leaf bouquet, the haughty chemical aroma of Vidal Sassoon, the smelly-foot smell of Johnson's Baby

Shampoo; and then came the refined aromas of the variety of big and small brands of day creams, night creams and beauty serums; as well as liquid soap for clothes, shower gel, skin protection creams, hairspray and Florida Water.

Both sides of the shop were lined with rows of glass shelves that reached the ceiling, every stack protected by a sliding glass door, as the products they contained were relatively high value: many different kinds of the more expensive or exclusive cosmetics. The bottom two shelves of the glass cabinets were wider and open, where general household goods were set out: plastic jugs, sticky tape (double and single-sided), mosquito spray, refills for electric mosquito repellent, air freshener, electrical extension cords, folding stools, buckets, potties, toilet brushes, plastic cups, toothbrush holders, sewing kits, electric scales, hot water bottles, screws, AA and AAA batteries, all crowded and closely packed, silent and unwieldy, waiting there, emitting a faint scent of plastic, leather and an odd stinky-sweetness that was hard to describe. Further in was an alcove of about eight or nine square metres, which contained all kinds of toilet paper in rolls, boxes and little packets of tissues, wet wipes, nappies for babies and adults, plastic-wrapped children's toys and photograph albums; suspended from the ceiling were purses, women's bags, leather bags, cloth bags and briefcases; behind them in an out-of-the-way location stood several rows of pirated DVDs, and from all around the ceiling and in the centre, small spotlights shone on these packages, colourful and bright, shiny things, encouraging their thick, rich, complex, conflicting scents to exude more densely into the surrounding air.

Countless smells embraced Caihong, leaping up, competing to be first, waiting for her nose and body to come and absorb them.

They had missed each other, though they had only been parted for half a day.

————

The first time Caihong smelled these scents was in the year her brother went before a firing squad.

In those days Caitang was a well-known juvenile delinquent. Whenever Caihong's mother and father spoke to each other it would turn into an argument, but they were remarkably consistent in spoiling their son. Caitang had never wanted in the slightest for food, clothing or anything else, and whenever he got into fights outside, was expelled from school or was the subject of complaints from teachers and parents, Caihong's mother would treat this as a call to arms and repel his attackers using every means at her disposal. After Caitang dropped out of school, he surrounded himself with a little gang known as the Flying Dragon Gang, which was in fact just a few teenagers who had teamed up together in the absence of anything better to do and got haircuts in the style of Hong Kong gangster movie stars like Chow Yun-fat. They went roaring through the town, letting out wolf whistles if they saw a pretty girl, and aiming flying kicks at any young man they did not like the look of.

The year he was seventeen, Wu Caitang, boss of the Flying Dragon Gang, and several kids under him, set off to start a new life in Beijing. The people of Wu Town had trouble making out what exactly they did there. It all seemed like a mass of opaque fog, sinister yet mysterious. All they knew was that he and a few other Wu Towners were illegally selling tickets at Beijing Railway Station. At that time the majority of the young people in Beijing who were from Rang County made a living as ticket touts. When Caitang first arrived, he had turned to a Wu Towner for assistance, and the youngsters who came after him went in turn to Caitang, making touting tickets their first activity in Beijing. Caitang was good at recruiting people to his gang and was violent and ruthless in his methods, and for a time his word was law among the other Wu Town lads.

Those other youths from Wu Town who were in the big city for the first time, young people who had found work as best they could in iron foundries and aluminium factories, cement plants, lime kilns and chicken farms, those young people from Wu Town, scarred from flying molten metal in the foundry, or lungs dark with infection from the lime kiln, those young people from Wu Town who had been caught at their illegal work and sent back home, came to Beijing and turned to Caitang. The first banknotes they earned would be sent back to Wu Town, after which they would go wild with drink and food and other amusements, before getting caught and beaten up, running away and then coming back again, living lives of inconceivable wildness and recklessness. It was said that their great crimes and sins had reached unimaginable levels; that they would corner strangers in dark alleys and beat them up; that they fought with cleavers, iron clubs, daggers, three-section metal staffs; that they suffocated people, sawed up their bodies and threw them into the river or on rubbish dumps.

Altogether more than twenty youths were arrested, all from Wu Town. The three ringleaders were executed, five more were jailed for life and the rest given fixed-term sentences. In the days that followed, Wu Town was eerily quiet since just about all of the villages had one or two children who were implicated, and almost every family was related to some degree to someone involved. All the relatives of those who were arrested were surrounded every day by many neighbours. Some put on a show of concern, others were seeking out the latest developments as a source of gossip, some were gloating over their misfortunes and there were even a few who were genuinely overcome with grief. The men tended to stay indoors, sighing, and the women stood in the courtyard, hands tucked into their sleeves, looking at each other until noon came when they would quietly prepare a meal and eat. In those days, there were very few telephones, so parents would write letters to their children in Beijing, asking if they were all right and warning them not to do anything rash, or better still, to come back quickly so they could see they were safe.

From her seat in the shop, Caihong saw people outside her door creeping along next to the walls with their heads bowed low, and she knew that their families were just like hers, one of their own had been put inside too.

It was Luo Jianshe who brought back the ashes from Beijing. When she heard that her son had been arrested, Caihong's mother took to her bed and stayed there. Her father took advantage of this development to move into his factory, which was several dozen kilometres away, and he never came back again.

Caihong's mother had set her heart on getting a different urn for her son's ashes. She went to Rang County and bought the biggest, most expensive one they had, to be a receptacle for the original container, only to find that it did not fit.

Who had suggested opening the urn to pour the ashes into the bigger one? Caihong could not recall. What she did remember was the smell that filled the air as soon as the urn was opened: a pungent, acrid odour with a faint reek to it, like a very slightly addled egg, the stink of a long-disused lime pit, or the smell that lingered in the air when Caitang had peed as a small boy. Caihong was stunned at what Caitang had been reduced to, and she choked and sneezed at the pungent stench of him, but the shock of her mother's weeping and wailing brought her back to herself, as her mother stretched out hands covered in sticky whitish-grey ash, and collapsed on the floor, keening, "My son, my son."

Caihong fled from the first floor to the ground floor.

She wanted to be sick, desperate to escape the sound of her mother's crying and did not want to be on the same wavelength as her. She hated the sound; she had detested this kind of performance by her mother ever since she was small.

———

The instant she stepped into the shop, she was surrounded by a hundred thousand different smells. Strong and faint, sharp and dull, lingering and brief, perfume, plastic, mothballs, cloth, nylon or concrete, the aromas all came rushing right at her, pushing forward and encircling her. The women who came to the shop to compare the merchandise, to look around or just to browse, each brought their own odour with them: women from the upper village whose neatly ironed outer garments concealed the greasy dirt and dust within, and whose hair always gave off an oily aroma accumulated over many years; people from newly built Liangzhuang, spanking new inside and out, who had acquired a certain status from their proximity to the main town, and whose bodies were lightly fragranced with soap; and the relatively small number of old women and men who came here to buy MP3 players, folding stools or torches, whose mouths gushed a sour, nauseating stench, strong enough to make you faint. However, Caihong did not faint, she looked at them as if on a member of her own family, or at least someone closer than her mother. As she was greedily absorbing and identifying the hundreds of thousands of different smells, she felt her body become relaxed and comfortable, her breathing calm and unhindered.

She immediately threw herself into the business of selling her products, taking money and keeping records. She patiently dealt with enquiries and tidied up goods that other people had moved out of place, while she was secretly conversing under her breath with those scents, saying words that only they understood, letting out sighs that they alone would comprehend.

———

When they heard that Luo Jianshe had broken his leg carrying on with another woman, Wang Hong and Yanzi hurried over. Caihong was sitting in the little stockroom at the back of the shop, busily checking the inventory and making a list of goods. There was a mountain of products piled up beside Caihong, every colour, shape and use, and she had to sort all of them out, mark them off on the inventory, make a note of the current price, selling price, price difference and quantity, then put them on the shelves, one at a time, and finally check them off again. Once she had gone through this process twice, she was able to remember the cost price and selling price of every single product with pinpoint accuracy.

In the light of the lamp, Caihong's expression was solemn and serene, not a hair out of place, no detail neglected. She sat in the centre of her realm, surrounded by the mountainous landscape of her territory, and she was its queen, busily and methodically ordering affairs of state. Her records were becoming ever more accurate and detailed. For the same type of product, toothpaste, for example, she could instantly recall the price of every variety, and could speedily calculate the price differentials, including previous prices, the amount by which they had increased, how much the suppliers took as commission, the quantity in which they sold, the likes and dislikes of the customers, and so on. Every fold and crevice, every cell of her brain was brought into full play, her head seething with the heat of ceaseless cogitation, and underpinning that bubbling heat was an enormous, boundless net, criss-crossing back and forth, densely packed, penetrating deeply, not a strand out of place, extending from all the different products, each number occupying its own position. This net would be comparing itself with another net, and many others, merging and splitting apart, each proceeding at its own pace. Her brain was a miniature universe, revolving in perfect order, endless, limitless and perfectly arranged.

Wang Hong and Yanzi felt left out. At that time the three of them were still on very close terms. The fourth member of their group, Caixia, had got into college in Nanyang, found a husband there and rarely came back. Wang Hong had also opened a cosmetics shop in the town and had become one of Caihong's business competitors, but no rivalry had fully developed between them as yet, so they stayed on good terms in every way that mattered.

Yanzi had married a son of the Wu family who ran a hot pepper soup restaurant renowned throughout Wu Town, and she could be seen standing every day in front of the wok, their very own Venus of the Soup.

"Stop working, Caihong, quick, tell us what's going on with Luo Jianshe! He's hopeless, he'll never change." The three of them had always shared each other's secrets since they were girls together, and even now Yanzi had kept up the habit of reporting everything to her girlfriends, drawing no distinction between major and trivial events, including her inharmonious bedroom relations with young Wu Shaobing. Wang Hong had always been the strong one, she would take the role of problem solver.

Caihong raised her head from her goods and seemed to be travelling back to join them from the mists of long ago, lifting her distracted but beautiful almond eyes to gaze at her two friends. These friends seemed to be eyeing her up greedily, wanting to extract her secrets and her energy, just like Luo Jianshe, demanding things from her with their unequalled talent for stirring up trouble. She knew that over half the people of Wu Town were whispering to each other, revelling in her misfortune, looking down on her and mocking her, fanning the flames, exaggerating and embellishing. Wang Hong and Yanzi were their chosen representatives.

"There's nothing much going on, he broke his leg checking over the house," Caihong muttered. She told Wang Hong and Yanzi to get themselves a soft drink and continued with her inventory. She had to finish it that evening and get everything on the shelves. The next day was market day, and any number of people would be coming to the shop, she could not fight this battle unprepared. It made no difference whether Luo Jianshe had broken his leg or not, none of this had the slightest effect on the running of the shop. For many years now, Luo Jianshe had left home early in the morning, returning around four o'clock in the afternoon, but if Caihong left the shop for as little as three minutes it would cease to function. At that time, it was not fashionable to stick price labels on the goods, so everything depended on Caihong's brain.

Wang Hong and Yanzi were discussing animatedly how to punish Luo Jianshe, and how to keep men under control. Wang Hong tugged at Caihong's sleeve saying, "Then why don't we go away on a trip, how's that sound?"

Yanzi clapped her hands and said, "Great, we can leave the family to our husbands for a while. Let's put some of the strain on them for once."

Travel? Caihong had been to Nanyang and Zhengzhou, and her impression of big cities was far from favourable: dizzying and dazzling, filthy and messy. Every time she went, she would go directly to her destination, select her goods, put in an order, and then turn straight round and leave. Later she wrote out lists and would send Luo Jianshe instead.

"What's the fun in going to those places? All the buildings, the crowded streets, it makes my head swim." Caihong raised her head to look at Wang Hong and Yanzi.

"Besides, going away for a few days, what with board and lodging and shopping, we'd be looking at two or three hundred every day, that would come to two or three thousand for a whole trip, buying things we don't need. And I'd have to shut the shop as well, so I'd lose several hundred in earnings every day. Taken all in all, I'd have to spend five or six thousand yuan. It's not worth it."

Caihong spoke seriously and clearly, and her logic was faultless. Wang Hong and Yanzi stared open-mouthed at Caihong the beauty with her delicate eyebrows and narrow eyes, and for a while, they did not know what they were supposed to say.

"It's not that I can't spare the money," Caihong explained, "but there really wouldn't be any point. It's not like the two of you haven't spent a few days away, looking at skyscrapers or going round shopping malls, and what's it all for? Don't we have everything we need right here?"

Luo Jianshe came back from the hospital with his leg in a cast, to find that Caihong was now sleeping in the storeroom at night. In the beginning, Caihong would go upstairs to get a nightdress or to pick up other little bits and pieces. At most she would say a word or two to Luo Jianshe as he lay there, explaining that she was too busy and was going to sleep in the storeroom downstairs. After a few days, she no longer went upstairs.

In the daytime, Luo Jianshe would listen to Caihong's voice, slightly gruff and very lacking in emotion: "What can I do for you?" "Two yuan." "One fifty." "Twenty," "No more than seventeen," "Then why don't you try some other places?" From eight in the morning until four in the afternoon, most of what Caihong said had to do with numbers, she rarely mentioned anything else. Even if somebody wanted to gossip with her, it would just be, "How's Luo Jianshe?" to which the reply was, "Oh, the usual". Or they'd say, "Your business is doing really well," to which came the reply, "Well? In what way?" and with that, the conversation would come to an end.

This was the first time that Luo Jianshe observed how little Caihong had to say.

Occasionally Caihong would bring Luo Jianshe a cup of water when she came upstairs or make minor adjustments to the position of his plaster cast, and then she would hurry back down. Luo Jianshe followed Caihong with his eyes, waiting for her to speak, waiting for her to raise her eyes and look at him, to scold him indirectly with hints and implications, or to weep silently, or tell him of her pain. Luo Jianshe was prepared for all of that. He fully intended to slap his own face to show his remorse. But Caihong did not give him the opportunity. She was so busy that she did not have time to spare him a glance in the first place.

One evening, limping on his plaster cast, Luo Jianshe appeared in the storeroom. The smells in there were dense and thick enough to make him feel faint. The goods were piled like mountains around a small bed and the little table at the head of the bed was piled with stacks of account books, inscribed with crowded masses of figures. Caihong was lying on her side on the bed like she had collapsed there, her eyes half closed, her face flushed. She seemed extremely tired and very happy and comfortable. He sidled up and squeezed in beside her. Her eyes still closed, Caihong turned over and took Luo Jianshe in her arms. Caihong did not refuse him, on the contrary, she seemed quite carried away, which both baffled and excited him.

Caihong was swaying above him, her eyes tightly closed, her mouth wide open, sometimes frowning slightly, nostrils flaring, as if she was trying to capture something, momentary relief, followed by a moment's tension, then a moment's excitement. Moving along with her, at first Luo Jianshe thought that Caihong was enjoying him, so he worked hard to go along with her movements, but he discovered that the two of them were not on the same wavelength at all. It was like he had no part in her excitement.

While Luo Jianshe needed to rest his leg, Caihong had telephoned her suppliers in Nanyang and Zhengzhou and got them to find her regular, dependable long-distance buses that could bring her products back, if she paid them for transportation. She discovered that the cost of having goods delivered was much lower than sending Luo Jianshe to acquire them. Not only this, every time the suppliers would send a few new products over for her to sell on a trial basis.

That was when she started selling high-quality cosmetics from Japan, Korea and Europe. She set up a new display cabinet at the entrance, where she laid out the newest and best products with their delicate packaging, the foreign writing that she could not read and their exquisite scents. Women who had spent time working away from Wu Town in the big city would scrutinise them and critique them with the air of one who had seen the world; women who had never worked away from home would stand behind them, listening carefully, and once the first women had gone, they too would approach and examine the merchandise in minute detail. In the end, these were the women who forked out for the goods.

These products were how Caihong made her mark; they represented taste and flowed into every corner of Wu Town. Owning a Caihong product was a symbol of conspicuous consumption and class, representing or at least hinting at a certain social status.

Caihong converted the ground floor kitchen into two beauty rooms and took on two young girls as beauticians. The cosmetics manufacturers sent staff to train them on the premises. On the day the rooms opened for business, the two beauticians, Jiaojiao and Lanlan, stood at the door of Caihong's Cosmetics, one on the right and one on the left. Caihong had not put up a sign, nor did she go and hand out leaflets. Just by having the two girls standing at the door in their pink uniforms, she had once again taken the lead in the fashionable life of Wu Town.

Once his leg had recovered, Luo Jianshe reappeared on the streets of Wu Town. But he felt that everyone was now treating him differently. He had not been scolded by his wife, had not been punished, nor backed his wife into a corner and given her a few slaps and then sauntered out with his head held high. This was like a boil of pus that had never been lanced, so he was still carrying the infection within him. Luo Jianshe found himself at a loss after his time of isolation, but he still had to wait it out until four o'clock came, and he could return home.

Caihong was still bustling about when she saw Luo Jianshe go straight up to the first floor without looking at anybody, frowning as if someone had angered him. After a while he crept back down again and stood behind the shop door, watching the customers. First-time visitors took him for the shop owner and approached him with questions about the goods, and he would reply.

When evening came, Caihong sprawled on her little bed as usual and waited for Luo Jianshe to service her. Luo Jianshe looked down at her almond eyes and enormous bottom, and was filled with fury, but also a submissive urge to ingratiate himself with her, as if the service he performed every evening was an inescapable duty demanded by some inexplicable kind of nightmare demon. Their nightwear, spare clothes, socks and slippers all gradually migrated into the storeroom. One day Caihong put in a partition across the first-floor bedroom and made two more beauty rooms.

———

At the end of that year, Luo Jianshe went to Korea and Japan and on a trip to France too. Caihong's Cosmetics' sales had exceeded a certain quantity of branded merchan-

dise every year, and the company that produced it
rewarded Luo Jianshe and Caihong with a free trip
abroad. Of course, Caihong did not go.

"There's nothing to see in Korea and Japan, it's all just
small houses and little people," complained Luo Jianshe.
"And you'd never credit how old and shabby Paris is.
Apart from a few half-decent buildings, on the streets it's
no better than our Wu Town."

Sitting in his doorway, Luo Jianshe spat into the street,
took a small purple clay teapot, poured a mouthful down
his throat, and said to Hongguo and Yizhi the doctor,
"They paid for plane tickets, board and lodging, right
enough, but the food? A few slabs of meat, some chunks of
potato, a dish of greens and that's your lot. I spent a good
few thousand with every trip, there's really no point in it."

Luo Jianshe was not showing off for Hongguo and
Yizhi, he truly could not see the point of it. It was all just a
few shabby old houses, and as for style, you could get way
more luxury in Zhengzhou. It was exhausting, being
cooped up in a plane for more than ten hours. Yizhi and
Hongguo looked at Luo Jianshe, and both expressed praise
and agreement, but then a while later exclaimed in disgust,
"That little bastard, he doesn't even appreciate he's gone
abroad, and he sits there bragging about it."

Luo Jianshe and Caihong set themselves up as a cut
above everyone else, yet they were also incomparably
vulgar. Everybody envied them. Being set apart like this
forced them to put on a united front, which, perversely,
made them into a devoted couple. They were diligent and

painstaking, and in that two hundred square metre shop they bought and sold, added, subtracted and calculated, united against a common enemy, at peace and content.

Wang Hong and Yanzi became obsessed with aerobics. Every evening they led a group of Wu Town women earnestly copying their movements along to the earth-shakingly loud sound system, like new leaders of fashion. At daybreak, Wang Hong would put on her eight-inch heels, carefully make herself up and stand in the shop, graceful and smiling artfully, flirtatiously greeting the men who came to buy cigarettes and spirits in the hope of earning herself a repeat customer. By now Wang Hong was in direct competition with Caihong and was devoting her intelligence and resources to overthrowing her.

Caihong was going nowhere. Her bottom was getting ever heavier, and droopier too, protruding even further. She waddled like a duck, flippers splayed outwards, her bottom swaying from side to side. Caihong's bottom was still the crudest strength of her body, a public declaration of her powerful lust for life and sexual desire. There was an almost unbelievable sluggishness to her movements, like she had fallen into some kind of dream world, from which she was unwilling to awake.

She sat there in her shop, dressed casually all in black from head to foot; she did not powder her face, nor did she wear eight-inch heels (just black flats), nor smile at her customers. Her hair was knotted carelessly at the back of her head. She wore a small platinum chain around her long white neck, which would glitter with shards of light as she approached, and her long almond eyes were becoming increasingly reserved with age, carrying within them a hint of sorrow, which might only have been exhaustion from her daily grind, but on Caihong it had become a part of her good looks. She was just this kind of natural beauty, at the forefront of all Wu Town's trends, drawing the local men and women to follow in her wake.

As far as Wu Town was concerned, Caihong, like her body and face, was a riddle: peaceful, mysterious and noble, but also ruthless, crude, a merciless driver of hard bargains and deeply inscrutable, and this simply added to her allure. Only Luo Jianshe knew that behind this enigma there was nothing at all.

Luo Jianshe, on the other hand, had become boorish and diminished. Thanks to premature baldness, the head of black hair in which he had taken such pride had become a black semicircle. This semicircle was remarkably round, U-shaped like a big wine glass with a wide mouth. There was something repellent in the softness of its lines, and something weak about it. Morally empty and ingratiating, it was becoming more and more in tune with the look in his eyes. Every time he saw someone go into the shop, he would incline his body and approach solicitously, staring fixedly at every move the customer made, or he would go and choose the products they wanted. The more attentive he was, the more false he became.

———

At four o'clock in the afternoon, Caihong could finally take a moment's rest. She lay down on the massage chair, ran her hand lightly over the product shelves beside her and took a deep breath, letting the scents of the shop fill her nose, mouth, body and mind. Her gaze swept automatically over the shelves of goods, and she at once became acutely aware that they were two rows short of Colgate toothpaste, and several Safeguard soaps were missing too, leaving an unsightly gap. This could not be tolerated. In her realm and her world, she demanded perfection.

Jiaojiao came out from the beauty room. Luo Jianshe's eyes slithered quickly over her bare legs, with no expression in them at all.

Caihong had long since caught on to the direction of her husband's gaze and observed the remnants of his unrelinquished desires; she almost felt a little bit sorry for him. There was no place for this man in Jiaojiao's eyes; he was too old, and although he appeared so earnest, he could not hide that air of ageing boorishness. A young girl would have no time for someone like that.

Luo Jianshe was spending longer and longer in the shop and was becoming increasingly familiar with its products, yet Caihong was becoming less and less aware of his existence. She disliked his presence in her world, smelling the scents she smelled, experiencing the numbers she experienced. The numbers, constantly changing yet something one could grasp, were her only truth in life, and the only thing on which she could really depend.

Sometimes Luo Jianshe would anticipate her

answering a customer's enquiry, and look back at her with a fawning glance, or the smug back of his head would pop up in front of her, and she would actually detest him a little. But this too was only a very faint, momentary emotion.

She glanced outside the door. This was the furthest she would look in a day.

Hard though it was to believe, for over a decade she had never even ventured as far as the open fields a kilometre from the crossroads. All of her life could be encompassed within a one-kilometre circle. Go out of the door, and three hundred metres to the left were people selling vegetables and meat; five hundred metres to the right were steamed bread and noodle vendors, and she had everything else for her day-to-day needs in her own shop. This two-hundred-square-metre shop and this crossroads had become all she needed in life.

Caihong went to sleep. Her half-open mouth formed an O shape, a capital O, without beginning and end, turning full circle and starting again from where it had begun, sucking in all brightness, impulses and fervour, without crack or seam. She was snoring, evenly, relaxed, and her face gave off a smooth white sheen, like a baby, pure and beautiful.

Luo Jianshe stared at the only customer in the shop. The man had been wandering about the place for half an hour already, picking up soap, cigarettes, razors, notebooks, taking careful note of every item for a while and then putting them all back; judging by his aimless behaviour, he would not be buying anything. But Luo Jianshe kept gazing fixedly at him anyway and made sure that he knew he was being watched. He stared at that man, at his walking, moving body, with all his heart and soul.

However, his body language was betraying his secret: he loathed this place, and his hatred was equal to the amount of attention he put into his stare. His body was growing a million hands and arms, which even now were sweeping through these endless, interminable products that pressed down upon him. He wanted to throw them away, to smash them, he wanted to pound the roof into a wreck, he wanted to charge into the beauty room and throw that old woman's naked, ugly body out, and take Jiaojiao and Lanlan with him, mount his horse and gallop away, to a place where nobody could ever find them.

Luo Jianshe sat there, watching this upheaval in his mind, and a faint, cold smile appeared on his face.

In the midst of her snores, Caihong's nose twitched briefly, greedy and determined, as if it had caught some unfamiliar smell.

7

Meatheads

THE MOST IMPORTANT PERSON in this story is Xiuqin. She's from the family who lived in the fourth house diagonally opposite ours to the right, on the side next to the main road. Nowadays Guo Hongyi's sister runs a cash-and-carry there. Xiuqin's surname is Wang, and she's from Wangying, like me. Her old father-in-law Cheng Xian'er ran a medicine shop on the main street, and he's pretty well-known. Xiuqin's husband is called Cheng Lin. Xiuqin and I are the same age, and you'd have to say that she's a pretty good-looking woman, unusually tall and slim. A gowk, as we say in the countryside, not the type to pay attention to detail, with a loud, cheerful way of talking. She got on very well with the neighbours on either side.

How did I find out about it? That day the weather was just like it is now, strangely warm. I was stripping corncobs when I saw Yang Xiuzhen charging over in a tearing hurry, shouting, "There's a fight, there's a fight", and all the neighbours came running out onto the street clutching their lunch bowls. I wasn't in a position to join in the fuss, your little nephew had a fever that day and wasn't at kindergarten. He was so clingy, he just wouldn't let me out of his sight, so I couldn't go running off.

The next day Yang Xiuzhen dropped by on one of her visits, and as soon as she was through the door she said to me, all mysterious, "There's a been a fight in Xiuqin's family." Yang Xiuzhen lives diagonally opposite us but on the left, and she'll drop by several times a day whether she's got any business with you or not. I said, "No wonder you were running so fast, you were on your way to break up a fight," Yang Xiuzhen said. "You've no idea, the state Cheng Lin beat Xiuqin into, she's lucky to be alive. Xiuqin's been having an affair."

I had no idea that things had got so bad between them. A day or two before the fight, I'd even been to their house to borrow a hoe for the sweetcorn. The pair of them were bickering then, but when they saw me, Cheng Lin gave me a nod and left. I had even said, smiling, "Xiuqin, what's this, the two of you falling out?" Xiuqin said, "Oh, that bastard, he's the worst."

Yang Xiuzhen told me, "Cheng Lin caught Xiuqin at it."

This is the first family.

———

First thing on Sunday morning, Yizhi's three sisters drove back to Wu Town. From Rang County to Wu Town is no more than half an hour's drive, but normally they were each busy with their own affairs and getting them all together for a trip home was very hard. Yizhi's eldest sister sold alcohol and cigarettes and the nearer it was to Sunday, the more she had to do; and his second elder sister kept a general store, which she could not leave unattended for an instant. His fourth younger sister, on the other hand, was a lady of leisure, a teacher in Rang County Teachers' College, but she spent most of her time dabbling in writing, essays and the like, or gathering material and taking pictures all over the place, like this hobby of hers was some mighty undertaking, so she was busy too.

But this time they had to go back. They had heard from their elderly father that Yizhi and his wife Xueli had spent the last two weeks in a state of cold warfare, during which time Xueli had actually left home for three or four days. Rumour had it that recently Yizhi had been spending money he could not account for, sums that had mounted up into the thousands, but nothing could induce him to say where it had gone. The sisters found Xueli a bit of a cold fish, someone who always seemed to keep them at arm's length, no matter how friendly or ingratiating they were with her. Yet they respected her and felt for her too, working so hard to keep the family going, with her clear principles and sense of duty, especially since Yizhi had been regularly embroiling himself in scrape after scrape for years. If all the sisters got together to scold Yizhi, that would at least be a comfort to Xueli. In any case, as Yizhi's eldest sister said, we might as well take this chance to get back the money he owes us all. At least that way he won't be getting up to who knows what every day. He's got no sense of danger, never looks ahead. His second and fourth sisters had small concerns of their own too; each would have struggled on their own to get back the money they had lent their brother, but if the eldest spoke up, this was justification for them too and would save a lot of toing and froing. So the three sisters all fell in easily with each other's plans and drove back to Wu Town.

It was a fine day, with only a slight wind. There was no market in Wu Town that day, and few people were on the streets. As soon as the sisters set foot in the clinic, they heard the rattling of mah-jong tiles from the annex. The players did not even raise their heads, just flicked an eyelid in their direction, and smiling said, "Oho, the sisters are back?"

As soon as he saw his elder sister and the others come in, Yizhi stuck his head out from the kitchen, looked ingratiatingly at Xueli who was picking over vegetables at the kitchen door, and let out a chuckle. "The moment you called yesterday to say you were coming, Xueli made me buy meat and vegetables, as she knows Big Sister likes dumplings. They'll be ready in a bit, sit back and later on we'll make dumplings together."

Xueli dusted off her hands and stood up saying, "Ah, you've come back."

The sisters secretly exchanged glances. Although Xueli was not looking in the direction of the kitchen, her expression was calm and self-possessed, and there was nothing more out of the ordinary than that, so they could let go of their worries too and started teasing each other.

Yizhi's big sister took the vegetable basket out of Xueli's hands and threw it on the floor, saying, "Xueli, don't bother with that, get Yizhi to do it. Let's talk for a while, and once the filling is all mixed and ready, all you have to do is make the dumplings."

Tea was made and melon seeds brought out. The women sat in the courtyard, and somehow the talk turned to Xiuqin, Cheng Lin and all the rest. This was a love affair that had shaken Wu Town a few years earlier.

———

Cheng Lin had caught Xiuqin in the act with a man. That man lived directly opposite our house, he was a teacher at the Number Five High School, five doors down from Xiuqin's house. As you can see, it's now been converted and sells Aima brand electric bikes. The man was called Yang Fengxi, he had a twisted neck, properly ugly, and he wasn't as young as he used to be either. And Cheng Lin was seriously good-looking, always clean and tidy.

I said I couldn't believe it, not even if you threatened to kill me. Yang Fengxi and his wife were both teachers at the Number Five High School, the two of them pretty much always left together and came back together, so they couldn't have had any opportunity to misbehave. Besides, Yang Fengxi's wife, Zhou Xianglan was her name, was very pretty and elegant. Yang Fengxi seemed a bit henpecked, and you wouldn't hear him say more than a few words all day. His comings and goings were all arranged by his wife, but they seemed to get along pretty well. When there was a mah-jong game in Xiuqin's family, Zhou Xianglan would always go there too, to watch the play. Figure it out, there just weren't any opportunities.

That's the second family.

The third family is over there on our street, the sixth house along past the coal yard. These two were school-teachers as well, in the central township primary school. The man of this family was called Qian Guofeng, his wife was Chen Na, and they had two little girls.

What sort of person was Chen Na? She was the talk-ative kind, there was no side to her, but a little bit flaky. And she was up for a bit of fun, she liked to watch them playing mah-jong in Xiuqin's house. After it all came out, everyone said that that was a sign; when they were playing mah-jong together, Chen Na was clearly partial to Cheng Lin.

Apart from Cheng Lin and Xiuqin quarrelling among themselves, there was no other gossip about their family. That family of Qian Guofeng and Chen Na's was far messier. What was messy about it? Qian Guofeng's father Old Qian. A long time ago, he was the headmaster at the primary school, and a man of status, and he used to have a thing with the female boss of the coal yard Chen Chunlian. Chen Chunlian was so tall and so pretty, and she really knew how to dress up. Her husband Shan Bin was a very ugly man and a simple soul, he used to run a jute sack factory. In those days, Chen Chunlian had a terrible reputation, so she got married to Shan Bin because she wanted someone to depend on. Who would have known that they'd barely been married any time at all when the jute factory went bust and they had to depend on Chen Chunlian? Chen Chunlian's and Old Qian's houses were just three doors apart, and they had a little door between them. I've been to Chen Chunlian's house, and I've seen that door open wide. The two of them were quite open about their relationship, everyone in town knew. It was an accepted thing.

Chen Na could be sharp-tongued, and after seeing her old father-in-law going in and out of Chen Chunlian's house, she said some things she shouldn't have outside the home. Qian Guofeng give her a talking-to, and she didn't dare to do it after that. The two of them often fell out because of this. All the same, it hadn't got to the point of divorce.

Out of these three families, Yang Fengxi was the oldest, Cheng Lin was in the middle and Qian Guofeng was the youngest.

Now it had all blown up. The gossips and idlers were hard at it every day, going everywhere in search of further scandal, it was all very pointless and nasty. The people who came to our place to play cards were saying such horrible things, and that Yang Xiuzhen was making her reports two or three times each day.

Rumour had it that Xiuqin sometimes told Cheng Lin she was going away for a break for two or three days, when actually she was with Yang Fengxi. That daft bastard Cheng Lin didn't know a thing. In the daytime, he would go to his dad's medicine shop on the main street to make up herbal prescriptions and see patients. His dad paid him a wage, and business was very good there, very busy indeed, so at noon he would not go home for lunch. By day Xiuqin would be at their own medicine shop, where she sold medicines, but if someone wanted a consultation she'd nip off and call Cheng Lin to come back.

Cheng Lin didn't suspect anything, so somebody else passed the gossip on to him. It was that wife of Wang Laoxiao's, she always has to be up to something. She used to tell people behind his back that Cheng Lin was a meat-head,[1] that Xiuqin was carrying on with a man outside the home, making a cuckold of him, and the wretched woman was excited like you wouldn't believe. Someone said they had seen Xiuqin slip into Yang Fengxi's house with their own eyes, through a crack in the door, and had waited for over two hours, and then saw Xiuqin coming back out.

Xiuqin was stubborn as a mule, she flat-out refused to admit she had something going on with Yang Fengxi. She said, "You lot don't know that bastard Cheng Lin, he's the worst of the worst, the kind of swine that goes and finds other swine to back him up.

He even called in people from my own family to prove I've been up to no good. Very sneaky. He'd never say a word about himself no matter what, covered with pig's bristles as he is, but he's happy to gossip about other people. Like *he* can talk, carrying on with Chen Na on the quiet!"

So Xiuqin took herself off to Chen Na's husband Qian Guofeng to say, you keep an eye on your wife. Once she'd spoken up, Qian Guofeng started to get ideas, and he checked Chen Na's phone. The first thing he saw was a call that Chen Na had made at eleven o'clock at night lasting for an hour and twenty minutes. They had a big row because of this.

Chen Na said, "I'm a patient, I called the doctor to describe my symptoms, it's totally normal."

"Who do you think you're fooling, you little cow," replied Qian Guofeng. "You're making phone calls at eleven at night to discuss symptoms? Do you take us all for fools?" And he threw Chen Na's phone into the cesspit in a fit of rage.

———

Yizhi, who had been making filling for dumplings in the kitchen, but had come out at some point, broke in, "Ah, fuck, this Cheng Lin business is the stuff of legend. When all's said and done, who knows whether he and Chen Na really were getting it on?"

Xueli did not look at him, nor did she respond to his

comment, but she kept on talking. The sisters exchanged glances.

Zhenguo, Wu Town's famous master of ceremonies, had been watching the game in the clinic annex. He came out with his cup to get some water, and on hearing them all talking about this key moment in history, he stopped and listened intently.

———

When a person is shameless, nobody can do anything about them. First it was quarrels in Cheng Lin's family, after that fights broke out in Qian Guofeng's family too.

Cheng Lin and Xiuqin quarrelled nastily, dropped all pretence at keeping up appearances and ripped each other to shreds. There was really no point to it, so shaming. They were competing in being hateful, and when they'd done those awful things, they'd stand at the door and fight over telling the people who'd come to laugh at them, like they were afraid someone might not know yet.

Xiuqin parcelled up all the medicine in the shop, returned it to the suppliers and took the money for herself. Cheng Lin got mad too, saying, "You've sold the family business." So he reported that the bank card for the account with all his wages in was lost, and he changed the number. Cheng Lin had always left his card with Xiuqin before. Up till then, Xiuqin had been living the good life all day long, as idle as a donkey, just looking after the kid and doing a bit of cooking, and always wearing brand names, really expensive stuff, some we'd never even seen before.

So Cheng Lin got Xiuqin's clothes, all those lovely patterns and colours, took the whole lot outside, dumped them at the gate and burned them. Xiuqin was even more angry, and she said, "If you're going to such lengths, and you're not giving me any money, how are me and your son supposed to live? And now you've burned my clothes, you're behaving like I'm already dead." She got all the furniture from the house, everything of any value, and took it home to her mother's.

The folk in the old town were talking themselves crazy over the business with Cheng Lin and Xiuqin alone. The Chengs were an old Wu Town family, with plenty of friends and relatives, and Cheng Lin's dad was a major local figure, his word carried weight. He'd been a doctor his whole life, he was on good terms with everybody and he got a lot of respect. Now the whole town was gossiping all over the place, and Cheng Lin's dad was publicly humiliated, he saw this as a major loss of face, so he ordered Cheng Lin to get a divorce.

Cheng Lin and Xiuqin had a boy, two years older than our Haohao. At the time he was at junior high school, and the lad was doing well there, though he was rather quiet. When the pair of them fell out so publicly, he stopped wanting to go to school, he felt ashamed. A few nasty class-mates were talking about it, pointing him out to everyone. He couldn't bear it and fought those kids a few times over it, but he would rather have died than go back to school, and in the end he just left. Now he's training as a hair-dresser, although he's only seventeen. The two of them basically ruined their son.

To all intents and purposes, this family is broken beyond repair.

Now let's talk about Qian Guofeng and Chen Na. The two of them kept their heads down and fought in silence, although they often came to blows in the middle of the night. For exact details, you'd need to get Yang Xiuzhen to come and tell everyone all about it. Yang Xiuzhen was their colleague, she said she often saw Qian Guofeng with purple and green bruises on his arms, and Chen Na with a black eye or a bad limp. That Qian Guofeng really went for her. Chen Na used to tell the other teachers in the school that he deliberately hit her in places no one could see. Qian Guofeng wanted to divorce Chen Na, but right at the start she refused. Not because she didn't want a divorce, but because Qian Guofeng wouldn't give her any money. She held out for a year, but it was only once he had given her 170,000 yuan that she agreed.

Cheng Lin and Chen Na never admitted to anything between them. Later on they actually got married, and people would ask jokingly, didn't you two have something going on before it all started? They still wouldn't admit to it. But everyone thought there was something fishy in all of this, and said there must have been something off about Cheng Lin. He'd argued so ferociously with Xiuqin, was desperate for everyone to know that his wife was carrying on with someone else, he put too much energy into it, more than was right. As for Chen Na, she was shamelessly grasping, and as soon as the money had changed hands, she divorced Qian Guofeng straight away. Yang Xiuzhen said that on the same afternoon she got divorced, Chen Na went with Cheng Lin to view a flat in the Imperial Vista Gardens in Rang County and signed the deal on the spot. As you know, you can't get your hands on an Imperial Vista Gardens flat for anything less than tens of thousands. There's this teacher in the Wu Town Number Two Junior Middle School, and when she heard that Chen Na had been to the county town to buy a flat, she made a special journey to check the documents, to see whether she and Cheng Lin went there together.

———

When they had got this far into the story, Yizhi's elder sister slapped her thigh, causing her bulky frame to quake. "Heavens above," she exclaimed, "all those people with nothing better to do! Spending money to get people followed just to prove some piece of gossip, these people really do live lives of leisure."

Yizhi's fourth sister, who had been listening as if hypnotised, called to her big sister to stop, "Shush, Older Sister, let Sister-in-Law talk or I won't be able to keep track of who's related to who."

Zhenguo said, smiling from the sidelines, "This is old women's gossip. Do you, a university teacher, actually like listening to all that?" He lowered his voice. "That wasn't what I heard. They said that to get proof that there really was something going on between Cheng Lin and Chen Na, Qian Guofeng got two of his country relatives to follow them everywhere. He even got someone he knew to visit the Telecoms Customer Service Centre to check the phone records. Even so, for a year or more they just didn't find any evidence. When Qian Guofeng learned that the pair of them had gone to town to buy a flat, he was so angry he was spitting blood. Who knows how they communicated with each other? You tell me."

At some point in all this, another person had joined them in the yard to listen to the conversation, and now they chipped in. "I heard that to catch Cheng Lin and Chen Na, Qian Guofeng hid behind the end wall of Cheng Lin's house, pressed himself up against it and listened in. Somebody spotted him and told Cheng Lin. When it was past ten at night, Cheng Lin pretended to be going out of the house and went to the yard, stumbled about there, then suddenly called out, 'Who's that?' and threw a brick over the wall, which nearly got him. Qian Guofeng was so scared that he ran off with his tail between his legs."

Everyone burst out laughing. "That's all just slander," Xueli said, "who would be so horrid?"

———

That Chen Na's as daft as they come too, the way Yang Xiuzhen tells it. After the divorce, she dolled herself up like a parrot every day, neat as a pin, really putting herself on display, oozing shamelessness. Some people asked Chen Na why she'd gone to all that trouble with her appearance. Chen Na said, "What can you do? I've got to make myself a match." After marrying Cheng Lin she was just the same, hair all done up to here, tottering about the streets every day in tight skirts and high heels, and she'd say to anyone she met, "I'm as happy as anything, honestly."

Then let's talk about Yang Fengxi's family. While the other two families were arguing and beating each other bloody, those two teachers weren't affected in the least. They went about their business as if it was nothing to do with them at all. They set off together to school first thing for their classes, and as soon as they got back home in the afternoon they'd close the door, have their meal and sleep, quiet as anything. Those idiots were kicking up a scene over here, while that couple were perched peacefully on their branch over there. Sometimes they would stand at the gate, think about it, just four houses away, where they could actually see Cheng Lin and Xiuqin fighting. They looked at them like they couldn't see anything.

As to whether there was anything going on with Yang Fengxi and Xiuqin, only the two of them know, nobody else does. Yang Fengxi didn't come out and deny it, and his wife Zhou Xianglan didn't start bawling people out in the street either, it was all very polite and civilised. As soon as the conversation turned to that pair it seemed to stop because there was nothing to talk about.

Later on, the Number One High School in Rang County was recruiting teachers. Yang Fengxi and Zhou Xianglan both got accepted, so they sold their house and both moved to the county town. And from then on, they vanished, never got in touch with anyone here at all.

What's the situation now? Yang Fengxi and his wife have gone to live in the county town. Cheng Lin and Chen Na are married, and they have a daughter, she's already a year old. Qian Guofeng got married again, to another primary school teacher, from the same school as Chen Na, and she had a child too, they're doing just fine.

It's Xiuqin I feel most sorry for. As soon as the divorce was final, she left Wu Town. I've heard she found herself a much older man and had a kid with him too, but he never married her.

Going back to Old Qian, that's another can of worms. About two years ago Old Qian's wife died. Everyone thought he was bound to marry Chen Chunlian. Chen Chunlian's old man Shan Bin is a soft touch, an old meat-head, Chen Chunlian could have given him the boot any time she wanted.

But Old Qian very quickly found himself a new wife, a decade or more younger than Chen Chunlian. People almost went mad cursing Old Qian, like he'd wronged Chen Chunlian by not marrying her. Some folk took to watching Chen Chunlian at that time, taking a turn or two round the coal yard whether they had any business there or not, just to observe Chen Chunlian's expression. Chen Chunlian really was a cool customer, she showed no reaction at all, and she kept her head held high, always so nicely turned out, hosting dinners, drinking and playing drinking games with the guests, she was still the image of a feisty boss lady. Yang Xiuzhen says she was barely holding it together, but she had a strong grip on herself, nobody knew how furious she was in private. All the same, it's common knowledge that the door between Old Qian and Chen Chunlian has been bricked up now.

Look at them, they'd been together for the best part of their lives, and at the end of it all, when at last it was possible, the man turned her down. That's a tragedy too.

———

Xueli spoke coolly and calmly, only occasionally when she raised her voice would she reveal a little emotion. Yizhi was wandering in and out of the kitchen, but whenever she got to a particularly ironic place in the story or a double meaning, he would nip straight back inside and pretend to be very busy.

The crowd heaved a collective sigh, there's nothing certain in life. Only Yizhi's fourth sister was jiggling up and down with delight, saying that all those people had found themselves a replacement and were living their best lives, there's nothing more to be said.

Yizhi's second sister was a silent type who had not had much education. All this time she had been listening intently with furrowed brow, trying to sort out the complex relationships between the protagonists, and now she finally voiced an opinion. "I just can't get my head around this, what's so good about all this swapping back and forth? Look at the horrible things people say about them on the street, what did they think they were going to get out of it?"

"Second Sister, you've got such backward attitudes," Yizhi's fourth sister replied at once. "There's no virtue in being unhappily married, quite the reverse. Besides, these days it's all about freedom and the rights of the individual. Parents are still independent individuals, you can't sacrifice yourself for a child. Those people could be said to be moving with the times, to each according to their needs and all that."

Yizhi's eldest sister suddenly flew into a rage. "Get away with you! What are you saying, you think you understand rights just because you're a teacher? Taking up with anyone that catches your eye, d'you call that freedom? Rights? That's having no sense of integrity, or responsibility. Moving with the times? What do you know about it? Coming here and showing off."

Yizhi's fourth sister saw that her eldest sister's face was flushed red with emotion, and was on the point of defending herself when she abruptly recalled that recently Eldest Sister had been angry with her husband. There had been rumours of some mysterious exchanges between her brother-in-law and a woman who played mah-jong, and Eldest Sister had been so busy running her business that she had only recently got wind of it. Fourth Sister did not dare to answer back, so she hurriedly changed the subject and turned to ask Xueli, "Who's this Yang Xiuzhen? How does she keep popping up everywhere?"

Xueli spat on the ground and said dismissively, "Oh, Yang Xiuzhen, she's a nightmare, in and out of everybody's house all day. Her one fear is a world without chaos. Whichever family has something going on, that's where you'll find her, a cradle of gossip, a professional, fully qualified scandalmonger and scandalmaker."

"You can't say that," Zhenguo said. "Yang Xiuzhen doesn't think like that, she sees herself as a woman of importance. You see, whenever something's happened in anyone's family, Yang Xiuzhen will always turn up and hand out money or give gifts, meet those arriving and take leave of those departing, she looks after everything, beavering away."

Xueli shied away and went off to the kitchen, saying, "She thinks she can get things done, but she just wants to peek and pry, it makes you sick."

———

The stuffing for the dumplings was all set out ready in a big basin. Its tempting aroma filled the yard: fresh green leeks and fresh, melting red meat.

A skinny woman walked slowly past the door of the clinic, peering inside as she walked. The wind blew through her clothes, causing them to flap around her.

Xueli called out, "Sister Xiuzhen, come on in and sit with us for a while."

There was nothing but brief, empty courtesy in Xueli's voice. This was just a greeting, no more, without any expectation that Yang Xiuzhen would actually come over. However, her body language showed that she had been waiting for an invitation.

"That's torn it, she's really coming," Xueli muttered in a low voice.

The sisters screwed up their eyes and watched like wolves as she approached. She had a straight, tidy appearance, with a painstaking air that had something of small-town petty-mindedness about it: shirt buttoned neatly all the way up, not a hair out of place, ruler-straight lines to her trousers; that style of dress unique to people in small towns who feel they have a position to maintain. But her glance was penetrating, and when it swept over you it seemed to illuminate all the rubbish that had accumulated inside over the years.

Yang Xiuzhen stared at the three sisters folding dumplings around the stone table, looking each over in turn. "Ai, you've all come back, tsk tsk, the sun's rising in the west today, as you might say. Look at that car by the gate, very impressive, you don't get one of those for less than a hundred thousand, two hundred thousand, even, that's properly wealthy. You sisters really are a bit much, your brother doesn't even have a car. You should all dig deep, and then you could get him one. What's all this? Looking down on us country folk, and on your brother?"

Yang Xiuzhen was seeming to smile without actually smiling, oozing sarcasm, as she was both praising the sisters for being rich and mocking them for not taking care of their brother. Although you could call it a joke, the sisters felt they had been wrong-footed and had to force themselves to smile back.

"Sister Xiuzhen, have a seat, do. We were just talking about Cheng Lin and Xiuqin."

Yang Xiuzhen went to the sink to wash her hands, rolled up her sleeves and started to fold dumplings. "I'll have to be quick, I reckon we're due a big wind before too long," Yang Xiuzhen said as she began to stuff the dumplings with a nimble rhythm. "Oh, Cheng Lin and Xiuqin, that was years ago, how did you get talking about them? All the same, I've been mulling it over and something's just come to me. It's that wife of Yang Fengxi, Zhou Xianglan. She's a meathead, such a wicked one, she set up a trap and got them all jumping into it. She's so educated and elegant, and when she speaks everyone believes her. For a while, she was always going to Xiuqin's to play mahjong, and sometimes she'd have little chats with Cheng Lin. I reckon that's when she started getting her nasty ideas. Cheng Lin saw her plot and got her with one of his own. He and Chen Na were already carrying on, so he was only too glad to start a row. And Qian Guofeng, he'd got sick of Chen Na long since, so when this business blew up, he turned their plot to his own advantage and dumped her flat. It was Xiuqin who was most hard done by, she's daft as anything and fell into it with her eyes wide open."

"How come there's yet another version? You mean to say that Cheng Lin knew beforehand that Xiuqin and Yang Fengxi were carrying on?"

"It's definitely Zhou Xianglan who planted the rumours that were going about. I know all about *her*. Back then her Yang Fengxi was already engaged to another teacher, but Zhou Xianglan had set her sights on him, so she spread ugly rumours about that woman all over the place, and broke them up, just like that. At that time Yang Fengxi was still pretty good-looking, he was the only one in the Number Five High School with an honours degree from a proper university, he could write and do maths, and play the *erhu* as well, so you might say he was a man of many talents."

Yang Xiuzhen suddenly switched the subject. "Ah yes, d'you know? Recently everyone's been talking about Chen Chunlian and that long-distance lorry driver. He parks his lorry at the coal yard every day, and Chen Chunlian doesn't think *he's* in the way, oh no, not a bit of it, if it was anyone else... just you try parking there and see what you get. That lorry driver's a proper flash Harry, you can tell at a glance that he's not a decent person."

In the middle of this rapid succession of bewildering threads and plot twists, Yang Xiuzhen suddenly got to her feet, as if she was about to leave. "Aiya, I'd better be going, my grandson's still asleep back home."

"Sit down, stay a bit longer, we're about to start boiling the dumplings, have some before you go." Again, Xueli was only saying this out of politeness, and again, Yang Xiuzhen sat back down.

"Wu Town's rotten to the core," said Yang Xiuzhen, "it's been that way for ages. Nobody has any morals, they get it on with anybody they please, men and women, the state of them! Family? Kids? Nobody cares about any of that."

"You look at those people opposite," Yang Xiuzhen continued, her lip curled in the direction of the photographer's studio on the other side of the road. "That photo studio's a nice little earner. There are some no-good kids, seventeen or eighteen years old, who get their marriage certificate photos taken at the start of the year, but by the end of the year they're back for more photos, and why? They go away to find jobs, and when they get back, they get divorced and need photos for that certificate. And that's nothing, do you have any idea how wicked the boss of that place Wang Xiuli is? When business is slack, she incites people to get divorced, just so she can earn money from a few divorce photos."

Yang Xiuzhen curled her thin, sharp lip again, this time to the left, displaying a blast of sudden venom. "You look at the people that sell Aima electric bikes opposite, Li Xiaozhen's family. Their dad died recently, and he put on a really good show for him at the funeral, but you know, when his dad was alive, it was his sisters who ran themselves ragged looking after him. That Li Xiaozhen is a no-good so-and-so, he's carrying on with Li Xiaogui's wife who lives behind them, his uncle's wife, no less."

Xueli's nimble hands froze at their work, and she stared wide-eyed at Yang Xiuzhen. "That can't be! That woman? She looks so clean and honest, how could she be carrying on with Li Xiaozhen, like a pig?"

"Well, you know," said Yang Xiuzhen, suddenly lowering her voice and leaning over towards Xueli, who involuntarily leaned in. "I saw it with my own eyes. Just the day before yesterday, at noon, I went to Old Wu's to buy some tofu, you know my grandson's only little, tofu's all he can eat, and I'd just turned past the end of Li Xiaozhen's house when I saw him and Li Xiaogui's wife coming out. I hurriedly turned my back and pretended to be going in another direction. You tell me, what would take them there, in the middle of the day like that? Li Xiaogui's out of the house all day long, playing mah-jong from morning to night, relying on the money his wife makes for everything. He's got no sense of morality at all, he's fine with being a meathead. And then let's talk about Wang Laoxiao. Never mind that, his wife's nothing much to look at, always yattering away about something or other, but I've heard that she's got a thing going with Wu Baoguo. It started when they were playing mah-jong, and having got her claws into him, she's sticking to him like glue. She built a house facing right onto the street, and she'll have got Wu Baoguo to sign it off, or how else would she be able to build in such a prime position? You think Wang Laoxiao doesn't know? He knows very well. He's doing just fine out of it, never mind him, one eye open, one eye closed. Besides, that Wu Baoguo isn't the kind that just anyone can cosy up to, what with his bribery and corruption, wining and dining, he's so rotten he's oozing pus. How many women has he ruined? Wang Laoxiao's wife, Li Xiaogui's wife, Old Zhang's daughter, that's Old Zhang who sells hardware at the south end of the main street, they've all been involved with him. Talking of Old Zhang's daughter, she's married to Li Minglun from our school, and they put on quite a performance there, complete with full-scale action sequences. One time when Li Minglun was teaching a class, Old Zhang's daughter carried their one-year-old son into the classroom, dumped him on the teacher's desk, scratched Li Minglun's face twice, tossed her head and ran out.

"And talking of our school, it's shocking the way they carry on there. Those intellectuals, they're no better than pigs or dogs. They take boarders there now, don't they? They say the young men and women teachers take it in turn to be on duty, and in the evening, they sleep together, bold as brass, you've no idea. Li Minglun even had a thing with Chen Na, then there's that Zhao Jiawei and Chen Deli, and Zhao Hui with Yang Jinhuan. Chen Deli's dad owns the twelve-storey block of flats at the east end of Wu Town, Leju Gardens. That family's rolling in money, Zhao Jiawei wouldn't look twice at Chen Deli otherwise, with those buck teeth of hers, who would? He wants to take advantage, to get a cheap house off her dad. And that Yang Jinhuan, with those dreamy eyes of hers, she was no better than she should be even as a student. That's right, wasn't Yang Jinhuan's brother at school with Yizhi? I heard from

Yang Jinhuan that a few years ago he was always round at your place."

Yang Xiuzhen nudged Yizhi's eldest sister with her elbow. "Sister, do you still remember her? Yang Jinhuan's thin and very tall, lots of curly hair, such a white face, she talks all soft, with slanty eyes that look like they can't open all the way, and the way she twines and twists her body. She'll be forty soon, and she's still carrying on like a siren. I heard she's been fighting with her husband, they're getting divorced, and they say it's not even because of that Zhao Hui. Oh, Yizhi, you're always drinking with her brother, aren't you, I'm sure you know all about it. The other day I saw some of you having a meal in the Roast Goose Restaurant. Ah, Yizhi, isn't that how it is...?"

Xueli suddenly stood up, turned away and went into the kitchen, where she stopped for a while, then took up a ladle, came out into the yard and said in a fierce, furious voice, "Time to boil the dumplings, Sister Xiuzhen! No, no! Don't go! Stay, do, and have some dumplings with us."

Yizhi's eldest sister felt like she was being led round and round in dizzying circles. Drawn in by the urgent tempo of Yang Xiuzhen's voice, she raised her eyes to see Xueli, one hand on her hip and the other holding a ladle, jabbing it forward, as though she was about to land a blow on Yang Xiuzhen's body. Her voice was not that of someone persuading a guest to stay, but rather driving her away. She looked round again. Yizhi had already slipped away to the counter in the clinic.

A glint of self-satisfaction and penetration flashed

across Yang Xiuzhen's eyes, as if she had finally proved something, or something had suddenly dawned on her. She smugly buttoned her lip, came to an abrupt halt and said contentedly, "Aiya, that would never do, I daresay my grandson's awake by now. I'll be on my way."

Yang Xiuzhen left the clinic and tripped away. Xueli went back into the kitchen, flung the ladle down onto the chopping board and stormed in and out of the yard, clattering noisily and slamming things around. Yizhi stood at the counter in the clinic for a while and then took quite a few minutes topping up the tea of the card players in the big room, apparently very busy. Sensing the tension, Zhenguo and some of the others slipped silently away.

Yizhi's fourth sister's mouth had been hanging open the whole time, immersed in Yang Xiuzhen's vast, convoluted array of gossip and stories that extended limitlessly outwards. Before their little circle had had a chance to compose their expressions, before they could contrive fake fascination or mockery to deal with Yang Xiuzhen, they found themselves subjected to a relentless bombardment. This woman had come prepared and forearmed; indeed, she did not need to prepare, for Wu Town was like a dish of food to her. She was familiar, even beyond familiar, with its every nook and cranny. She had all her material at her fingertips, picking out a bit here and another piece from over there, throwing them all into her stew pot, spotting things that seemed to have nothing in common, then bringing them together into an organic whole.

"Goodness me, that's an information overload," Yizhi's

fourth sister said in genuine amazement, having failed to notice the expressions of the others in the yard. "If you were to draw the relationships between the people she described, what a complex thing it would be. It's a web of a thousand knots, a great ball of tangled thread."

"Pah," said Xueli, letting out a cold, derisive laugh. "Don't talk to me about her. Li Xiaogui's house is at the back of Li Xiaozhen's house. If she was going to Old Wu's to get her tofu, how'd she end up there, with all those houses between them? She's just a long-tongued woman, digging a cesspit and shoving everything that comes near her into it. Out of her mouth, anybody and anything ends up in the cesspit."

Yizhi's eldest sister had long since become aware that there was something off about the situation, and she sharply changed the subject in order to state the sisters' attitude. "You can't say that it's completely wrong either. Call it gossip, call it chasing the wind and clutching at shadows, but if there's no wind and those shadows don't exist, if there's no dung on you, no matter how much dung people throw at you, it won't stick. If you want to live a decent life, you have to act in an upright manner."

Xueli gave her a sidelong glance and looked meaningfully at Yizhi who had reappeared in her line of sight. "Well that's true enough, if you don't want anyone to find out what you did, don't do it in the first place. But if you've got a dedicated creator of dung who wants to cause trouble, it's not that easy. All the same, some people are just base, and they insist on causing that trouble and setting everybody's tongues wagging."

Yizhi set down his bowl and chopsticks and chuckled, and without looking at Xueli he said, "Ah, I'll go and put the dumplings in the pot. First we'll have the dumplings, second noodles. There'll be a little bit more in the first pot."

Something else occurred to him, and he turned round to face Xueli. "Hey, I've heard that Yang Xiuzhen's husband has come back."

Xueli raised her head in surprise and looked at Yizhi. "When was this? I didn't hear about it." This was the first time all morning that Xueli and Yizhi had looked directly at each other.

"I heard it from Hongyi. He's been back for several days now, skulking at home, never going outside all this time. Poor man, he's little better than a beggar. That pyramid selling scheme of his got broken up, the big fish all ran off long ago, leaving nothing for people at his level, so all he could do was come back. Yang Xiuzhen had told everybody, As far as I'm concerned that man no longer exists, and if he does return, I'll never take him back. And the result, guess what? That Yang Xiuzhen went running to the head of the school he used to work at, with flattery and gifts, crying and wiping away tears, wanting to get her man to teach at the school again. The head said, 'That's absolutely out of the question, if you're a state employee you can't just disappear into thin air for two years and then

turn up asking for your job back. We can't justify something like that."

"Serves her right! She's no better than she should be,
slandering people all day long when she's up to her neck
in it herself. Just look at her, putting it on so convincingly,
making out she's oh so very capable," Xueli said viciously,
following Yizhi into the kitchen, where the water was
bubbling noisily. Yizhi picked up the board with the
dumplings on, and Xueli put them in the pot one by one,
both busy about their work as they discussed Yang
Xiuzhen. After a while the conversation became heated
and intense, so their heads were touching as they
muttered to each other in low voices, cursing and
laughing.

Suddenly a wind came up, a little whirlwind that
came rushing in from nowhere, whipping past the grape
trellis in the yard, snatching away all the leaves of the
Chinese white olive tree with the broken branch and stripping the trellis bare, leaving just a few warped, twisted
vines. A sudden, deadly silence fell on the yard. The dust,
scraps of cloth, stones, bits of paper and other oddments
that usually collected in the corners were lifted away from
the earth in the whirlwind and scattered all over the
ground.

Yizhi came running out of the kitchen and hurriedly
started to move the bowls, chopsticks and cold dishes set
out on the table into the kitchen. Yizhi's eldest sister
shouted, "Don't bother, just put something over them, it'll
be fine. It's already blown over anyway, usually whirl-

winds come and go in a flash, in a moment there'll be no sign of it."

Sure enough, a few minutes later it had stopped. The yard looked like a flood had swept through it, washing up all manner of things, strewn chaotically all over the ground. Everybody picked up the things that had been blown around and put them in their proper places, and very soon all was back as it was before.

———

The dumplings were brought to table. Gusts of delicious smells came wafting over. The green of the leeks showed through the thin white wheaten skins, whose surface was appealingly dimpled, a sign that the filling inside was firm but supple.

Rubbing his hands, chuckling with his mouth watering, Yizhi summoned his sisters. "Come on, get 'em while they're hot. Whatever we say is just idle gossip, but eating is real. Once you get these down, they'll warm you right down to your stomach. Ah, human life is like fog, like lightning, or an illusion, in the end, it's all for nothing."

Off to one side, Xueli curled her lip. "Humph, all for nothing, is it? Then don't eat, don't have kids." She turned her head away and said to the sisters, "Just recently, he's become obsessed with that damned Diamond Sutra. Every day at four o'clock he gets up, copies bits out, reads them out loud too, a string of bastard prayer beads in his hand, rattling them back and forth until he thinks he's become an immortal himself. But come the afternoon, when the clinic's at its busiest, you can't find the man. He's taken himself off for a nap."

Yizhi did not defend himself, juggling the bowls and chopsticks, while calling out to his fourth sister, "Bring the vinegar, quick, and two cloves of garlic."

As if something had suddenly occurred to him, Yizhi picked up the vinegar and garlic, then took a quick look at the plate of dumplings and started to laugh uncontrollably. Everybody urged him to say why, but he was laughing too hard to speak. Xueli gave him a rebuking shove and slapped his broad back a few times. Yizhi cringed in fake agony and ran off to hide in the yard, crying out, "I'll talk, I'll talk! It isn't even that interesting. But tell me this, aren't people just like this garlic and vinegar? They're all seasonings for other people. Which of us isn't Yang Xiuzhen?"

At the mention of Yang Xiuzhen's name, the whole yard roared with laughter. Yizhi held up the chopsticks, picked up a dumpling and popped it whole into his mouth, followed by a clove of garlic, which he chewed vigorously. A burst of strong flavour surged up into his skull and he started to cough, muttering to himself until tears streamed from his eyes.

This was noon at the beginning of autumn.

The sun shone down through the empty grape trellis in the yard, forming areas of superficial shadow, which had a blurred radiance around the edges, giving a feeling of something intangible and beyond one's grasp. The ground was warm and comfortable; this was the best time to enjoy a meal in the warmth of the sun. Yizhi's whole family clustered round the stone table, cheerfully eating dumplings, calling back and forth to each other, laughing loudly, debating, harmonious and happy, long-lasting and secure.

---

1. In Chinese, this word is made up of two characters: 肉 (meat) and 头 (head). However, the meaning is not quite the same as the English term "meathead": in Henan dialect, this word can be used to describe a person whose spouse has been unfaithful.

8

That Bright, Snowy Afternoon

ON THE JOURNEY BACK, they lost their way.

Snow was falling in big flakes, layer upon layer, slowly, steadily and heavily. When they raised their eyes to look upwards, all the differences and irregularities of the plain had been wiped away. The brown, dry, cracked and naked earth, the feeble, yellowish-green wheat, the tough, dried-out, low bushes, the hard, solid road and the shallow ditches on both sides, had all been covered by thick whiteness. Only smoothed undulations remained.

The land around was deathly still, living things had shrunk back into their holes. Voices returned to their throats, houses sunk into the earth, and the plain was like an immense graveyard, mourning ceaselessly.

Liangguang was pushing the bike, with Haihong following behind as they forced a way forward together. They did not look at each other or speak, just focused all their attention on walking, listening to the creaking of their footsteps. The snow enveloped them and hid them, yet it became a protection and a shield. The heartfelt words they had exchanged on their way out, the crying and laughing, stories and tentative exploration, all had become superficial and skin-deep. It was no longer possible for them to say these things out loud.

The image of Qingfei standing at the door as he saw them off remained in Haihong's mind, and she did not dare look back. She could sense that Qingfei was still standing there, watching them, now black spots in the distance, his eyes like those of a drowning man. The black cavern of his house was behind him, broken and crooked, entire mud-brick walls eroded by wind, rain and sun until they were thin and weak, tottering and ready to fall. With just another push, or another snowfall, gale or thunderstorm, they would give way.

The snow was starting to fall in earnest now. The slanting roof of the house was covered with a thick layer and seemed to be on the point of caving in. Haihong had left that house in the grip of almost physical pain and concern.

What had Qingfei said to them? Coming out of the door, Haihong could not remember clearly. She and Liangguang had ridden about ten kilometres on their way here from Wu Town, and they had enquired at a good number of villages and looked in a lot of houses before they found Qingfei's. But Qingfei had not been welcoming at all. His home was what they called "empty and echoing", no other words could fittingly describe the scene in the house. Qingfei's father walked about the room in a desperate attempt to find anything with which to entertain their two young guests. His mother was curled up on the bed in the inner room, head hanging low, not moving a muscle. His two younger brothers were playing on the bed. One of them was sticking his head out from the battered quilt, looking curiously at them both.

This poverty-stricken, empty, echoing dwelling that appeared before them had come as a great surprise to Haihong and Liangguang. They had never been aware of this aspect of Qingfei; he was always full of smiles when he appeared at Wu Town's Number Two Junior High School. He had very fair skin and tiny eyes, which would scrunch up into a wavy line when he smiled, radiating kindliness and simplicity. Every day he came and went in a hurry, spent most of the school day sprawled over his desk dozing, and in the evening he would hastily depart. It had never crossed Haihong's mind to wonder where he lived, and she had never taken any notice of what he ate, or what he wore. She and Liangguang had homes in town, where they lived and took their meals, so she had never been aware that this was an issue.

They did not dare encourage Qingfei to go to school after that. They just sat down gingerly, wondering when they could leave.

———

Haihong was a girl whose heart constantly overflowed with maternal love. Her concern for the studies of the two boys in the row behind far outstripped any concern for her own learning.

Tall, thin, delicately handsome Liangguang clung to her. Being short-sighted, he could not see what the teacher had written on the blackboard, so Haihong would copy it out for him an exercise at a time. He was always getting nosebleeds, so she tore up her homework jotter, rolled up the pieces neatly and put them in her drawer, ready to stop the next flow of blood. When Qingfei went to sleep in class, Liangguang would urgently call from behind her, "Haihong, Haihong, he's dozed off again." His voice was very light, very needy, with a hint of the indulged child about it. Sometimes he would poke her in the back with a finger, or tweak her hair, to show her how deeply Qingfei was sleeping. Motherlike, she would calmly call out to Qingfei, who would always open his eyes at the sound of her voice, smile blearily at her, straighten his back and pretend to pay attention to the lesson. Qingfei claimed to suffer from "napping sickness", which meant that he was always nodding off. He had dropped out of school and come back again several times, but once there he went to sleep just as before. Haihong had thought that Qingfei was being lazy, finding excuses to sleep instead of studying.

To Qingfei, Haihong was like a mother, caring about him, protecting him and worrying about him, but she found herself baffled by Liangguang's black eyes, captivated by the vague, bewildered and yet vulnerable expression in them. Every time she saw him peering through the window, the tips of his toes just touching the ground, hands stuffed in the sleeves of his bulky cotton-padded jacket, with red-and-white balls of paper stuffed up his nostrils or walking towards the other side of the classroom as if there was no one else there, the sight always warmed Haihong's heart. Even when Liangguang was just prodding her in the back with a finger, a strange feeling surged up from the part that had been poked, filling her heart with a secret joy.

She saved things that Liangguang had written, a series of scattered words and phrases on little scraps of paper ripped from books or carelessly thrown away, which she would gather up and carefully press in a book, to be read over and over again. Even today it was like she could see every single character, as clearly as if they had been printed, including the shape, style and content.

She took to wandering around the slope leading to the Tuan River at the south end of Wu Town. Liangguang's home was at the far end of the vegetable plots on the slope, on the very edges of Wu Town. He lived there with his widowed mother. She hoped to see him leaving the house so she could pretend to be just passing through and say "Hello", but she never saw him. In truth, she was frightened that Liangguang would come out. Her home was not in this part of town, so it was very unlikely for her to be just passing by. She was afraid that Liangguang would see through her. Haihong only saw his mother walking about in the vegetable patch, digging, planting, weeding. She saw the severe, stubborn face of someone who put her heart and soul into her crop of vegetables, as devotedly as she guarded her son. Haihong did not dare to approach a step nearer.

Liangguang spoke and walked like a well-behaved little child. The feelings between him and his mother were delicate yet robust. He seemed to be constantly observing his mother's expression. He knew she was toiling and suffering for his sake, and because he was afraid of going unwittingly against her wishes, this made him uniquely vulnerable. It was this innocent vulnerability that Haihong liked in him. He and his mother meant everything to each other. Haihong wondered what kind of feeling this might be. She wanted to squeeze between them, to experience this mysterious connection.

———

The snow was falling harder and harder, but not only had the sky not darkened, it was actually becoming lighter, shining bright, blurring Haihong's vision. The snowflakes struck them with real weight and rapidity, turning them into large, ambulant balls of snow. The pair had not spoken, they were just struggling to free their feet and walk. They still seemed quite shaken from what they had recently seen, as if that pitch-black cave of a house was pursuing them like some dark, heavy, unknowable truth.

Haihong suddenly realised that they had somehow turned around and come back once again to the small bridge. This bluestone bridge was now covered in snow, the withered grasses on the slope and the naked stones exposed in the little river were all topped with thick white hats, but the shallow river water was still moving slowly and placidly on, giving off wisps of steam.

Haihong remembered that bridge. On their way out, a strong wind had been blowing. She was sitting on the back seat of the bicycle, watching Liangguang wobbling laboriously over the bridge's uneven surface, and she could not hold back an involuntary giggle. There was a sudden drop in the road ahead of them. With a cry of "Aiya, aiya", Liangguang squeezed the brakes hard but failed to slow down. Haihong felt the wind whooshing past, her bottom was suddenly flung up into the air, and she instinctively threw her arms round Liangguang in front. Through the thickly padded cotton clothes on his back, Haihong could sense his body immediately go tense. In confusion, Haihong loosed her grip, but her bottom missed its place, and with an "Aiya" she was thrown off onto the hard ground.

That momentary embrace stayed in Haihong's feelings. Her cup was overflowing, and her heart was beating madly, so she forgot the pain, forgot that she was half lying on the ground in an uncomfortable, embarrassing position. Liangguang steadied the bike, hurried back and pulled her up, asking in a panic, "Are you all right? Are you all right?" She raised her head, and he saw her face, blushing so hard it was almost purple.

Liangguang was supporting Haihong with one hand

and pushing the bicycle with the other, as they slowly walked forward. The grit carried by the wind scraped over Liangguang's face and blew into his eyes. He could not get a hand free to rub them, so he blinked deliberately in a way that was quite adorable. Haihong, heedless of all of this, was leaning on him, emotions surging in her heart, trying as hard as she could to find something to say, but what came out was, "Actually, I've seen your mum."

Her voice was as thin as a mosquito, but Liangguang gave a start. "My mum? Where did you see her?" He straightened up almost imperceptibly, as if trying to protect himself. He was quite uncomfortable when other people mentioned his family.

Flustered, Haihong hurriedly changed the subject. "I really envy you, you've got such a good mother. My mum passed away a long time ago." As soon as she mentioned her mother, fourteen-year-old Haihong went straight back to that eight-year-old little girl, crying in front of her mother's bed. Mum's body had been covered in a white cloth. She wanted to pull away the cloth from her face, she wanted to see her face, she could not believe that she had just gone, like that. But her father, her aunt and all the adults held her back and would not let her look. Just like that, Haihong, who had been happily hopping and skipping all the way home, would never see her mother again.

Tall, skinny Liangguang saw Haihong's tears and did not know what to do with himself. "Don't cry, don't cry, you're better off than me," he said. "I've never even seen my dad." Haihong looked encouragingly at Liangguang with tear-filled eyes, willing him to continue.

Liangguang lowered his gaze as he walked ahead on tiptoe. "My mum told me that when my dad died, this man wanted to take the site of our house for himself, and force my mum to get married again, but she refused to leave. She started a market garden by herself, growing vegetables and selling them, so she could raise me and send me to school. I've known ever since I was small that things are hard in my family and that some people pick on us. I have to study hard and make something of myself, to make her proud."

Haihong listened quietly. Liangguang's voice was pure and sweet, bright and clear, with just a hint of sadness and softness, and Haihong liked it immensely. The road in front of them was pure white and unobstructed. By the side of that bridge, Haihong's heart had been full of happiness.

Haihong recalled a three-way junction just beyond the bridge. There was a large courtyard house at the junction, far from any other habitation, a solitary building with piles of discarded machinery, and tall, straight weeds had pushed their way up through the machines, like in a graveyard. Outside the courtyard, three roads split away from each other. She chose the road to the right.

When she saw the broken remnants of an iron pot in the yard, a vivid memory of her stepmother's son flashed before her eyes: her little stepbrother Xiaofeng, tumbling backwards as he staggered towards the pot of boiling porridge.

She told Liangguang that she had a stepmother, who had come with a five-year-old child. "He's called Xiaofeng. He didn't dare play with my big brother or big sister, he only played with me. Poor little thing, he couldn't speak the way we speak here, none of the kids where we live would play with him. My big brother and sister couldn't stand him either. At the start he didn't realise, he used to throw himself at them, but he kept getting pushed away, so he stopped trying. In the summer holidays this year, my stepmum and my dad went to Xinjiang for the grape harvest, and I was the only one taking care of him at home."

Liangguang glanced at Haihong and smiled like he could see it all. "You've got such a nice personality, he must have really depended on you."

"His bum, his bum got scalded."

Haihong was trembling all over as she spoke. She and her elder sister and brother had splashed him with cold water, rubbed him down with a towel, then wiped him with their hands, and the child's skin all fell away like rotting paper. She, her seventeen-year-old brother and sixteen-year-old sister had knelt in front of the injured, bleeding Xiaofeng, his skin hanging from their hands, bawling like they were babies.

Liangguang tugged hard on Haihong's arm. Even through his thick gloves, she could feel this gesture of warmth and his desire to protect her.

Haihong did not tell him that after summer ended, her stepmother had taken Xiaofeng away, scars and all.

Her stepmother's family had found her. They stood at the door of Haihong's home, shouting and causing a commotion, coming to claim back their own and demand compensation. Her stepmother had another husband back home, and that man had come too. His shoulders were drawn back, his eyes staring, he had picked up a brick and was making as if to use it to bash the mass of onlookers, fury shining in his eyes, but he was eyeing Haihong's father greedily. Father, Haihong's father, decided to play his trump card. Heedless of everything he sat down on the ground, flailing in the dust, weeping loudly, "Aiya", and he let matters take their course. His face was covered in dirt, and repeated applications of tears had plastered his face into a clown's mask.

Her short, slight, but strong stepmother, her tough and capable stepmother, stood there in the centre of the crowd. Her luggage had been knocked onto the ground, her brightly coloured clothes thrown all over the place. She looked to the left at her ugly, covetous real husband, and to the right at her fake husband with whom she had spent several years of true devotion, and her face was full of alarm and indecision. She spread out her hands, not knowing what to say for the best. Haihong's elder sister and brother were clutching hoes and fragments of tile, standing there, shouting and crying, cursing their step-mother's family right back.

She could not tell who was the first to call out, "Get her trousers off, the money's bound to be hidden in the crotch."

The onlookers laughed raucously and shouted, "Get those trousers off! Trousers off!" and pointing at Haihong's elder sister, added, "She led your dad by the nose like an ox, she must have earned herself a fair old sum."

They were laughing, pushing Haihong's sister and brother towards their stepmother. Repeated roars of laughter, rolling like waves, interspersed with whistles, spitting and jeers. Haihong felt humiliated. If there had been a hole in the ground, she would have burrowed herself into it. If there was an object that could have swallowed her in an instant, she would have paid any price to get it, but all she could do was stand up straight in a far corner and let the tears course down her face. She knew that these people were enjoying watching her family make fools of themselves. They would have been happier still to see them argue more violently, fight more viciously, keep their quarrel going for longer. She thought that from then on, she would never be seen in this place again, would never come back, had seen enough of this horrible life, this filthy place. She could not stay here another minute. She had to get into college, no matter what, anything so long as she could leave this family and this place.

Before she left, her stepmother took Haihong's hand and said to her in a low voice, "You were the best of them." Haihong's tears poured out in a silent stream. She could not see her stepmother's face clearly, nor that of her father, sister or brother. Neither could she see her stepmother hemmed in on all sides like a trapped beast, nor the savage, hideous faces of the spectators.

"You were the best of them." Many years later, thinking of these words, Haihong still felt ashamed. It was not goodness, not at all, it was treachery to her family, betrayal of the sisters struggling and weeping loudly in the mud. She was weak and cowardly, and that was all. She knew what she was, she lacked the courage to fight for herself. She would take orders from anyone who wanted to give her orders, even over her beloved Liangguang. That one look from Liangguang's mother had been enough to make her flee.

————

There was no courtyard, no village, nor was there the three-way junction that Haihong remembered. White snow had covered all traces and signs. Haihong gazed out at both sides of the bridge, and she was reminded of the general in Chen Zi'ang's poem: "In front she could see no sign of the ancients, behind she could see no sign of those who follow after." Even the road could not be seen clearly. That spring, all the trees on either side of the road had been chopped down: the white poplars that lined the road, so thick you could barely get your arms round them; the thin Lombardy poplars beside the dirt country roads; the rows of scholar trees protecting ditches and fields from the wind, all had been felled. Without the rising and falling of the trees and the protection they offered, it seemed like the plains had been stripped of their clothing and left empty and forlorn, alone and helpless.

In the endless white, several ancient trees stood there silently, and a number of tombs stuck out in the distance, with a handful of five-coloured flags dancing above them in the wind, bright and bleak. A short figure was leaping about in front of one of the tombs in the whiteness of the reflected snow, appearing rather evasive and unsteady. As if they had seen their rescuer, Haihong and Liangguang threw aside the bicycle and rushed towards him.

The man's hair and beard were wild and matted. A piece of bright yellow brocade was wrapped round his chest; a dense, elaborate icicle of drool was hanging from his wide-open mouth down to his chest in a straight column; greying cotton wadding was leaking from his padded jacket and trousers and his bare feet were black. He was crying out "Ah, ah" in front of a grave dotted with flags, dancing, throwing himself to the ground, kowtowing, praying, going round in circles. For a while he would stoop to look at the grave, then he would lift his head skyward, his mad gaze sweeping over Haihong and Liangguang, yet somehow passing through them, reaching out towards empty places far away. Haihong was drawn in by this maelstrom of frenzy and fervour, like a road linking the underworld and the heavens, mysterious and terrifying yet deeply enticing at the same time.

Liangguang plucked up courage and asked in his soft voice, "Uncle, what's the way to Wu Town?"

The man's movements suddenly stilled, his gaze drifted back from wherever it had been, and he turned it on Liangguang. After a long while, he took a step forward and approached Haihong and Liangguang, his eyes still fixed on Liangguang. All they could hear was the crunching of the snow beneath his feet, blood-curdling between the quiet skies and the far earth. He reached out, grabbed Liangguang's hand and pulled him next to the tomb. Liangguang struggled to retreat, but he was power-less to free himself, his feet scraping a track on the snowy ground that led directly to the tomb.

When they got to the tomb, the man fell with a flump to his knees, beating his head hard against the earth, the spittle from his mouth dangling down to the snowy ground. He gestured to Liangguang with an anxious expression, tugging at him and pointing at the tomb, digging with his hands. Then he rubbed his hand roughly over his face, so that tears, snot, mud and spittle all combined to form a solid layer, before he knelt once again and kowtowed. The grief and the tracks of mud on his face were slightly ludicrous, but they added to the horror of the spectacle.

While the mourner was prostrate, Liangguang took his chance to break away and struggled to run back. The man looked up and saw that Liangguang had gone, at which he let out a long, crazed howl and ran off in pursuit.

Haihong did not move, her hands clenched round the branch of a tree. As he rushed past her, she swept out with the branch at his legs and left him sprawled on the ground. She dodged out of the way, clutching the branch, but Liangguang rushed back, snatched the branch and lashed out madly and randomly at his pursuer. The man was struggling but he had no concept of how to evade him, he just clutched his head and cried out pitifully. His head was wounded, blood leaked down from his hair crowned with white snow, a mix of snow white and blood red. He opened his eyes wide to look directly at Liangguang and Haihong, full of bewilderment and hurt, like a child wrongly accused by its parents.

Tall, skinny Liangguang's eyes were wild, the snow on his hair was steaming and he lashed out again and again with that black branch against the man's body like he was possessed, no longer himself. The poor fellow had no place to hide from the blows Liangguang rained down on him, and finally, whimpering and sobbing, he turned in the snow and crawled away towards the grave.

Haihong stood there stupefied, open-mouthed, watching in disbelief. Slender, refined, sweetly spoken Liangguang was waving the branch around like a wild beast, chasing the mourner and beating his back. There was something in his eyes that Haihong had never seen before.

She began to push the bicycle away, calling out Liangguang's name. He seemed to come back to himself, threw down the branch and ran over. Once they had gone quite a long way, Haihong looked behind her and saw that that man was still dancing crazily at the tomb. The five-coloured flags on the withered branches hung silently down, unmoving.

Haihong and Liangguang stood bewildered between the snowy sky and the white ground. There was no wind, no sound, snowflakes beat against their bodies like ghosts, getting denser and denser. The inauspiciously grey-white sky and the fluorescence radiating from the snow were tinged with yellow and crystal clear, as if shining out from the depths of the remotest past. In the midst of that man's wild, animal ululations, dismal and bizarre yet full of sweet memories, all the hundreds of thousands of ghosts buried deep in the landscape were climbing out, mumbling and muttering, harbouring no good intentions, coming closer, surrounding them, seeping into Haihong's body. Haihong was overcome by a blast of bone-piercing chill that seemed to come from the inside out. She moved closer to Liangguang, terrified, and the instant she came into contact with him, she could sense that he was shivering too. The snow was enveloping their bodies, heavy and icy cold. Liangguang steered the bike by the handlebars as Haihong pushed from behind, holding on to his padded jacket with one hand, and they moved forward in silence, relying on instinct alone.

Haihong wanted to cry, but she saw Liangguang's tightly closed lips, and she did not dare. She could sense that he was blaming her. She had been the one who first suggested going to see Qingfei, and it was she who had wasted time at his home, asking all those questions. Liangguang's mind had been elsewhere the whole time as he looked outside at the increasingly heavy snow, while she, blissfully unaware, had forced herself to talk to Qingfei and his father, to demonstrate her kindness and concern. While she would not have had the presumption to regard this journey with Liangguang as an assignation, Haihong had imagined every detail over and over again: sitting alone on the back seat of Liangguang's bicycle, hands clutching his clothing, chatting, looking into each other's eyes, as she waited in sweet anticipation for Sunday to arrive.

The snow was dense, blocking Haihong's view like a curtain. She wanted to pull it back and see what was happening further away, but it was like the curtains came in many layers, there was no end to them. They seemed to be in the centre of the world, extending forever; but they also seemed to be stuck at a single point, however far they moved they were still in the same place.

She did not know how long they had been walking. The sky was neither light nor dark, the snow was neither rapid nor slow. Time had come to a halt. Fourteen-year-old Haihong and Liangguang had been cast away in a confined infinity.

At last, a village came into view. Haihong and Liangguang made a staggering rush for the door of the closest house.

Inside, the room was roiling with thick smoke. Someone was coughing and laughing loudly. Haihong stood at the doorway, stamping her feet hard and shaking herself. As she waited for the smoke to thin a little, her eyes became accustomed to the darkness of the room. She saw several young men and a young woman clustered for warmth around a burning, bright red log of wood. Their wolfish eyes were opened wide as they looked at Haihong standing in the doorway.

"Come on in and sit down, little sister," a man called out flirtatiously to Haihong and Liangguang. Haihong did not know how to respond, so she went in obediently and sat on a high stool.

"Warm yourselves by the fire. Tut, tut, you're wet all over," said the woman, who was wearing a bright red down jacket and bright red lipstick, like a ray of light shining on Haihong. She could feel the snow rapidly melting away and leaking into her padded jacket and hair, and the heaviness of the melted snow was pressing down until she could not catch her breath.

"How old are you?"

"Fourteen."

"Which year at school?"

"Third year of junior high."

"What were you and him up to together, on a snowy day like this?" said a young man, pointing sarcastically at Liangguang in the doorway. The youths behind him laughed and whistled in shrill, mocking voices. The woman laughed coquettishly, thumped the man and told him not to scare Haihong, which brought on another outburst of mad, high-pitched laughter and wolf whistles.

The woman walked over to Haihong and told her to stand up. She looked her up and down, tipping up her lower jaw with her finger so she could examine her face in detail. Then she turned back and gestured to the men to come and take a look for themselves.

The men came over like they were picking out an animal at the market, surrounding Haihong and speculating at length, before gathering in another part of the room, muttering in low voices, occasionally bursting into shouts of wild laughter.

They were pushing and shoving Haihong back and forth. The heavy, damp smoke caught in her nose, and she could barely keep her eyes open. Two of the men who were crowding round pinched her face, lifted her hair and even squeezed her chest. The other two looked at her with indifference and went back to the fire, where they talked among themselves.

The dim room was oppressive and stifling, and the expression in these people's eyes was unlike that of locals. Their conversation had nothing to do with the villages or the heavy snowfall, it was all monstrous and strange, inaccessible, as if they had been airdropped here from somewhere else, as they plotted over their prey, whose arrival was both unexpected and yet somehow inevitable.

Fourteen-year-old Haihong was terrified, staring in bewilderment as she hunched over, weighed down by her sodden padded jacket, allowing them to do whatever they wanted. Her frozen toes in soaked cotton-padded shoes gradually softened out, but every time she put them on the ground, she felt a stabbing pain.

Where was Liangguang? At one point, Haihong thought she saw him still standing doltishly in the doorway, his long, skinny body curled in on itself, eyes innocent and vulnerable, his face so pale that she could not make out its features.

The woman called out to Liangguang to come into the room, to stand by the fire and warm himself. He did not respond but just slumped there, exhausted, with water flowing from his hair into his eyes, down his cheeks, to the bottom of his ears and mouth. He blinked but did not dare to raise his hand to wipe the water away. The young man behind him walked over and pushed him forcibly towards Haihong. Liangguang's jaw smacked into Haihong's head, and his arms flung out to collide with her chest. Liangguang immediately jerked his arms away, his expression terrified and tense, as if he had bumped into something he was forbidden to touch, causing the crowd to stamp their feet and sneer.

The young man suddenly held up both hands and shoved their heads together, grumbling, "Didn't you want to get close to her?"

There was a "crack", as if Haihong's head had been hit with a rock. Stars appeared in front of her eyes, and she retreated to the fire, stumbling, head in her hands. Somebody pushed her this way, someone else pushed her that. She could hear Liangguang crying like a child. She did not raise her head to look at him, as tears drowned everything in front of her eyes.

One man in particular was holding her upright, dragging her over towards Liangguang, who himself was being held up. They stood the pair of them up straight and ordered them to turn face to face and kiss each other on the mouth.

Haihong desperately twisted her head away, unwilling to move in towards Liangguang's mouth. His neck was held rigid, but they could not evade the combined strength of all those men. Liangguang's lips were crushed up against Haihong's, ice cold, damp and smeared with the sticky, salty, slightly pungent liquid from his tears. She closed her eyes very tight and would not look at him.

The sound of hysterical laughter, whistles, jeers and the woman's amused scolding felt loud enough to lift the roof right off, straight up into the sky bearing down with snow.

Perhaps because he was disgusted by the gang's mean prank and the ugly picture the two of them made, the face of the man who had been sitting close to the fire the whole time darkened. He waved an impatient hand at the laughing, joking mob and said, "Set them on their way, and be quick about it."

The young man said to Haihong with a smile, "Let's go. I'll see you off."

His voice was like an elder brother speaking to his little sister who was heading out, indulgent and relaxed. Haihong looked at him in bewilderment, unable to believe it was that easy. She didn't move.

"Silly girl, she really doesn't want to leave," said the young woman, laughing out loud.

The young man pushed the bicycle, and Haihong and Liangguang limped mechanically after him.

The snow had stopped. There was a solemn, still brightness to the sky. At that moment, Haihong understood what was meant by "a brilliant expanse of white snow". You could not use that phrase to describe the landscape when the snow was falling. Only once the snow had stopped and the sun just appeared to be shining, could this hazy glow be called "a brilliant expanse of white snow".

The young man saw them to a small junction and stopped.

"Take this turning and go straight ahead, then you'll see the main road, turn right and keep going until you get to Wu Town." He paused for a moment and smiled. "If I hadn't told you about this junction, you'd definitely have taken a wrong turning." This young man's eyes were sparkling in the snow-light, and when he smiled there was something childlike about him.

Haihong and Liangguang each struggled their own way forward. Haihong did not dare to look directly at Liangguang again, afraid of how she would appear reflected in his eyes. At last they saw the red brick, three-storey building that stood at the west end of Wu Town: the dormitory for Wu Town's tobacco depot, which served as accommodation for many of Wu Town's secondary school students. Not much further along was Liangguang's house.

Haihong suddenly experienced a moment of panic. The words she had waited so long to say to Liangguang, the things she had wanted to ask him, seemed now to be impossible to force out. They were almost at his home and she was going to lose her chance. Something lost along the way slowly returned to her. She sneaked a glance at Liangguang, but his eyes never strayed from his path as he concentrated on walking, his face full of rage. His sticky hair, matted with mud and snow, hung down as far as his eyebrows in a pitiable, childish way. Haihong swallowed her words back down again.

As they stood at the doorway of Liangguang's house, and before he could push open the door, his mother opened it, as if she had been waiting there the whole time. She stared intently at her son, her eyes sweeping over his sticky, filthy hair, his face covered in mud and dirt, and his red, swollen eyes. She turned and gave Haihong a look, bitterly cold and full of accusation. Haihong hung her head. Liangguang said nothing at all but went inside as fast as he could.

The door shut.

Haihong turned back and gripped the bicycle handlebars again, preparing to leave. They were icy cold.

In the murky whiteness of Wu Town, cooking smoke was rising from someone's roof, turning in the great expanse of sky to follow the wind, perfectly silent and still. The snow was falling again. Haihong was pushing her bike, listening to the crunching of her footsteps on the snowy ground.

She was shivering all over. She had been wanting to pee all afternoon, but the opportunity had not arisen; there had been no room for peeing in her relationship with Liangguang. The excess of pent-up liquid in her lower abdomen suddenly dropped directly into the region of her bladder, which felt like it was about to explode. The pain was almost unbearable and she could not take another step. She bent down to untie the cloth belt of her trousers with stiff, frozen hands, but they were shaking and trembling so much that they would not obey her, and she could not get the knot of her belt undone. Haihong pressed her legs tightly together, clenching her bladder closed with an effort, as she shoved her hands through the gaps between the buttons of her padded jacket, hoping to warm them up a bit. The softness and warmth of her breasts were startling, so she pressed down strongly with her hands, hoping she could squeeze some of their heat into her hands. Her nipples suddenly stood erect in her palms, small and hard, and her hands pressed down hard, as a strange, numbing, tingling shot through her whole body, an inexplicable kind of shudder.

Haihong withdrew her half-warmed hands, undid her belt and slowly squatted down, watching as the snow beneath her gradually became soaked through and then caved in to reveal the dark earth beneath. Her abdomen was suddenly, disagreeably empty.

She felt extremely awkward, extremely ugly, bereft of everything.

———

In the end Qingfei never went back to school but left for somewhere else, nobody knew where. Two months after that, Haihong started to receive letters and all kinds of books from an unknown address. Her form teacher looked over her letters and bulky parcels with a censor's eye, but the sender was marked innocuously "Elder Sister Haihui".

Haihong and Liangguang stopped speaking to each other, for no apparent reason. Liangguang moved to the back row of the classroom and started to fool about with boys he had never played with before, talking loudly and joking. He had become oddly boisterous.

Haihong sat in her seat, reading her book with her head lowered. Tears fell in streams, and she could not see a word. When she took up a pen, the tears would flow before she had a chance to write a word on the white paper. When the teacher asked her a question she would stand up, but found herself unable to say a word, only tears came gushing from her eyes.

There had been no quarrel, nor had there been any offer or refusal to speak, but they had parted company. There was a thick wall between Haihong and Liangguang, and now its existence had become clear. They were each standing on a different side of the wall, not knowing what to do for the best. In the end, they truly became estranged.

Before Qingfei returned, she did not even know if Liangguang had made it into high school.

Six months later, summer had arrived, and Qingfei came back to Wu Town again.

Haihong seemed not to have paid much heed to where Qingfei had gone or what he had been doing, though she liked the books and letters he had sent anonymously. Like other girls who receive love letters, she had been deeply moved by them, and she hid in the toilets to read the letters over and over again. She did not understand that much about the warm, ardent feelings in the letters, or the descriptions of his own life, and they did not greatly interest her either. But the fact that someone had written to her was in itself enough to make her happy. This was the first time she read *Anna Karenina*, *War and Peace* and *Jane Eyre*, the first time she was the object of another's envious gaze, and the first time she got some vague idea of the hopelessness and the greatness of love. However, there seemed to be a vast distance between her and Qingfei, and she overlooked him in a way. He had dropped so quickly into a grey, meagre reality. The path he had taken was not for her. Her future was not in Wu Town, but neither was she going to drift around with no fixed destination.

At Wu Town's large corner building on the crossroads, Haihong saw Qingfei waiting for her. This was the first time Qingfei had appeared in town since he dropped out of school. He had changed, although she could not say for sure whether it was a certain stylishness or degree of maturity, but something about him was strange to Haihong. The first thing she noticed were Qingfei's lips, red, smooth and moist, so small, so plump. Every time she looked at his face, she could not stop herself staring at them, then her eyes would quickly shy away. His few patches of thick, black stubble also made her restless and uneasy, a fleshly feeling that was almost nauseating.

In the hospital dormitory, Qingfei took off his long

trousers in front of her and changed into a pair of knee-length shorts. This took her aback, but she did not know where to hide or what to say, so she blushed and let him get on with it. Her idea of Qingfei had not included this kind of thing. In front of Haihong, he kept blushing, smiling at her anxiously and a little ingratiatingly. It was only a very long time afterwards that Haihong realised that Qingfei was even tenser than she was and that he was struggling to get into those shorts. He seemed to be playing out a ritual of some sort, to make Haihong aware of the existence of a certain relationship between them.

In a blur, Haihong followed Qingfei. They came to the veranda on the roof of the dormitory building.

Qingfei slowly moved closer to Haihong, softly, experimentally embracing her waist, pressing his lips to her face, licking lightly. Haihong felt like a small, soaking wet animal was crawling over her face, its sticky, cloyingly damp hair and tongue moving about on her eyebrows, eyes and nose. Very slowly it extended sickeningly to explore her mouth. Haihong struggled to pull her face away, keeping her lips tightly closed. Qingfei's movements gradually became more forceful, and he prised apart Haihong's teeth with his tongue, which then nimbly explored Haihong's mouth, churning about inside. Its tip would sometimes go as far as the back of her mouth, at other times it would straighten out and extend into the empty space. Haihong pushed at Qingfei with her hands, hoping to shove him away, but it was like a devil had taken possession of her body, and she felt weak all over, with no strength at all.

They did not know that at that moment Dequan was walking up, step by step, preparing to descend on them, to rescue Haihong. As for Qingfei, he was about to incur punishment from a symbolic figure from the ancient past, after which he would fall into a dark place. In those days, Haihong seemed to have tumbled into a hallucinatory dream. In her bewildered daze, that emaciated, ramrod-straight holy man was constantly by her side, his Bible clutched in his hand. Although she did not see the book clearly, she knew it for a Bible. He was vague and indistinct, both remote and real, watching her.

She could not see his face or eyes, but she could feel his sternness and his censure.

Haihong did not dare leave the house for a very long time. She was afraid of being recognised and that someone might blackmail her. That man knew where she lived. He had led her home by the hand without the slightest hesitation. He knew the way so well it would seem that he had been watching her for more than just a day or two. But nobody ever came looking for her.

As the summer was nearing its end, Haihong saw Qingfei again, at the side of the main road that led to the county town. He was pulling a cart stacked full of coal, coming towards her from the other end of the road. The ropes on the cart were stretched taut, slanting across Qingfei's shoulders, leaving deep imprints, and the battered flipflops he wore could not get a proper grip on the ground, making every step forward an exaggerated stride, which caused his ragged singlet and shorts to sway as he leaned in. His hair had grown long and dishevelled, and the deep black coal dust on his face glistened. She looked at him, almost unable to bear it. This was not *Anna Karenina*, this was not *Jane Eyre*, nor the scorching words of those long letters, this was nothing at all.

As for Qingfei, the instant he saw her, his face flushed a deep red, and she could not tell if he was laughing or crying. He was straining away at his cart, but his legs kept getting tangled up, as if he had been drinking, and the cart rocked back and forth, shedding black lumps of coal onto the road. Haihong and Qingfei looked at each other, at a loss. Their mouths opened a few times, but neither spoke. Haihong felt nausea creeping up from her chest. She thought of that roving tongue, the bright red lips and the traces of coal-black stubble, and she wanted to be sick. She swiftly averted her eyes and looked towards the other side of the road.

After that, Haihong never saw Qingfei again.

———

This is just how things are. You never know what it is you have lost. Sometimes, even before your losses and pains have begun to truly live and grow, while they are still just revolving inside your mind, they can vanish and all trace of them is gone, like the snowfall that winter, which covered the sky and blocked out the sun, concealing all traces of humanity, emotionless and solid.

The fourteen-year-old Haihong knew nothing of this. She was still squatting on the snowy ground, tears falling in streams onto the thick, thick snow. Through the blur of tears, Haihong saw a series of little holes, each one spreading and staining and opening up, linking together with the moisture that had just fallen on them, caving in and spreading outwards in all directions, revealing more of the colours of the damp earth, forming a deep, dangerous cave. She felt as if a chunk of flesh had been cut out of her heart, and it hurt badly. She wanted to cry out, but this snowy day was so silent that she could not bring herself to shout.

She stared dumbly at the ground, and that deep hole of urine and tears looked back at her.

9

The Exercise Ground

THE STORY OF THE BIG EXERCISE GROUND, now that's a long tale.

My father told me that my grandmother died in the last month of the lunar year in 1953, and before she died she went to the exercise ground to watch the public sentencings and executions. For the last few hundred years, the exercise ground behind the schools had always been used as an execution ground. At that time it boasted a stage there for the opera, and whenever there was a public execution you would generally first watch an opera, then came the sentencing, then the firing squad. At such times, residents from miles around Wu Town would treat it like a festival. Women would put on their best clothes and come to see the show, bringing stools and carrying their children. That day, Wu Yan'er's house by the side of the exercise ground was the most crowded, and someone would always be there keeping everyone up to date with the latest news.

That day they had been performing plays with "Huang Shiren" and "Liu Wencai" in them, in which both protagonists ended up being executed. The audience cheered and applauded, deeply moved by the performance, and then the village leaders took to the stage and called out with their loud hailer, which echoed horribly, the sound scattering outwards in waves, "Bring up the criminals... up... up..." and two men were hauled up. Just like in the opera, the convicts' hands were tightly trussed behind their backs with a further loop of rope around their necks and tall hats describing their crimes on their heads, and they were made to kneel on the ground. The leaders' hands waved and danced, and their spittle flew as they denounced these men as "big landlord", "bad element" or "counterrevolutionary", and the spectators set up a clamour, concerned only with trying to identify the convicts, who they were related to and what they had done. Anyone who knew anything about it would share their knowledge passionately with those around them. The town leader's voice would suddenly increase in volume, and the loud hailer screeched so that it hurt your ears, "This man is guilty of the most heinous crimes, even death could not expiate all his wickedness. He will be executed at once by firing squad!"

It was hard to distinguish true from false, in the opera and outside it. They heard two gunshots, bang, bang, and the men fell to the ground. My grandmother gave a cold shudder. She said to my grandfather that before those two men were shot, their heads had been held in a firm grip, they had been staring huge-eyed into the crowd, and they had seemed to see her. At that moment her entire body went cold, as if something had come surging across and overwhelmed her.

After returning home, my grandmother became ill and ached all over. Without having bumped into anything, her flesh came out in patches of green and yellow bruises as if she had been brutally pinched. My grandfather took her to a doctor, but he could not find any cause. Some folk said that something bad must have got into my grandmother's body and suggested bleeding her so that it could flow out; others reckoned she had been possessed by a ghost, so they bought paper money and firecrackers, and went to the crossroads to burn the money and set off the firecrackers, pleading with the ghost to leave her. My grandmother cried out in her daze, "That's not it, that's not it." Only then did my grandfather recall the shudder she had mentioned, and he hastily found two pieces of white paper, had someone write down the names of the two men who had been executed, hurried to the exercise ground, burned paper money, prayed and made his apologies, and then put the men's names into the fire. By the time he came back, my grandmother was already dead. The people said that his apology had come too late.

My dad can still remember the names of those two men: one was called Deng Xiangting, the other was Han Lige.

———

One evening in winter, four men were drinking and eating sesame seed cakes at Bald Wu's little restaurant: Yizhi the doctor, Hongzhong who had a non-job in the local government, the new-made real estate tycoon of Wu Town Wu Hongxing and Wu Town's renowned fortune-teller Lao Li Ge. Those cakes were a local speciality, crisp on the outside and soft in the middle, bursting with flavour. Yizhi was treating them all and had invited Lao Li Ge specially.

Wu Hongxing had made himself a fortune and had instructed Yizhi on how to make a pile of his own, saying that now was the best time for real estate in China. Any place could earn you money, anybody who wanted to buy or build a house should do so quickly, and those with more limited means could sell one house in order to buy more. Yizhi did as Wu Hongxing said. He borrowed six hundred thousand yuan behind his wife Xueli's back at the ruinous interest of two per cent a month and bought a small two-storey building opposite the exercise ground.

That little house was already crooked and tumble-down when he bought it. There were cracks in the foundations and walls, and the interior had never been touched since it was built. Yizhi spent another hundred thousand yuan redecorating it, hoping to sell the place on at a good price. Three years passed, and not only had it failed to sell, but the few elderly families who lived around it also moved away. There had always been something oddly sinister about this patch, and now it was becoming increasingly deserted.

Wu Hongxing, whose main residence was in the Rang

County town, came back on Sunday for a game of cards at Yizhi's place. On hearing Yizhi grumbling about his property problems, he pondered the matter carefully but remained baffled. Hongzhong, who was an avid reader of the *Book of Changes*, said hesitantly, "Is it a problem with the feng shui in this area?"

Wu Hongxing slapped his thigh, as if he had finally found a rational explanation. "That's right, there's that exercise ground right next door."

On the slope from the south end of Wu Town to the Tuan River, an old road passed through a patch of ancient woodland; to the left was the Number Two Junior Middle School, and in the hollow ground to the right was Wu Town's notorious exercise ground. The exercise ground was about a third of an acre, square in shape, and at the other end was the main north-south street of Wu Town, with an almost sheer slope leading to it. Yizhi had heard from his elders that this exercise ground had been a place for execution throughout its history: sentencing, imprisonment, death by dismembering, beheading, firing squads, who knew how many heads had rolled there? When he was in junior middle school, Yizhi lived with his elder sister in Wu Town Hospital. To get to the hospital you would turn right out of the main gate of the Number Two Middle School, and then go past the exercise ground and the Wu family's hot water shop. On windy nights a moaning and whistling would issue from that old wood, blowing over from somewhere far away, sinister and terrifying. Yizhi would get a feeling in the back of his head like he was being followed, and he would break into a run, afraid to stop until he reached the main gate of the hospital.

"We must get Lao Li Ge over," Wu Hongxing said, "have him take a look, see if there's some problem with the feng shui." On the phone, Lao Li Ge said in a mysterious tone that he was in a certain place inspecting a residence, but any affair of Hongxing's was his affair also, and he would certainly come that very afternoon.

At five o'clock in the afternoon Lao Li Ge arrived, all in a rush. Lao Li Ge was about sixty years old, recently retired, with a big bouffant hairstyle, a large purple face and a bookish manner. He first went all the way round Yizhi's little two-storey house, inspecting in front and behind, left and right, staring fixedly at the exercise ground in its hollow for a very long time, then scrunching up his eyes and looking at the Wu family's hot water shop to the front and right. Finally he said, "That'll do."

They drove in convoy to Bald Wu's little Muslim restaurant, where they took their seats, poured tea and passed around cigarettes. Lao Li Ge lit a cigarette and inhaled deeply. Knitting his eyebrows and wagging his head, he said in a low voice, "Well that's a turn-up, after all these years it still hasn't dispersed."

Then, turning to Yizhi, he said, "I'm to blame for this, I truly am, you're Hongxing's friend, I'm his friend too, so that makes us friends as well. Back then I did know something about you buying this house, but you didn't tell me and I wasn't involved, so I didn't give the matter much thought. Looking at it now, that was an oversight on my part. I had forgotten the matter of that exercise ground."

After Lao Li Ge had told his grandmother's story, he concluded, "The negative energy of this exercise ground is too strong, there are too many wronged ghosts, they'll cling to you. See this little house of yours, it looks directly onto the front left-hand side of the exercise ground." Lao Li Ge drew a plan on the table in water: the exercise ground, the stage and that little two-storey house on the slope, pointed them out and said, "Just here, that's where the stage used to be. I've heard the old people say that all the killings were on the front left of the stage. The condemned would kneel down facing slightly to the left, facing the onlookers, in what just so happens to be the direction of the main gate of your house."

Chills ran down the backs of Yizhi, Hongxing and Hongzhong, like a gust of cold wind. All of them were born in the 1960s or 1970s, which meant that when he was young, Yizhi had seen people paraded through the streets, struggled against and displayed as a warning to the masses, and he had heard the powerful loudspeakers reverberating through the whole town. Every time a death penalty notice with names crossed out in red appeared at the gate of the township government, there was bound to be a large-scale parade through the streets a few days later. A big lorry would drive slowly down the streets, with officers of the Public Security Bureau in their peaked caps standing solemnly on it, along with criminals, backs bent, heads forced downwards, placards hanging from their chests inscribed with the words "rapist and murderer", "hooligan" or "robber". All along the route, which ended at the exercise ground, the men with the loudspeakers would read out the crimes of these people in a piercing but matter-of-fact voice. But nobody would have ever thought that those who had died on that exercise ground would crawl up and attach themselves to live bodies, using their powers to trouble the living.

Yizhi was no great believer in such things, but neither could he say that he did not believe in them. Calling in a feng shui master when building a house was a matter of custom; although you might say it was just to get rid of any lingering, nagging feeling in your mind, neglecting to call one in would always leave you feeling mildly uneasy. He had met plenty of folk who had had strange encounters that defied explanation. The old branch Party secretary of Wu Town had believed in Buddhism and in fate, and he was always burning incense and praying to the Buddha. First his grandson suddenly fell to the ground and died, then his son got run over, after that his wife died of a stroke, and a year ago the old Party secretary himself died too. Everyone said he must have offended some kind of god or spirit. Yizhi did not believe in this sort of thing, but he did think it was very mysterious.

Yizhi hurriedly poured wine for Lao Li Ge. He downed two cups, then asked, "Is there any way to break the ill luck?"

Lao Li Ge drank a mouthful of tea, raised his chopsticks, picked up a large slice of beef cooked according to

Bald Wu's secret family recipe, stuffed it into his mouth and chewed for a while. He said slowly and deliberately, "Well, there is a way, but I don't know if he'll agree."

Yizhi, Hongzhong and Hongxing all leaned in towards Lao Li Ge, listening attentively.

"Have you seen the Wu family's hot water shop? It's located exactly on the right corner of the exercise ground, like a nail driven firmly in there, keeping the evil influences at bay. Never mind that it's not far from the exercise ground, that place has won victory from the jaws of danger. The closer it is, the more firmly it nails down those wronged ghosts. Actually, it's a good location. Look at old Wu Yan'er's son, Wu Chuanyou, who now runs the hot water shop. See how he always appears so ill and sickly, yellow-faced and skinny, he's been seeped in that all day, fighting with those ghosts. The ghosts have all been sucked into the man himself, so his house is fine. If he were to move into your two-storeyed house, the negative essences on his body would keep the ghosts at bay, he'll be fine, and that little house will be fine too. It's a win-win situation. Perfect."

After Lao Li Ge had said that last sentence in a meaningful tone, he raised his teacup again and drank a mouthful with relish, took a Zhonghua cigarette from the soft pack Yizhi offered him, inhaled deeply, blew out a smoke ring and regarded Yizhi with a half-smile.

Yizhi, Hongxing and Hongzhong looked at each other and understood what Lao Li Ge was telling them.

Hongxing said, "Oh, Yizhi, wasn't Wu Chuanyou in

the same class as you at school? He was seriously ill for a while, so they took him out of school, that's how he ended up a year below us."

Hongzhong shook his head. "This won't be easy, he's a strange-looking chap, a bit scary, and he doesn't have that much to do with anyone else. I'm guessing it might be tricky to talk him round."

Yizhi suddenly recalled how all those years ago Wu Chuanyou had fallen ill and left school. A rumour had gone round that he had been possessed by ghosts, and the teacher had criticised them all in class, calling it feudal superstition. Wu Chuanyou had been small-featured, thin and frail, with a slightly hunched back and a worryingly pale face. At break all the other children used to charge around, jumping and yelling, but anyone who ran near him would automatically give him a wide berth. After Yizhi bought that little two-storey house, he caught sight of Wu Chuanyou from time to time, standing at the door of the hot water shop on the other side of the road. His back was still hunched, as if something heavy was pressing down on him, his appearance depressed and melancholy. On seeing Yizhi he would greet him from far off and they would say few words, but it seemed he was unwilling to come into closer contact.

'It's not a rumour," Lao Li Ge said. "Wu Chuanyou really was possessed by ghosts. I witnessed the whole thing first-hand. The year was 1983, the first 'Strike Hard' campaign, it was properly scary. They said they wanted to tackle hooligans and street toughs, but once it all got going there was no limit or end to it, who knew what might get you arrested? A friend of mine from the army was sentenced for hooliganism because he'd kissed a girl on the mouth in public, and a man from my home village who was a just bit light-fingered got more than ten years.

"That year I was just shy of thirty. The Party secretary at my work unit liked fortune-telling books and things of that sort. I'd just been posted there after leaving the army, and the Party secretary often had me round to his house for a chat. He'd talk about his own experiences, and when he was in a good mood and he'd had a drink, he'd tell people that I had a gift and send them to me for readings. Once the Strike Hard campaign got going, the Party secretary stopped coming round, and I burned all those books straight away in a panic. If anybody came to me for a reading, I'd act like I knew nothing.

"It was at this juncture that folk said that the Wu family's son Wu Chuanyou had been possessed by a ghost. As soon as I heard this, I hurried over to take a look. There were people everywhere at Chuanyou's home, standing three deep inside and out. Chuanyou was lying on the bed, his face bright red, his eyes were sometimes rolled right up in his head, then they would roll down and close. Then suddenly he gave a start, raised himself, sat up on the bed and cried out, 'Ding Shengbo, Ding Shengbo, come in.' The voice was nothing like that of a young child, it was an old man, coarse, hoarse, full of anger. A man came in from outside, agitated and flustered, and sure enough, it was

Ding Shengbo from Ding Village. He was already fifty at the time.

"Chuanyou had been possessed by a distant relative of Ding Shengbo's, an uncle. Chuanyou, no, Ding Shengbo's uncle said, 'I've been calling out for you for two days, brat, and you never came, don't think I'll forgive you. Your dad was carrying on in secret with the widow, so tell me, why did he have to frame me instead? What's it to do with me if that widow hanged herself! You're all liars, and you just a boy of ten!'

"I worked it all out. This was something that had happened back in the nineteen forties. Ding Shengbo's uncle was beheaded in the exercise ground for having a secret affair with a widow and forcing her to hang herself. They said Ding Shengbo had been a witness, he'd seen his uncle going into the widow's house. That Ding Shengbo was shaking all over with fear, he grovelled on the ground kowtowing desperately, saying, 'Uncle, Uncle, forgive me, I'll burn paper money for you, I'll set off fireworks, I'll hire musicians, I'll cook you fresh steamed bread and pour you strong wine.'

"When he heard these words, Chuanyou, no, Ding Shengbo's uncle, fell back on the bed and went to sleep, his face was still that brilliant red. His dad Wu Yan'er was beside him with a damp facecloth, which he held to Wu Chuanyou's forehead.

"Those in the room and those standing outside were shaking all over with fright. Some wanted to leave, but they didn't dare, for fear they might get chased by a ghost when they were halfway home.

"An hour and a half passed. Wu Chuanyou gave another start and his eyes snapped open, this time it was two people's voices, speaking in turn. One was a young lad with a crisp, sharp voice, the other was middle-aged and powerful. 'Tell me, has Wang Qiankun come here?'

"A white-haired old man squeezed in from outside and went down on his knees with a thump.

"That middle-aged powerful voice said, 'Wang Qiankun, we took a life in payment for a life, so why did you tell the government to take us both, father and son?'

"That was a big murder case from before Liberation. There were two powerful families in the village of Wangying, and a quarrel broke out between them over land, one side went after two people from the other side with meat cleavers, and the other side did the same to two people from the first side. It had caused a huge stir at the time, mainly because one of the murders had been widely witnessed. The man had been running away when he got cut in two at the waist, his legs were still running forward while the part above the waist was drifting backwards, and blood was spurting upwards. A father and son from one of the factions fled to the army and enlisted as soldiers. As they said, it had been a life for a life, and the thing was pretty much over and done with. Then several years later that army unit came marching back to Wu Town and settled there to fight the Japanese, and every day they did field training on the slope of the Tuan River. That father and son didn't even dare go home. When they went out on manoeuvres, they would hunch their backs and lower their heads for fear that someone would recognise them. And in the end they were recognised anyway, by Wang Qiankun from the other faction. At that time the army was strengthening discipline, so they carted them both off to the exercise ground and had them shot, father and son together.

"That old man got such a fright that snot and tears were running down his face and he couldn't speak, all he could do was kowtow.

"There were others, too, who reproached their family members for not burning paper money for them, who scolded their sons for disloyalty. That afternoon Wu Chuanyou was possessed by at least five people, speaking in five people's voices, talking about five people's affairs. Those near him spoke in shock and amazement: that's so-and-so's own voice. By the time dusk was coming on, Wu Chuanyou's face was no longer red, he'd gone white, like a corpse. He collapsed with exhaustion.

"I could see that something was not right. I took Wu Yan'er discreetly outside and said, 'Uncle, you daren't carry on like this, not in times like these. They're arresting people on the streets. If you keep this up, the pair of you will get taken away, father and son.'

"Wu Yan'er gave a start. He grasped my hand and shook it. I knew what he was trying to say.

"A few days passed and they said he was cured. Wu Chuanyou became an ordinary kid again.

"You can call it incredible and indeed it is, I've seen so

many witch-women pretending to be spirits or messing around with ghosts, talking in different voices, you'd know them for fakes as soon as you clapped eyes on them. But there'd never yet been a child who'd been possessed, and the voices were spot on, he could never have imitated them under normal circumstances. The facts were highly accurate as well, all those tiny, irrelevant details from years ago, even the people involved had forgotten them, how could he know?"

It seemed that Lao Li Ge was still feeling the fear from those days. He drank several cups of wine in succession and said, "All the same, once that business was over and done with, the evil influences in that place basically all went away."

Hongzhong broke in. "Once he'd told all their wrongs, they all left the exercise ground. They got themselves reborn and started again."

The whole group burst into loud laughter.

———

This was how the matter was arranged.

First would come a visit and a chat from Yizhi, to get to know Wu Chuanyou, then Wang Hongxing and the others would invite him out for a meal, to slowly win Wu Chuanyou over. Finally, they would suggest a house swap. Ideally Wu Chuanyou would give Yizhi some compensation. When all was said and done Yizhi's house had two floors, and Wu Chuanyou's was just a shabby three-room, single-storeyed property. Failing that, a simple house swap would do. The hot water shop occupied a larger area than the little two-storeyed house, and if they swapped Yizhi could at least build a new four-up-four-down building, he would not stand to lose out.

After a big snowfall, Yizhi went to check up on the little house. The path in front of the gate had been blocked off by snow, so Yizhi went to Wu Chuanyou's house opposite to borrow a shovel.

Outside the end wall of this one-storey building was a small lean-to of ten square metres or so, which they had used to heat the water when the place was still a hot water shop. The holes for the stoves were still there, more than ten of them, pitch black like wide-open eyes staring, looking quite forlorn. In the old days, the hot drinking water for the Wu Town Hospital had been taken on as a job lot by the Wu family. Every morning just past six o'clock, Yizhi would go to the hot water shop with his coupons and two big thermos bottles to collect hot water for his family. The dozen or so stove holes inside were glowing red, from time to time a kettle would let out a long, shrill whistle and steam would come spurting out of the spout, all the way up to the ceiling, wreathing the entire room in steam. Wu Yan'er was bustling about, stooping over the stoves. Wu Chuanyou's short, stocky mother kept nipping in and out, busily topping up the kettles with water and collecting coupons.

Yizhi went into the main room of the hot water shop. It was unexpectedly simple and clean inside, with barely any traces of human activity. Against the centre of the main wall was a big square table from the 1970s or 80s, on both sides of which stood a pair of old-fashioned wooden armchairs. In the precise centre of the square table was a tall, bulky statue of the folk hero Guan Yu, with his red face and long beard, a large knife in his hand, armour-clad, stern and awe-inspiring, glowering furiously at anybody who entered the room. An incense burner had been placed in front of Guan Yu, and several sticks of incense were smoking in it.

Without quite knowing why, Yizhi hastened forward, took up a stick of incense lying on the table, lit it and stuck it in the incense burner. He then took two paces back and bowed solemnly several times to the glowering Guan Yu.

Wu Chuanyou led Yizhi towards the carved armchairs, and told his wife, who was waiting in the inner room, to pour a cup of tea for Yizhi. Wu Chuanyou's wife was skinny and small, quiet and calm. She filled his cup and returned to the inner room.

In the course of their little chat, Yizhi mentioned his boyhood illness. He did not expect Wu Chuanyou to chuckle softly and say, "That was made up by my dad. The high fever was real, the possession was fake."

Wu Chuanyou made no attempt at evasion. "I said what my dad primed me to say. Living beside the exercise ground since he was small as he had, where people got killed all the time, and listening to all the gossip, was there anything he didn't know? My dad, my granddad, my great granddad, everybody had been keeping stock of who died and how they died, why they died, who were their enemies, when they were beheaded, when they were shot, all as clear as you like. They all went round and round our house every day, the ghosts from the underworld, and they would never disperse.

"My dad said, make use of my fever to speak out their grievances, let their families and enemies take their spirits away so that they wouldn't have to keep circling the exercise ground any more.

"I didn't have a clue what these dead people were like, or how their voices sounded, how could my voice be like theirs? I was burning up with fever and my mind was wandering, I was beside myself, I didn't know anything at all."

"Did you really not know? The people who saw it all said that you imitated the voices so well that it was just like that person." Yizhi did not entirely believe him.

"I really didn't know. I got that high fever because of the fright I'd had."

When Yizhi saw Wu Chuanyou speaking with such conviction, and thought of the words he was saying with such conviction, the hairs on his arms stood up on end.

Chuanyou looked intently and meaningfully at Yizhi. "That fever has something to do with you as well."

How could that be? Yizhi did not understand what he was trying to tell him, he could not even remember having anything to do with Chuanyou in the past.

"Have you forgotten? At that time we were in the same class in Junior One, you were living at your sister's in the hospital, and when you were at a loose end you'd come and play with me. The loudspeakers were calling out every day on the streets, those big trucks were driving towards the exercise ground for public sentencings, first one and then another, it was only later that we knew that this was the Strike Hard campaign."

Yizhi knew of the Strike Hard campaign, of course, but he really could not recall when he might have had any dealings with Wu Chuanyou. He thought it was unlikely that they had ever played together. Wu Chuanyou's face was so sinister, so pale, they belonged to different worlds. At eleven or twelve years old, he had been bursting with latent energy, playing tricks in class every day. As soon as he heard the loudspeakers, he would get excited and run everywhere following the trucks, jumping up and down, running around and making a nuisance of himself on the crowded exercise ground.

"I saw *you*, though." Wu Chuanyou stared stubbornly at Yizhi, waiting for Yizhi's reaction. In that instant, Yizhi felt that Wu Chuanyou was like a wronged ghost who had been waiting a long time for his anticipated revenge.

"I saw you."

Yizhi was starting to find the way Wu Chuanyou stared at him quite unsettling.

"You've forgotten? That evening, a few days before I got my high fever, the evening self-study period at school had finished, you'd gone home, and so had I. And where did you go after that?"

Yizhi could not see what Wu Chuanyou was hinting

at. His memories of the fever were hazy enough, how could he remember some small stupid thing from a few nights before that? However, the insistence with which Wu Chuanyou was imparting information about their youth had piqued his curiosity and stimulated his stubborn, perverse streak. He looked at Wu Chuanyou, encouraging him to keep him talking.

"Do you still remember that girl hooligan Zhao Xiaoyan? She was a hospital employee, from Shanghai. She had a very rough and ready way of speaking, she had flared trousers and a big, fluffy perm. The one that got sentenced to death."

"Yes, I remember," Yizhi said, becoming excited all at once. On that occasion, everybody in Wu Town had gone to the exercise ground to see Zhao Xiaoyan. Her hair was curling loose about her shoulders, she was wearing a white dress with pink polka dots that showed her long, white legs, trussed up like a convict with her hands behind her back and a loop around her neck. The spectators were both cursing her and clicking their tongues in admiration at those white legs.

Yizhi could vaguely remember how the boy standing next to him had nudged him and told him to look at Zhao Xiaoyan on the stage, saying mysteriously, "Do you know what her crime was? She kissed two men on the mouth."

"Do you still remember the little hut in the old woods behind the hospital?"

As if a floodgate had suddenly opened, Yizhi recollected a certain night. In the blurry darkness he saw light shining from that little hut, heard sounds of music and laughter that made his skin creep. He saw inside: men and women embracing each other, heads touching, faces pressed together, swaying like they were drunk. Zhao Xiaoyan seemed like she was being held up by two men, her body twisted, skirt swinging and swaying, mouth half open. In the eyes of the teenage Yizhi, her expression was hideous, sickening.

Yizhi let out an involuntary "ah", and on realising he had cried out, he turned and ran. The people in the security office at the gate saw that he was flustered and upset, and asked him what had happened. Yizhi made no reply but ran like the wind.

"You don't remember a thing?" Wu Chuanyou was staring at Yizhi, searching for some trace of evidence in Yizhi's eyes.

Yizhi could not quite meet his eye, so he asked Wu Chuanyou in return, "Zhao Xiaoyan got a life sentence, didn't she? How did it get changed to a death sentence?"

"After that it was all 'Strike Hard, Strike Fast', so they sentenced her to death. That evening I was there too. They got me to buy snacks for them, and once I'd bought them they wouldn't let me leave. I saw you. You were peeping in at the door. I was sitting right opposite the door.

"When you shouted 'ah' like that, I heard it. You ran off, and not long afterwards the hospital security staff turned up. After that, officials came from the Public Security Bureau and took them all away."

Yizhi stood up with a clatter and said furiously, "I most certainly did not give them away."

These words were from the heart. For all that he was over forty, Yizhi swore to himself the way he had as a young boy: I'm a dog if I did any such thing, I'm a pig! Only a dog or a pig would do something like that!

"Then are you saying that I was the one who gave them away? That evening I got taken away as well. They got me to identify them. I was scared out of my wits. I told them everything, I was afraid they'd sentence me too. And I said enough for them to be sentenced to prison. Actually, if I hadn't said anything, I'm guessing they would have got away with it." Wu Chuanyou laughed softly, as if mocking his childishness and simplicity.

"Just a few days later, they held the public sentencing. I wanted to go and see, but I didn't quite dare. So I stood right at the very back of those big trucks. They'd got them all tied up, facing the crowd, all I could see was their legs. I could recognise Zhao Xiaoyan's legs, white and straight, it had to be her. When they announced the sentence, I saw that Zhao Xiaoyan's legs were shaking the whole time. If it hadn't been for the two people next to her in big peaked caps holding her up, she'd have collapsed. When they were being moved, Zhao Xiaoyan's eyes turned to where I was, I could sense that she'd seen me, she'd recognised me, she knew that I'd given them away. I fell to the ground in a faint, and I didn't know anything after that.

"Later on, it was my dad who put that performance together."

Yizhi could sense that Wu Chuanyou did not require any confirmation from him, he was just recounting something that had happened all that time ago. Those past events had been bottled up inside him for too long, and he had nobody to tell. But Yizhi did not care at all for Wu Chuanyou's tone, as if the death of that young woman had something to do with him. He did not like those associations and that feeling of guilt. That excessively clean and tidy room was the expression of that guilt.

Yizhi involuntarily gave a cold shudder like Lao Li Ge, as if someone was watching him. The source of that feeling was Wu Chuanyou; with the pride and self-respect of those who bear a burden of guilt, he was using this same guilt to intimidate Yizhi.

Yizhi hurriedly changed the subject. "Just think about it, how many people must have died on this exercise ground of ours."

"Just so. All the same, after that the public sentencings and shootings here at our exercise ground seemed to stop. After it happened, I said to my dad that I didn't want to live here. My dad said that the generations before us had lived in this place, neither could leave the other. If we did leave, something bad was bound to happen."

Wu Chuanyou sighed lightly, stood up and topped up Yizhi's tea, saying, "Sometimes I think that my dad believing in ghosts and spirits had a lot going for it. My own fate is bad too, it has to be something to do with the evil influences of this exercise ground. And then sometimes I feel that it's all a load of rubbish, are there ghosts there? All those ghosts, if they'd really come to haunt me they'd have haunted me to death long since."

Yizhi waved a hand in the air and laughed loudly. "How could that be? If you really did move away, who's to say that your luck wouldn't improve?"

———

Once he had escaped from the oppressive glower of the Guan Yu statue and was breathing gulps of the freezing air outside, Yizhi turned round to see Wu Chuanyou standing reverently in front of Guan Yu, lighting a new stick of incense. Yizhi suddenly felt that that house was too quiet, Chuanyou's voice was too soft and his actions too cautious, he was constantly shrinking inwards on himself, as if in fear of disturbing something.

Yizhi reckoned that if the house swap succeeded, he would have this tumbledown property pulled down straight away. Negative energies? It was all down to the eyes on that Guan Yu statue, the way they blazed with fury, as if anybody they looked on was a ghost or a monster. As soon as the house was pulled down, as soon as the light shone in, any negative energies would be burned away by the sun.

In the days that followed, Yizhi would often pop in and out of the hot water shop for a chat with Wu Chuanyou, and the two of them gradually got closer. One day Yizhi, Lao Li Ge, Wu Hongxing and a few others went out for a meal and invited Wu Chuanyou to come along too.

Lao Li Ge sat in the seat of honour, not a hair out of place, neatly dressed, and when he saw Wu Chuanyou arrive he stood up, held out his hand and shook Wu Chuanyou's heartily several times. "Chuanyou," he said, "you don't know who I am, but I know who *you* are. I was a bosom buddy of your father's. Back in the day, that business with your high fever and getting possessed by spirits, if I hadn't restrained your dad, he might well have got himself arrested. Just think about it, in times like those, they were desperate to catch someone and make an example, and your dad insisted on throwing himself at the barrel of a gun."

"Lao Li Ge," Yizhi said, "Chuanyou said it was a trick to chase the ghosts away, it wasn't real."

Lao Li Ge pursed his lips and smiled, saying seriously, "With things like that, you can't believe in them completely, but you can't discount them either. I was listening from the sides, the voices you spoke in were truly the voices of those people. Your dad only called them in for you, but once they were inside you, they were real. Those people were actually there, in your body."

Everyone in the group fell silent. Eventually, Lao Li Ge said, "Look, Chuanyou, I'm not ill-wishing you, but nobody in your family is long-lived, your forefathers lived there for several generations, and in such an atmosphere, the stink of blood alone, it's too much. That house of yours has been no fit place to live for a long time."

Everybody involuntarily looked at Wu Chuanyou. They could sense that sinister influence radiating from his eyes, his hair and his body, and the temperature in the room plunged several degrees. Wu Chuanyou sat up straighter, he seemed to be fighting back against this scrutiny.

When Lao Li Ge had reached this point, he suddenly stopped. The talk turned to other subjects, such as drinking and gossip.

Wu Chuanyou seemed mesmerised by Lao Li Ge's poise and style, and he very much wanted to make Lao Li Ge finish the conversation he had left unfinished. Whenever Yizhi proposed a toast, he invited Lao Li Ge to join them. Having finally found himself a loyal listener, Lao Li Ge started talking to Wu Chuanyou, seemingly at random, about "integrity".

"In this line of business, the most important thing is to consider your integrity, that's to say we can't go around selling ourselves. What does that mean? You can't stand at a man's door, bold as brass, and come right out and say that you want to tell his fortune. You have to consider your dignity, and you must have integrity. For example, people will invite you to work on houses for the living and tombs for the dead, to calculate how to succeed in examinations, how to get rich or to get married, all of these are fine, but you can't show them ways to work against people, to hold them back or harm them. Especially when looking at tombs for the dead, sometimes a good place for this family will be harmful to the feng shui of a neighbour. At these times, you must remember your integrity. You can't hurt another family because this family's asked you to work for them. You have to consider balance."

Lao Li Ge enunciated the word "integrity" in a vibrant, carrying tone. In the dialect of Rang County, this word retains the old pronunciation from classical Chinese, so that *de* becomes *dai*, uttered in a strong voice with an open mouth, a heavy, clumsy, powerful sound that is somehow also loaded with sarcasm.

When the talk turned to Wu Chuanyou's hot water shop, Lao Li Ge just kept shaking his head, as if there were too many problems that were best left unspoken, leaving Wu Chuanyou a little bit concerned. After a while, he poured out another round of drinks for Lao Li Ge and asked him to do a reading for his house.

"This house of yours is like a gatehouse," Lao Li Ge said, "and your family are the gatekeepers. My guess is that back in the day your earliest ancestors must have been selected specially for the task. This is the fate of previous generations in your family. The gatehouse is stuck here like a nail, and so those ghosts can't get out, but wander back and forth every day, half yin half yang. Never mind your Guan Yu statue, the Jade Emperor of Heaven himself couldn't hold them back. They are too familiar with the people in your family, they're climbing all over you, taking advantage. This place of yours urgently needs to be passed on to people with strong positive energy, to keep them down."

"Then I still need somewhere else to go," Wu Chuanyou remarked.

Hongxing said, as though it had just occurred to him, "Oh, but Yizhi is wanting to sell that two-storey house of his, isn't he? You can go and live there, it's just over the road. That doesn't count as leaving the exercise ground."

Li Lao Ge slapped his thigh and exclaimed, "Well that would be ideal. That place is highly desirable. But if we were talking about really leaving the exercise ground, I would guess that wouldn't do either. This exercise ground can't be cut off from its guardians."

Everybody was looking at Yizhi. Yizhi was silent for a while, before he said, "That's all very well, I'll sell the house to anyone so long as it sells, it's just... I'm going to need ready money. The thing is, I've got loans to pay off."

Wu Chuangyou's eyes had filled with hope, but now they darkened. He had no ready cash.

"Don't you want to build more houses?" Lao Li Ge asked Yizhi.

"And so I do. I'll definitely build more if there's a suitable place."

"So if the two of you were to swap?" Lao Li Ge was looking at Wu Chuanyou as he said this, as if he were presenting Wu Chuanyou with a marvellous, heaven-sent opportunity.

"But won't Yizhi lose out?" Chuanyou said, looking at Yizhi.

Lao Li Ge paused for a moment, sat up straight and said solemnly, "How about this, if the two of you give me face I'll be your middleman today. Let's put our cards on the table. Chuanyou's hot water shop has a good, open location, facing the exercise ground, and an area nearly twice the size of Yizhi's little house. Yizhi's house is only half the area, but it's newly refurbished, you can pack your bags and move straight in. Yizhi will lose out a little, but in the long term he'll still do pretty well. Taken all in all, Yizhi will have got himself a good piece of land, and Chuanyou will have saved himself the cost of building a new house. It counts as working out for the best to both parties."

Wu Chuanyou was half believing, half disbelieving. He had thought that all this was just idle banter. Once it was all confirmed, he was delighted. He drank a big mouthful of wine without waiting for an invitation and clinked glasses with Yizhi, saying, "So long as you aren't afraid of losing out to me, I'll be only too glad to swap. My dad wouldn't let me move house, and before he died he urged me again and again never to move away, no matter what. As soon as I moved, there would be disaster in my fate. Even my death would be sudden and violent. I don't want to stick around here any more. If I stay here, the poverty will kill me anyway."

Yizhi's heart gave a thump, and he looked over towards Lao Li Ge. Lao Li Ge was absorbed in his drink and did not meet Yizhi's eyes. Hongxing was wholly taken up with talking to Hongzhong, and neither of them gave any sign of having heard what Wu Chuanyou had said.

Wu Chuanyou noticed that there was something

peculiar about everybody's expressions, and thinking that he had said something out of turn, hurriedly added, "All the same, this is all my affair, and my family's. I'll take the evil influences away with me, and this house, this place, you'll go and live there, and everything will be fine. Wouldn't you say so, Lao Li Ge?"

Hongxing, Lao Li Ge and Hongzhong stood up and clinked glasses with Wu Chuanyou and they all shouted, "Yes, Yes! With this exchange, there'll be no evil influences for anybody."

Lao Li Ge slapped his chest and said, "If you move into that two-storey house of Yizhi's that would be absolutely ideal, not too far and not too near, keeping your distance from those wronged ghosts, but when they want to hurt you, you'll see them more clearly."

As the guests departed the banquet, Lao Li Ge muttered drunkenly to Hongxing, "This Chuanyou is no pushover, his words are half truth, half lies. The way he goes back and forth with his words like this, there's a goal in it, he's got a very big goal."

Yizhi wanted to take the matter further and asked, "Then those evil influences that Wu Chuanyou says are so great, are they actually real? Let's not swap a two-storey house for a shabby plot of land, only to get big problems in exchange."

"That's just a manner of speaking," Lao Li Ge replied in a slurred voice. "Besides, if there really is a disaster, then it's his disaster and not yours."

———

So it was that Yizhi's two-storey house was exchanged for the Wu family hot water shop just before Spring Festival. Once they had sorted out the title deeds, Yizhi again invited Lao Li Ge for food and wine, and gave him a red envelope containing five hundred yuan. Lao Li Ge politely refused a couple of times, and he accepted.

Lao Li Ge chose a lucky day, and on that day Wu Chuanyou moved his family to the little two-storey house, and the big table, the carved wooden armchairs and the red-faced Guan Yu statue moved in with him. That day, Wu Chuanyou invited Yizhi, Lao Li Ge and a big crowd to his house for the traditional housewarming feast to celebrate the move. Yizhi couldn't stop looking at the red-faced Guan Yu, and he kept thinking that something was missing from his eyes. He no longer appeared as imposing or as lifelike as he had been at the hot water shop.

Having moved into the new house, Wu Chuanyou seemed to have lifted the curse. The ice was broken, and his expression became considerably brighter and more cheerful. Sometimes when he was free, he would go to Yizhi's teahouse for a drink and some chat and to watch the play. Once New Year was over, he decided for the first time to find employment away from home, leaving for Shandong with his wife's brother to work as a labourer in a quarry.

Yizhi went behind the back of his wife Xueli and privately borrowed another hundred thousand yuan through Hongxing. He made plans to start work once the first month of the new year was over: to pull down the hot water shop and build two courtyard houses, which could be sold separately.

On the last day of the first lunar month, Yizhi was sitting at the counter in the clinic, drinking the Baisha tea that Hongxing had brought back for him from Hainan Island, crunching numbers on his computer and dreaming of property deals. Hongxing had gone to Hainan for Chinese New Year and came back raving about the place, saying that he and the rest of the gang should all buy houses there for their old age and live like gods, enjoying the sea breeze, playing cards and drinking coconut chicken soup. Yizhi had started to dream of this too. He was doing his sums, thinking how once he had built the house and sold it he would buy a few more small houses and sell them on too. A few rounds of this and he would have enough for a flat in Hainan.

At midday, Wu Shuangxi who sold hot pepper soup in the north street came charging into the clinic and stuttered, "Something's happened." But he was wheezing and choking so much that he could not say the words that should have come next.

Yizhi said with a smile, "What's got you in this state, you daft sod? Come on now, sit down and have a glass of water."

Still wheezing and coughing, Wu Shuangxi said, "Wu Chuanyou's had an accident."

Yizhi's hands shook for a moment, and he stared at Wu Shuangxi.

Wu Shuangxi stared back at Yizhi and said, "He got dragged into one of the machines."

"He's dead?"

"Yes, he's dead. Covered in blood. His body wasn't even in one piece."

Yizhi froze. He stood up, his face slack with shock. "So Wu Chuanyou's had an accident," he said. "Why did you come running over here to tell me about it?" He turned on his heel and went inside.

Yizhi's hands were shaking violently, and he was chilled to the bone. He pulled out his mobile phone and went through the list of contacts. Several times he was on the verge of calling Lao Li Ge, but he hung up every time.

They brought Wu Chuanyou's ashes back home. His wife went to Shandong, hoping to take his body home to bury on the western slope near the exercise ground, as his ancestors' tombs were all there. Her brother said it was best not to see him, some things you shouldn't see, just get him cremated quickly, enough is enough. Some folk from Wu Town went to negotiate with the manager of the quarry, who initially had refused to pay compensation, saying that Wu Chuanyou worked for them for less than ten days, so they had no right to demand compensation for his death. After that, some unknown person had a word with a contact in the local Propaganda and Communications Department, who put the frighteners on that arrogant quarry manager. The manager was forced to concede and grudgingly paid out thirty thousand yuan. Wu Chuanyou's wife returned to Wu Town carrying his ashes, which they buried on that river slope, watching over the exercise ground. She locked up the two-storey house and went back to her parents' home, taking her daughter with her.

All that time, Yizhi at the south end of the street was unconsciously listening for the sound of weeping from the north end. He waited for the noise to come, to bring resolution to the matter. But resolution never came.

In March Yizhi paid a visit to Mount Wutai, where he burned incense and prayed to the Buddha, and brought a buddha statue home with him. In spare moments he would light a stick of incense, stand it in the incense burner and pray.

He never did work up the courage to renovate the Wu family hot water shop. That old single-storey house had been old and dilapidated to begin with, and with no one living there it soon fell into decay. After a few summer storms, the roof caved in. Yizhi did nothing about it. He no longer felt any desire to dabble in real estate, and he virtually cut off contact with Wu Hongxing. Hongzhong, who usually went off to drink tea at Yizhi's once he had clocked in at the local government offices, was also waiting to see whether anything had happened, and where. Wherever something did happen, there was certain to be a good dinner.

One time when they had all been drinking, Hongzhong saw Yizhi lighting his incense and could not stop himself from saying, "Yizhi, what the hell, if you keep this up you'll do yourself a mischief."

Yizhi burst out laughing. "What the hell are you saying? What are you even thinking? We all have our own fates, I'm just getting rid of this nagging feeling in my mind. So as not to have him hanging around us."

People still regularly requested Lao Li Ge's services as a diviner. Several times when he was passing by the door of Yizhi's clinic, he slowed his steps to peer inside, saw Yizhi sitting idly at the counter and started to approach. Yizhi would get to his feet and heartily invite him in, but this heartiness seemed to be a little bit too much, a little bit fake. So Lao Li Ge would retreat, saying, "I've got to go, they're waiting for me, I'll be on my way."

After the summer was over, an outsider who had made his fortune came to Wu Town, boasting to one and all of his intention to buy himself a house there. When this man was young, he had got into university from the Number Five Senior School, he had eaten Wu Town's hot pepper soup and thick lamb noodles, and he had taken a liking to the high slopes behind the town. He said that he wanted to escape from the chaos and racket of the big city, to find a patch of pure earth in the country where he could return for a holiday, to grow vegetables, look at the scenery and feel the breeze. He went to the Number Five Middle School to visit his teachers from his school days and talk at length on the subject to anyone he could find, and one day he ran into Yizhi's old class teacher Teacher Zhao. Teacher Zhao, who spent his days at Yizhi's annex playing cards, told the man that there was no more suitable place in all of Wu Town for him than the Wu family's hot water shop.

A price was speedily agreed, and before the outsider had had time to think too much about anything, Yizhi dragged him to the Property Management Office to transfer the ownership.

Six months passed, and a European-style garden villa appeared beside the exercise ground. White marble columns, pink and white three-dimensional tile cladding in a diamond pattern, bright blue window frames, golden yellow pointed dormer windows, cheerily and elaborately decorated, bright, clean and new, standing there on the slope to the river. The exercise ground was still there, set deep in its hollow, yet it had almost become a back garden to this villa. That outsider built a set of wooden steps into the precipitous slope to the exercise ground and planted a ring of different kinds of roses that extended all the way to the edge of the old woods. When he came again in summer, the exercise ground was full of blossoms, pink, white and red, cheerful and lively, even the noises of heavy breathing emitted by the old woods in the evening seemed to sound softer, warmer, more pleasant.

The residents who had moved away all slowly moved back again, and villas started to proliferate along the road, creeping out towards the hospital. Weeds were cleared, courtyards were tidied up and new houses rose one by one. Very soon this area had become the most expensive real estate in Wu Town. Only Wu Chuanyou's small two-storey house remained, still sitting slumped there, nobody took any interest in that. The lock hanging from the gate was now a mass of rust from the wind and sun.

Soon afterwards, rumour had it that Wu Hongxing had located the widow and daughter, and bought the two-storey house for fifty thousand yuan. Lao Li Ge checked it over for him, determining that he would have to buy the land behind the house as well, as this was the only way to cut off the ill luck. Wu Hongxing bought that family's house too, at a high price, and set preparations in motion for a large-scale construction project: a twelve-storey high-rise building. By this point, the outsider's garden villa was no longer regarded as anything special.

10

The Good Man, Lan Wei

NIGHT WAS FALLING.

Lan Wei sat on a boulder, feeling the chill in his backside. His back was facing the workers' shack and the bed of the Tuan River as he watched the roads on the river slope that led to Wu Town, winding and crossing and tangled.

The riverbank was low and flat. The black, gaunt trees and the white reeds were lonely and silent. Dusk came without even a single crow. Lan Wei sat there, looking around at intervals, left and right, rubbing his smooth chin with his hand, jiggling his legs, chuckling. His laugh was peculiar, a little roguish, but with a hint of feebleness and of something concealed from view.

Lan Wei pulled out his mobile and stared at it for a while, but the phone did not respond. He read a text with great attention. Soon he had finished. He set the phone on the ground, put his hands together in front of his chest, closed his eyes and muttered something to himself. Then he opened his eyes, squatted down and moved his feet apart into a horse stance, manipulating his inner forces with his hands and wrists, before pushing the forces in the direction of the phone, at which he emitted a short, sharp cry, "Hai! Ha!"

The phone did not move a whisker.

A file of ants was walking along in a solemn procession, bearing an object on their shoulders. Lan Wei squatted down, earnestly scrutinising the steps of the ants as they walked, his head nodding along with them as they marched, his mouth unconsciously emitting the words: Left, right, left! Left, right, left! After a while he lost interest and spat at the ants, swamping them in his spit as if in a raging ocean, causing their march to become disordered and the ants to stagger about.

Lan Wei raised his head and continued to look in the direction of the road. His head was tilted upwards, his eyes slightly raised. He would not let himself cry, he was just a bit lonely, that was all.

A black speck in the distance, getting nearer, was accompanied by the put-putting of an engine. Lan Wei sprung to his feet, staring at the growing black spot as it gradually resolved into the outline of a man.

Yizhi was riding a motorbike, his face swollen and eyes black from the wind. A pot was secured with rope to the front footplate, and a bulging white bag was tied to the back seat. Yizhi untied the things from the motorbike, sucking in his breath. "Fuck, this weather," he said. "It chills you to the bone."

Lan Wei sniggered off to one side. "What made you think to come over?" he asked Yizhi in a stuttering, unclear voice.

Yizhi passed the tightly sealed pot to Lan Wei. "Here are some of my stewed turnips, they're still hot. There's enough here to last you for several days."

Yizhi's turnips were first-rate. Exactly a week before Chinese New Year, on a day called "Lesser New Year", the majority of families would buy food at the market and bring it home to cook on the hot flue. Yizhi's main task that day had been to stew the turnips. He thickly sliced the white turnips with a few chunks of pork, the back legs or the hooves, or belly pork, and he mixed them all together and put them into a big pot to stew. When we say "stew" it is because the meat has to be cooked just so far and no further so that it holds its form outside but will fall apart at a touch inside, and the turnip still has some proper texture to it but the delicious flavour of the meat has completely permeated it. On first eating it is not so very special, but after three days the turnip acquires a slight sourness and a unique fragrance, making a light, refreshing and long-lasting dish, an unusually savoury delicacy.

The workers' temporary shed was horribly messy inside and seemed even colder than outside. A small camp bed was set up next to the wall, on which a quilt had been left unfolded, and some books were scattered at random over the surface. The stove had gone out and there were lumps and fragments of coal piled up on the floor beside it, together with a handful of unwashed pots, bowls and spoons.

Lan Wei snapped a few dry branches for kindling, relit the stove and set Yizhi's turnip dish on top. Yizhi found a cardboard box, spread a couple of pieces of paper over it and started to pull things from the big plastic bag: piping hot baked wheat cakes, pressed sheep's head mixed with garlic, a bag of deep-fried tofu and chunks of fish, and a bottle of Old Luzhou wine, as well as a bunch of dried bean noodles, a huge white cabbage, several onions, a few handfuls of wheat noodles, a chunk of fresh pork...

As Yizhi kept producing more items, Lan Wei said from beside him, "I've got bean noodles here, Hongxing brought me some last time. I've got wheat noodles too, and cabbage, I've got everything."

Yizhi curled his lip and said, "You have everything, yes, only you're all by yourself."

"Come on, have a drink of this, Old Luzhou is still the mellowest of them all." Lan Wei held out a cup of the fermented sorghum wine and greedily swigged a mouthful. He picked up several chunks of mutton, chewed forcefully and swallowed them, saying, "There's nothing like Bald Wu's pressed sheep's head. Hey, Yizhi, do you still remember when we were at high school and we'd pool our money to go and eat Bald Wu's flat noodles? They were absolutely delicious. We used to eat a big portion each, then a small one. Xiao Zhou really knew how to pack it away. Every time he'd order a big one and a small one, and then he'd ask for another small bowl on top."

"Of course I remember, how could I forget? One time Lao Guo was treating us and insisted on bringing his new girlfriend along. He was boasting that he was going to give us all a wonderful surprise, that the girl's eyes were so big, and she was so beautiful. When we got there and saw her, we all doubled up laughing, that girl's eyes were tiny, though there was a nice curve to them, pretty cute really. The point was that she had a big bowl and a small one too, and then she ate up Xiao Zhou's small bowl as well, just like that."

Yizhi spluttered with laughter, and the wine that had just entered his mouth spurted out. Composing himself, he said, "Afterwards we all had a go at Lao Guo about it, and that so-and-so tried to wriggle out of it, saying, 'I just think that her eyes are the biggest.'"

"Last year I went to Shandong Province to see Lao Guo. He took me out for a hot pot, and we talked about that girl, he actually said that her eyes *were* big, I don't know where Lao Guo even keeps his eyes! All the same, Lao Guo's current girl isn't bad, she may not be well-educated, but she's his, heart and soul, and she's a lot better-looking than that girl."

"Yes, back when Lao Guo left Wu Town to find work, he promised to be faithful till the mountains wore away and the seas ran dry, and they wrote to each other for ages. But by the time Lao Guo came back from Shandong, she'd already got married to a man from the army camp."

Lan Wei was drinking the wine, chuckling, and occasionally smacking his lips, savouring it like a connoisseur, and a rosy, greasy grin crept over his face. He was more nostalgic than anyone for his high school days. That skinny, quick, clever youth, his smile bright like the sunlight, endlessly full of life.

In middle age, Lan Wei was starting to run to fat. His face was an unhealthy white, overlaid with a flush and a permanent oily sheen, and his eyes and eyebrows were squashed together so that it was hard to tell them apart. There was something slightly pitiable in his appearance.

Everybody said that Lan Wei was a good man.

As soon as he arrived in high school, Lan Wei's goodness was brought into full play. Throughout his three years there, plus the two years he retook the final year, he was class monitor and an enthusiastic participant in all kinds of community activities, encouraging and helping everybody, without prejudice, never forming factions or cliques. Two classmates who did not get on could both become friends with Lan Wei, and he would always come up with ways to resolve the conflicts between them. Lan Wei also won great popularity among his classmates' parents. During the summer wheat harvest, he would lead his classmates to each family in turn to help cut the wheat. In summer they would go to the roasting-hot tobacco fields to pick tobacco leaves, and in autumn they would help harvest maize and soybeans. A crowd of young people would pop up wherever they were needed, and although they were tired from their labour, they were happier than they had ever been. Some of the town students' families had no farmland of their own, but they still followed Lan Wei everywhere.

Many of his classmates' parents treated Lan Wei like their own son, and their dependence on him exceeded that of their own children.

Everybody respected, admired and liked Lan Wei, describing him in fine terms such as keen, unselfish, earnest, altruistic, unstinting in a just cause, idealistic and cheerful, none of which seemed excessive when applied to Lan Wei. In turn, Lan Wei knew that everyone liked him and approved of him, and his goodness kept on increasing.

In the second year of high school, when the class had their spring outing to Tugu Mountain, there was just a hint of some special feeling between Lan Wei and his classmate Yanchun.

Tugu Mountain was about forty kilometres from Wu Town, a dusty hill of earth that was neither tall nor beautiful, but living on the plains as they did, it at least gave them something to climb. A mighty contingent of them rode there on their bicycles, but once they got there they encountered an army unit stationed at Tugu Mountain. Negotiations took place, after which the young soldiers not only showed them their weapons and equipment and took them on a tour that included the restricted areas, they even provided a meal. Everybody was cheering and jumping for joy.

Dressed in a blue-and-white checked skirt, Yanchun sat in the cockpit of an aeroplane, wearing a flight helmet that left only her round, tender face exposed. She tilted her head to look at Lan Wei and said with a coquettish smile, "How do I look, Lan Wei? Does it suit me?"

Lan Wei suddenly saw Yanchun's eyes, and he noticed a hint of reproach in her coyness. In those days Yanchun was a delicate-featured girl, a gifted essay writer but proud and cold with an acid tongue. None of her classmates quite dared get close to her, but all this lent her an aura that was difficult to put into words. Yanchun was responsible for the wall posters in the classroom and was head of the school's Literary Society, so she often had occasion to discuss business with the class monitor Lan Wei, or to show him essays written by herself or other students. But Lan Wei had been keeping himself busy all day long, and he had barely noticed Yanchun.

That day Lan Wei was unusually excited. On the way up and down the mountain he bustled about, back and forth, arranging rest stops and photographs, making sure nobody had fallen behind, thanking the army leaders, he was everywhere.

After lunch the lads from the army base held a basketball match, a friendly, by way of a farewell ceremony. In the match, that gaggle of schoolboys were thrashed. Even Zhang Sheng, who was over six feet tall and Number Five Middle School's star player, could barely withstand them. Another classmate twisted his ankle, and a substitute player was urgently required. Lan Wei rose to the occasion and volunteered.

Lan Wei tucked his white shirt into his belt and entered the fray, glowing with pride. Everybody had thought him a highly skilled basketball player, but once he got moving, they discovered that his footwork was rigid, exaggerated and awkward, weak and laughable. He was leaping and jumping blindly in the wake of the other players, like a fly without a head. Everybody realised for the first time that there had never been the least method to Lan Wei, and he had no judgment at all of the situation in front of him.

They took a great many photographs on that spring outing, but not one came out well. The classmate who had taken the pictures had not understood about focus, and the subjects were all blurred.

Lan Wei did not get together with Yanchun. She got into university ahead of him and started going out with somebody else. Lan Wei fell silent for a while, then laughed and asked about Yanchun's boyfriend, saying that he sounded like a good sort and he wished her well.

As for Lan Wei, he did what he could to diminish any sense of loss, and he tried not to care one way or the other. He was simply too busy. Yanchun had gone, only a very faint feeling of regret remained at the bottom of his heart, and soon another girl student caught his eye.

Two years later Lan Wei got into university, and Yanchun and her boyfriend split up. Yanchun sent him a quite remarkably aggrieved letter, reproaching Lan Wei for not getting in touch more often, forgetting an old classmate just like that, and so on. Reading the letter, Lan Wei chuckled, and he wrote a very long reply, full of deep emotion, the gist was that he had never dared to aim so high as a girl with such good looks and brilliant mind, he had hoped that she would explore all the opportunities available to her, but he had always kept a fondness for her hidden in his heart, and so on and so forth.

There was an element of exaggeration in his writing, but since he had written it down himself, a word at a time, in the action of writing he had made it true. Besides, he was intoxicated by his own powers of expression and the beautiful words and phrases in his letter. He therefore made a copy of the letter for himself, which he passed among his friends or read out loud to them, telling them how he had taken a liking to Yanchun from the first time he saw her.

———

"We really could eat in those days." Lan Wei filled a bowl with turnips for Yizhi. "This bowl wouldn't have been enough for Zhixin. I remember when Lao Guan's family were harvesting the wheat, and that big pot of theirs, which was full to the brim with noodles, with two big fried dishes on the side. We had three bowls of noodles each, filled to overflowing, we scoffed the lot. It wasn't until we'd eaten it all up that it occurred to us that Lao Guan's mum and dad hadn't had anything to eat."

"That Lao Guan, he's got no loyalty, he never got in touch after he finished school. When we held get-togethers and invited him, he wouldn't come even then."

"He's divorced as well, took the kid. He didn't like his teaching job, the pay wasn't good enough, and it was only after he became a lawyer that things took a turn for the better." Lan Wei was eating, and the steam rising from his food hid his face and concealed his expression.

"Divorced?"

"He wouldn't let me tell a soul. I went to Ping County to see him, you wouldn't believe how fat he'd got." Lan Wei heaved a sigh. "The kid's just four or five, always at Lao Guan's heels, it all looks so sad."

Yizhi looked at Lan Wei, whose expression was remarkably calm. He asked curiously, "When did you go to see him? Can you leave this sand pit?"

Lan Wei's legs quivered briefly. "Aiya, there was no telling him, he had to go away on business, and he couldn't find anybody to take care of the kid. He said I didn't have anything important to do and insisted that I came over. I had a word with Hongxing, and Hongxing agreed, we're all old classmates, so I went. We had a glass or two before he left, and we ended up getting drunk together, laughing and crying all at once."

Yizhi's expression was pained, like he did not know whether to laugh or cry, there was reproach in it, but also frustrated resignation. Tentatively, he asked Lan Wei, "Talking of which, how long's it been since you went back to Rang County to see your Xingyue?"

"What would I see her for? Her mother looks after her just fine." Lan Wei downed another mouthful of wine and chuckled again. "If I don't see her for a long time I stop wanting to see her, and if I just showed up out of nowhere it'd disturb her. Besides, I can't leave here."

From Lan Wei's neutral expression, he had no intention of letting the conversation go any deeper. Yizhi did not know what to say either, as they had had many similar exchanges over the years, so he raised his wine cup and downed a mouthful.

———

Deep in the night a few years earlier, Lan Wei had come banging on the door of Yizhi's house. Lan Wei's clothes were dishevelled and there was a wild look in his eyes, it was like some great disaster was drawing near or even that his last hour was at hand; there was an obscure sense of imminent collapse. Shortly after Yanchun came hurrying over too, looking deeply agitated and concerned, and when she saw Lan Wei drinking tea with Yizhi she heaved a deep sigh. Yizhi and Lan Wei drank their tea in the outer room, listening to Yanchun's muffled voice, sometimes loud and sometimes soft, sometimes laughing, sometimes crying, and to the brief, quiet responses of Yizhi's wife, Xueli. Lan Wei did not say anything, and when urged to go and sleep he did not reply.

After they graduated from university, Yanchun and Lan Wei both went to work in the county town. Lan Wei was at the Supply and Marketing Cooperative, Yanchun was in the finance department of a government-run work unit, and Lan Wei's parents looked after their child for them. Lan Wei's career got off to a very promising start, and soon he was made secretary to his boss, whom he accompanied on business trips to all kinds of places, and his word carried considerable weight in the organisation. Yanchun, on the other hand, was pitiless and exacting, her eyes could not tolerate so much as a mote of dust. She had a string of complaints against Lan Wei and his family, and quarrels frequently broke out between them. Yanchun was no longer popular with their classmates. To them, Lan Wei was like a god, their elder brother and the best of all good men, he would make arrangements for anything with such enthusiasm, yet at home he was treated so harshly, it was not fair. However, whenever anybody commented jokingly on this, Yanchun would always curl her lip in scorn.

By the following morning, after listening all night to Yanchun, Xueli's view of her seemed to have undergone a great change. She treated Yanchun with great solicitude, but when she saw Lan Wei, she did not spare him so much as a glance.

Yanchun and Lan Wei each had a stone stool in a corner of the yard. Lan Wei was hanging his head and kept avoiding Yanchun's eyes.

Yanchun was interrogating him in a loud voice. "Well, did you do it or didn't you? Give me a proper answer, it'll be easier for me to process." Her voice was wounded, and there was rage in it. Lan Wei shook his head wordlessly as he slumped lower and lower. Yanchun kept on asking, again and again, her voice rising, and there was more in her questions than simple grievance and rage. It was like she was not truly unaware of what she was asking, but she was unwilling to believe it. She was clutching at a thread of the vaguest hope, hoping for a reply in the negative.

Lan Wei's silence was an admission in itself. Yanchun sat down on the ground, grabbed Yizhi's hand as he came to help her up and started to choke with sobs.

Lan Wei's brain was a roaring mass of confusion: Yizhi, Yanchun, that dark red, seedy room, that garishly dressed woman and the policemen too, were all wavering back and forth in front of his eyes, like distant ghosts and demons, yet all their eyes were staring at him. He seemed to see the dark waters of a lake, he was walking above it, on the point of toppling down into it, and at last he fell. He was terribly afraid, he wanted to open his mouth to call for help, yet he could not make a sound, and he did not know where to go.

Yizhi told Yanchun to sit herself down and have some tea, whatever was wrong they could talk it through, everybody would help them find a solution. Yanchun glared at Yizhi, and her rage slowly shifted away from Lan Wei. "Those dodgy friends of yours, spending all their days plotting and scheming, trying to make an official of him, teaching him their ragbag of tricks, currying favour with this man, sucking up to that one. And now look at the state of him, he's in a mess. Who'll carry the can for him?'

Lan Wei waved a hand in Yanchun's direction, saying, "Let's talk this through like adults, why do you have to drag Yizhi into it?" Yanchun was looking at Yizhi with an expression that said, There he goes again. Yizhi knew that the words that would come after this must have formed part of their quarrels any number of times.

"Yizhi, look at him, as soon as I say anything about his friends he's unhappy. I can be as miserable as you like, that's all fine, but let one of his friends be the tiniest bit sad, or let the smallest thing happen in that friend's family, and he'll go haring over there quicker than that man's actual parents, or his brothers and sisters. When Xiao Zhou's mother was ill, he was running about all over the place. I was away on business, and his daughter had a high fever, but even then he didn't go back home. Was that man's mother his own mother? And while we're on the subject, does he take proper care of his own parents?"

Lan Wei could not see what this woman was thinking; he had never thought that he had been wrong to do this. Through the feverish fog that filled his mind, he weakly justified himself, saying, "Xiao Zhou was in Guangzhou, he couldn't come back. If I didn't go and help make arrangements on his behalf, his mother wouldn't even have been able to get into hospital. I could hardly just watch her die, could I?"

"Did you actually do any good? It's because you helped him that he wasn't willing to come back, not until his mother was dead. But for your help, he might well have returned much earlier! It was you helping that made him put off coming back, in fact you forced him into a position where he was disloyal and unfilial."

Yanchun smacked down every statement of Lan Wei's with a sneer. Lan Wei sat furiously back down on his stool, his head on one side, not saying a word. Yizhi too was like an aubergine hit by the frost, hanging there limp and deflated. Xueli was standing off to the side, watching all of this with a quiet pleasure in Lan Wei's misfortune.

Yizhi was indeed one of Lan Wei's dodgy friends, and the closest of them all. Whenever Lan Wei went back to Wu Town, his first stop was always Yizhi's, and together they would make plans and preparations, mapping out a route for his official career, pondering on the best way to get along with leaders and colleagues. Lan Wei had gone to the hospital to help care for Xiao Zhou's mother and made phone calls to any number of old classmates, getting them all to come and visit her. Xiao Zhou did not reach Rang County until after his mother had died, and he was not entirely happy about it, but he had certainly not considered matters to the level that Yanchun had.

"You're forever ingratiating yourself with other people. Whatever they think, you take their thoughts a step further, and things they would never even have thought of, you'll think for them. Do you truly just help them out of the goodness of your heart? Not you. All you think about is getting people to say that you're good, you need their affirmation. You're acting a part, and you care more about this part than for your wife or your child, and a lot more than for your mother or father."

At that moment Yanchun sounded like an irate philosopher. The more she spoke, the deeper and further she went, following her ideas to their logical conclusion.

"And let's talk about you, Yizhi. Just why did you end

up owing so much money at the end of the year, why didn't you give your folks a proper explanation? What did you do with all that money? You had Xueli in tears, you made Uncle and Auntie Wu cry too, but you just wouldn't say. Is that the way a son should behave?"

Xueli was almost in tears again. She scowled at Yizhi and her fingers groped for Yanchun's hand, like she had finally found someone she could depend on. Yanchun glared at Lan Wei too, as if her glare could set him on fire.

"When Yizhi was in difficulties, you didn't even stop to think, you bastard, you went everywhere borrowing money on his behalf, you did everything short of kneeling on the ground. You never asked anything, you took no heed of whether he'd eaten, drunk or whored it away, or what he'd been up to. All you cared about was getting him more loans. Are you actually helping him or harming him? You cover up for one another, you each know what the other one has been up to, for sure!"

Yanchun was flaying Lan Wei and Yizhi with her words, covering both men in the mud she flung at them, as they each sat in their own corner like a pair of primary school students getting told off.

"You're the worst. Cold, selfish, no feelings, a classic appeaser. You're fine with everything, with everyone, whatever life gives you, you accept, you'll never take a stand on your own, never break ranks. Whatever things come your way, you turn them into filthy mud, as if they'd been that way all along, and then you fake being a good man, fake innocence. But are you really innocent? I know how our old classmates see me, I know, I know they say I'm a bad daughter, they call me harsh, they say I've become a vulgar woman. But did I want to turn out like this? Isn't it only because you don't turn a hand to anything that I ended up this way? Isn't it true that the only reason you went off whoring is because you wanted to do it? Did that leader hold a gun to your head, force you to go in? You'll always be someone else's lackey, always!"

When Yizhi heard the word "whoring", he gave a start and looked over towards Lan Wei. Lan Wei had hunched his back and twisted his head away to one side, unable to meet Yizhi's eyes.

"You don't tell, you'll never tell, you're embarrassed to say the sordid things you got up to. You're dirty all over, through and through, the whole lot of you are filthy."

Lan Wei rushed over to Yanchun and slapped her face twice, crack, crack. He would not permit her to speak about Yizhi like that. She could say anything else, but not have a go at his friends.

Yanchun stared at Lan Wei, then shoved him out of her way, grabbed a chair and dashed it against his body. Lan Wei was running all over the yard, his arms wrapped round his head.

"Lan Wei, you're just like the appendix you're named after,[1] bad enough that you're no use to anyone, but now you're causing real harm."

Seeing Yanchun ranting and raving like this, the depths of her resentment and her cravings for a better life, Yizhi suddenly felt quite grieved for her.

Yanchun left. Lan Wei stood wordlessly in the yard, his body shrunk in on itself. That basketball court in Tugu Mountain and that white-shirted, leaping figure now seemed like a foreshadowing: weakness, inner emptiness, drifting with the tide, doing things with no aim in sight to please others. That prancing figure was so laughable that it would grieve you.

Yizhi walked over, patted his shoulder and said, "It's as well she's gone, the two of us can have a drink." Yizhi did not enquire whether he really had done that thing, and he had no plans to seek out confirmation either. They were the best of friends, they understood each other. Whether he'd done it or not would make no difference to the feelings between them.

———

Lan Wei was still a good man.

He was loyal, devoted and true. He never exposed the leader, nor had a bad word to say about him. The leader, on the other hand, told all, no details omitted. Lan Wei was transferred from the head office and was relegated to outside staff. Yanchun left him, taking the child, and very soon she married again. Not long afterwards the Supply and Marketing Cooperative where he worked went bust, and its staff were relocated to various townships in the region. Lan Wei found himself back once again in Wu Town, where he was employed, at least nominally, in the local government, drawing only a basic salary of a thousand or so a month, his sole income.

His life went downhill and then downhill again, a straight and easy downward slope, it truly could not have happened any more quickly.

When Lan Wei came back to Wu Town, it was like the prodigal son had returned. Although he did not have a penny to his name, he enjoyed great popularity. His old classmates who had been living in Wu Town the whole time slowly started to gather around him, and the parents of those old classmates often got their children to invite Lan Wei to their homes. Lan Wei soon became a vital link in Wu Town's day-to-day personal networks. He could get you in touch with anybody.

Lan Wei walked the streets of Wu Town, all smiles, constantly greeting passers-by, looking at the familiar faces with a peculiar feeling of satisfaction. He often stopped for a chat at Hai's meat stall. He would squat down beside an old man selling vegetables and help him call out his wares, then when he was done the two of them would drink a few small measures of cheap wine in a little wine shop, chatting and smiling. He would go to Luo Jianshe's Caihong's Cosmetics, or to Old Wu's hardware store, or he would visit Weirdo Wang in the Civil Affairs Office for a cup of tea and spend the whole afternoon there. Of course, the place he visited most was Yizhi's teahouse, where he would talk to Yizhi about everything and anything.

Everybody still trusted Lan Wei. As soon as anybody needed help, he was sure to be the first to appear. When classmates came back to Rang County from outside, the first person they got in touch with was bound to be him. When there was a business dinner, Lan Wei was naturally their first choice to accompany the guests. At weddings and funerals, Lan Wei would always be the one taking an inventory of the gifts and money at the door. He had become an emblem and a symbol of a tragic life. When his name was mentioned everybody would feel sad, but he was at the very heart of this big family.

When Yizhi's new house was built, he invited everybody to a banquet. Lan Wei organised a gang of their old schoolmates, put together a sum of money and bought a large sheet of decorative glass from the best interior decorator in Wu Town, to be hung on the main wall of Yizhi's living room. Towards noon, when the glass had just been cut, it was set out flat on the ground, and Lan Wei took a big brush, dipped it in vermillion paint and inscribed it with words from Chairman Mao: "I stand alone in the autumn cold, On the tip of Orange Isle, The Xiang River flowing northwards..."

Lan Wei's characters were powerful, poised and natural, especially the final strokes, with their slight upward flourish, which made them seem full of optimism, positivity, spirit and presence, very much appropriate to the words of the poem. The onlookers all cried out in praise. Lan Wei's face was flushed red, cheerful and moved, and for an instant it was like he was back in the days of high school and university, when he was always surrounded by people. He was at the heart of everything, he was the sun, shining on himself and on those around him.

A crowd of them carried the glass through the streets of Wu Town, and some asked, who did this calligraphy? To which the response was, Lan Wei, that's Lan Guodong's second son, from Lanying. People would think, and then it would dawn on them, and they would say to those beside them, "Ah, Lan Wei, I know him, he's a good kid, very bright. He got into some university or other, he's quite the guy." Others would respond that he had been back in Wu Town for quite some time now, doing a non-job in the local government.

Lan Wei walked at the front of the group, greeting everyone. His back was straighter and the smile on his face had deepened, radiating pride and nostalgia for his past glories.

That great sheet of glass with its bright red calligraphy hung in the living room, baring its fangs and brandishing its claws, presenting an unusually bombastic and exaggerated appearance. Many times Xueli had wanted to take it down, drag it outside and smash it, to get back her nice clean white wall, but she was determinedly opposed in this by Yizhi.

Life in Rang County and his former flourishing career had vanished into the far distance. Lan Wei never discussed it with anyone else, he could not even be sure himself that he could remember those things. Since that evening when the police had twisted his arms behind his back and dragged him from the bed of that girl he did not know, ordered him to squat in the corner of the room and forced him to confess, part of his memory and spirit seemed to have been damaged. He made a conscious choice to forget those scenes, although many times later he had returned like a sleepwalker to that place, to look for that girl again. Whether he wanted to console her, or whether he was seeking some kind of titillation, he could not even say for sure himself.

But he really did like this place, this Wu Town. Seeing any one of its inhabitants would fill him with delight. He even regarded the plots, schemes and anger that spilled into every corner of it with great joy. He was an onlooker, an omniscient watcher from a great height, loving everybody with the kind of detached delight one takes in a moonlit landscape. He felt that he belonged to this place, and to the people of Wu Town it felt like he had always been living here. Only those who had seen him in his glory days would feel any surprise at his low spirits and inactivity.

Lan Wei took to playing mah-jong, then borrowing when the money ran out, and he started to get into debt, leaving him unable even to pay maintenance for his daughter. Yanchun sent his daughter to demand her maintenance several times, and had Yizhi chase him up for it as well. Lan Wei only laughed and did not say a thing. Many times he arrived unannounced at friends' houses and headed straight for the kitchen where he would enthusiastically set about preparing a meal, which he would eat, toasting everyone present, and then he would take a friend's place at the mah-jong table for a few rounds. Finally, he would collapse in an untidy heap on a bed in the friend's house and sleep.

Seeing Lan Wei asleep was a disheartening experience, sprawled out with his shiny face, his rounding, softened body and his oily, dishevelled clothes. He would shrink into a ball as he slept, and his head would jerk from time to time as if something was chasing him in his dreams.

———

"I'd better be going. With all the relatives I've got, I'll need to cook another two pots of turnips if there's going to be enough."

Yizhi stood up, took up the big sack and pulled out several things from inside: a few books, two notebooks, a pile of paper and several ballpoint pens.

Yizhi handed the books over to Lan Wei, one at a time. "*Study of Tang and Song Poetry*, the *Diamond Sutra*, *The Book of Songs* and *Anthology of Classical Prose*. I couldn't find a copy of *Free and Easy Wandering*, but tomorrow we're sweeping the rooms for Spring Festival. I'll go to my study and have another rummage through my books."

In their years at high school, after studying the philosopher Zhuangzi's *Free and Easy Wandering*, Lan Wei had given himself a nickname, "The Free and Easy Idler", and written himself a couplet that went, "The Free and Easy Idler is a free and easy man. / Like the Great Sage, Equal to Heaven he dares to reach for the sky." In those days he had believed himself to be free and easy. He loved everything passionately, he looked lightly on all he encountered, for the world was in his hands, through which he could move freely as the whim took him.

"These two notebooks and this manuscript paper you can use to copy or write. Jot down a few lines when you've nothing better to do, it might be fun. Back in the day, you were a pretty good hand with a pen. Every time you wrote an essay, it was held up as an example."

Lan Wei took the books and exercise books, laughing, as if Yizhi had made a joke.

How many years was it since Lan Wei had been heard fully expressing his thoughts? Back when Yizhi was at middle school in Lan Wei's village, by day the lean, wiry Lan Wei would take Yizhi around the villages in search of people to play Chinese chess with. They worked their way through all of Xiaying and Liangzhuang, then in the evenings they would go over to listen to the men talking about the classics, like the *Three Heroes and Five Gallants*, and he would always be ready with village legends, or stories that others had forgotten, right there on the tip of his tongue. People would look at clever, eloquent Lan Wei and click their tongues in admiration, saying that the lad would really be somebody in future.

At university, Lan Wei had once debated with a classmate the topic of what constitutes a righteous life, and they had fallen out as a consequence. This heated argument had created quite a stir among his old classmates from Wu Town because Lan Wei was just not the kind of person to break off a friendship. Besides, that classmate was just a young fogey who habitually poured cold water on everything.

That classmate came back once on a visit to Wu Town, and he got Yizhi to invite Lan Wei out for a drink with him, and at the table they resumed their heated debate. That classmate maintained that Lan Wei was too much of an idealist; he appeared proactive and enthusiastic, but actually he did not have any position of his own. Moreover, he had no interest in anything complex, he was not pragmatic, and this meant he would be constantly hitting a wall, and in the end it would lead to his undoing.

"All pragmatism is playing the hooligan," Lan Wei retorted. "Because this implies a betrayal of the spirit, that you're turning a blind eye to social phenomena, that's not a man, that's an ostrich."

Lan Wei's words were powerful and impressive, there could be no comeback, and his classmate indicated that there was nothing he could say to that, but he did not endorse this view. In senior high school, Lan Wei had always been class monitor, and he also held that position at university, in addition to his roles as head of the Students' Union, liaison for the Wu Towners' Society, head of the debating society and head of the calligraphy club. You could see him everywhere, labouring away tirelessly. He seemed not to be doing all this purely for the sake of gaining office or being a leader, but from a kind of inborn enthusiasm and a personality that delighted in being busy, any time and anywhere.

Who would have thought that someone like this, in the prime of life, would be reduced to guarding the sand in a sand quarry, solitary and lonesome, rejected by the world?

Just where does the change in a person begin? In the course of this transformation from an eager, ambitious man to the appeaser Yanchun had named him, had there been some hidden connection all along? Could there be some underlying, innate common factor at work here?

Perhaps what Yanchun had said was right. When a young couple start tearing each other apart, their inner weaknesses are all suddenly exposed.

Yizhi walked out of the workers' shack. The bone-piercing cold wind blew over and instantly seeped right into them. Yizhi shivered and said to Lan Wei, "Come to my place on New Year's Eve to watch the Spring Festival variety show with us on the telly. What's worth guarding in this place, who'd steal this sand? That Hongxing's bloody impossible, he won't even let you have your New Year."

"It's not like that," Lan Wei replied. "Hongxing didn't actually insist on me staying here, but someone's got to keep watch. It's not like I've got anywhere else to go, I'm fine here."

"Then he can't even discuss it with you properly? He knows fine well that if he doesn't say anything you're bound to be here guarding it. He's an unscrupulous merchant, a profiteer. People who go into business all end up like that. He's got no consideration for an old classmate's feelings. And talking of which, has he paid you your wages?"

"Yes, he's paid me," Lan Wei replied feebly. "He takes good care of us, really."

Yizhi started up his motorbike, a loud sound that rang out sharply. At almost the same moment, a muffled sound came over from the distance and a ball of colour exploded in the sky. They had just entered the Lesser New Year, seven days before Chinese New Year, and some folk who could not wait for the main festival were starting to set off fireworks. One explosion followed another, the noise carried as far as the empty river valley, exceptionally startling, like the sound was drilling up from the depths of the Earth, straight into people's hearts. One cluster came, then another, one soaring up as the previous one fell. Viewed from this broad, low, flat river slope, those fireworks were extraordinarily magnificent and graceful.

Yizhi switched on his headlights and drove away. The beam pierced the blackness into the far distance, pencil-straight, bobbing around from time to time, carving randomised slashes of light into the slope.

Lan Wei stared at the light, watching it recede into the distance and disappear into the blackness. He raised his head and jiggled his legs vigorously, humming a song, watching the fireworks burst into the sky all around.

The wind from the riverbed blew over, carrying sand with it. It blew past the woods, past the dried clumps of reeds and past the tin hut, causing the thin metal walls to emit a howling sound as it rushed past Lan Wei's body and seeped into his eyes. The glorious fireworks, a contrast in light and dark, illuminated the houses on the riverbank, the cross on the church, the round and pointed roofs of the mosque, and then they were covered by the darkness, blurring into a mass of gentle silhouettes, rising and falling.

He was all alone in this chilly weather and wild country. Lan Wei thought about the residents of the town, of all their different expressions, and his mouth twitched involuntarily and he laughed. He loved this place, and every human being living here.

He was thinking of Yizhi simmering his turnips; Hongzhong teasing his children in that shrill voice and making cutting remarks to his wife; Hongxing, who was sure to be at the card table with another girl at his side, which one was anybody's guess. He saw Aqing, Dequan, Haihong and every one of them walking towards him. He saw their tears, their sorrows and the smallest details of their innermost thoughts.

Aqing, Aqing, don't be unhappy, that's just the way life is, there will be always something to make you sad. If you knew what Grandmother Ahua had been through, you'd forgive her. I know, Aqing, I know, you feel that the image you held in your heart has been ruined, that Grandmother Ahua in her black clothes should have been the representative of an ideal, of strictness, abstinence and persistence, which can be a source of inspiration to a young boy, something to aspire to in future, in the spirit and in life. But Aqing, do you know how happy it made Grandmother Ahua to share a meal with her younger son?

She would have gladly eaten anything he told her to eat. She could be unsmiling, she could meditate, she could commune with the spirits, but in front of her younger son, none of that meant a thing. She only wanted to make her son happy and safe. Not all persistence is a beautiful thing, or the right thing, compromise is beautiful too.

Yizhi, you must not blame yourself. In this world, people die every day for no reason at all. How many die halfway through their journey, how many leave their homes and never come back again? But, Yizhi, you shouldn't have bought Chuanyou's family hot water shop. In life, there are some lines that should not be crossed. You can't say that Chuanyou's death was directly connected with you, but, Yizhi, do you truly not feel like there's a corner missing from your heart? There'll be a gap there forever now, it can never be mended.

Haihong, forgive your father, it's not that he doesn't love you, he's a man too. Forget that holy man, he never set out to cast a shadow over your life, he knows not what he did.

Caihong, Caihong, you have to leave home. Go to the beach and sunbathe, treat yourself to the Western food you longed to eat as a young girl, buy yourself that long, strappy sundress you set your heart on. You are so pretty, when you walk on those boulevards there will be countless Luo Jianshes to whistle at you.

Lan Wei's thoughts turned to his own Xingyue, his lovely Xingyue. She was thirteen already. Those who had seen her said she had a startling beauty, having inherited his thin, delicate face and her mother's fair skin and black eyes. He often went to Rang County to loiter at the side gate of Rang County Number One Middle School, waiting for classes to finish and his Xingyue to come out so that he could steal a glimpse of her. But as soon as the bell rang for the end of school, he would scurry away.

Lan Wei's eyes blurred and his tears fell, creeping where they would all over his face. He rushed back to the hut, fumbling in the dark, found the pen Yizhi had given him and wrote:

"A shining cloud, moving over the skies of Wu Town."

---

1. Lan Wei's name 蓝伟 *Lán Wěi* sounds like "appendix" 烂尾 *lánwěi* in Chinese

About the Author

Liang Hong (b.1973-) is a writer, essayist and professor at Renmin University of China. Growing up in a village in rural China, Liang Hong's talent and work ethic drove her to pursue writing and academia in the city. However, it is her determination to hold on to the memories of her rural upbringing that sets her apart from the crowd. Narrativising rural China, she has been heralded by critics as a trailblazer, focusing on the lives of ordinary rural people and exploring something other than the metropolis.

In addition to her novels, Liang is also a prolific writer of short stories and literary criticism, inlcuding the non-fiction study of Liang village, *China in One Village*, which has been translated into French, English and Japanese. She has won a number of prizes, including the Seventh Wenjin Books Award of the National Library of China and the Second Zhu Ziqing Prose award.

About the Translator

Esther Tyldesley is a translator and a teacher of translation and Chinese. She graduated from Robinson College, Cambridge with a degree in Chinese, after which she spent four years teaching English to trainee teachers in rural Guizhou Province. During those four years, the things she had learned about China at university started to make more and more sense, and when she got back to the UK she was able to translate her first book: Xinran's *The Good Women of China*, released in 2001. She gained a Master's degree in Applied Translation Studies at the University of Leeds in 2002.

Esther now works teaching Chinese Language and Translation at the University of Edinburgh. In her spare time, she reads far too many books and dreams of China. Her published translations include *Sky Burial* and *China Witness*, also by Xinran, *Confucius from the Heart* by Yu Dan and *Little Aunt Crane* by Yan Geling.

ABOUT **SINO**IST BOOKS

We hope you enjoyed these short stories surrounding the reality of rural life in Wu Township.

SINOIST BOOKS brings the best of Chinese fiction to English-speaking readers. We aim to create a greater understanding of Chinese culture and society, and provide an outlet for the ideas and creativity of the country's most talented authors.

To let us know what you thought of this book, or to learn more about the diverse range of exciting Chinese fiction in translation we publish, find us online. If you're as passionate about Chinese literature as we are, then we'd love to hear your thoughts!

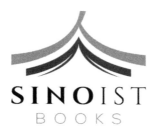

SINOIST
BOOKS